A
Simple
Death

Carolyn Morwood

First published by The Women's Press Ltd, 2001
A member of the Namara Group
34 Great Sutton Street, London EC1V 0LQ
www.the-womens-press.com

Copyright © Carolyn Morwood 2001

The right of Carolyn Morwood to be identified as the author of this work has been
asserted by her in accordance with the Copyright, Designs and Patents Act 1988.

British Library Cataloguing-in-Publication Data
A catalogue record for this book is available from the British Library.

ISBN 0 7043 4727 X

Typeset in Plantin 11/14pt by FiSH Books, London WC1
Printed and bound in Great Britain by Cox & Wyman Ltd, Reading, Berkshire

To Margery
First (and best) storyteller

And to

Norm
Who taught me how to run over rocks

Acknowledgements

Grateful thanks to:

Denise Page, Manager and Law Clerk for Searchwide, Melbourne. For once again giving time out of her busy working day to help with details of the workplace.

Gary Storey, Forensic Document Examiner. For generous time given in regard to document and fabric analysis and other forensic matters.

William Reilly, Senior Legal Executive at the Office of Public Prosecutions, Victoria, for information on the legal process.

Celia Bridle – for guided tours of material shops, love of bright fabrics and expertise in shot silk.

And – Women's Cricket Australia – for information on cricket and schedules.

Chapter 1

Small things set the fear off. Simple things like Harold pausing suddenly in the flow of conversation, listening and alert. Something about his sudden tensing makes me stop too, my mind leaping with possibilities.

The sounds around us are mixed. A thin note of birdsong from the Flagstaff Gardens. The hum of traffic on surrounding streets. A tiny crack of noise, like a stick breaking underfoot. And in the distance the sound of running rises up clearly for a moment and fades. Small inconsequential sounds that are carried on the still air and give no clue as to the reason for Harold's sudden pause.

In the park, lights shine palely along meandering pathways and I catch a momentary glimpse of the runner on the winding, middle footpath. A dark-clothed figure against a paler darkness. Despite their speed, there is an impression of awkwardness, a heaviness to one side, as though they are weighed down. And then they are gone, swallowed up by a distant plantation of trees.

'Marlo!' Harold has moved and stands some distance off, an

1

amorphous shape in the gloom. A shape I distinguish into separate components as I cross the icy grass towards him. Part Harold, part park bench and something else. Someone else. Someone who lies awkwardly, body slumped, head twisted against the metal rail. The air is cold but my skin is suddenly clammy, sweat prickling under my arms.

'Call an ambulance, Marlo. It's Bill. The old man . . . I heard him call out just now. I don't know . . .' He trails off.

Bill's body is engulfed in shadows but his face shows clearly in the park light and I see the trail of blood on his face, the stain of it in the stubble of his beard and on the grass beneath him. His eyes are open but only one is visible, pale and staring.

I fumble in my bag for my mobile phone, with hands that are uncharacteristically sluggish. The call made, I turn back to Harold. 'They're on their way. How is he?'

Harold shakes his head. 'I don't know. He spoke to me just now, but . . . I can't feel a pulse.' I put my hands on Harold's shoulders to reassure him and feel, not the familiar bulky overcoat that I expect but a layer of polyester that I recognise as one of his waistcoats. He has covered Bill with his coat and taken his hand, offering up his own warmth. He must be freezing.

How long we stand there linked in this strange tableau of stillness, I don't know. The air is sharp with cold and mist and Bill Diamond lies as still as death. Around us, no voices break the silence, no movement erodes the sense of isolation. Save for the hum of cars around the park and the restless glitter of their lights, it feels as though we are only people on the planet. When the sirens sound in the distance, they seem plaintive and disembodied.

'I'll go and meet them Harold, bring them over.'

He shifts and stands up. 'Yes.'

Above me, his face is pale and expressionless, but I can tell by the downward slump of his shoulders that he has given up hope.

Chapter 2

Torches and a brisk efficiency. We stand out of the way and watch the flurry of activity give way almost immediately to something more orderly and routine. There is no need for haste. Harold was right but I had known it too, felt it in the set of Harold's shoulders and the absolute stillness of death.

The police arrive next. More activity and voices. Next to me Harold is unmoving and unspeaking. When I put my hand on his arm, I feel his coldness with a little jolt of shock. The practical part of my brain kicks in and I remember that Harold keeps a spare jacket at work, and work is just across the road. There is nothing more I can do here anyway.

After the stillness of the park, my footsteps are loud on the wooden staircase leading up from the street. Inside, the office is warmer than I expected and there is a faint spring-like scent that surprises me. I don't switch the lights on as I don't intend to stay long and there should be enough light from William Street to see by. This is a mistake, though, because I collide heavily with Irene's chair, for once, not pushed in with its usual precision. Irene's desk is office legend. She always tidies it before leaving – documents filed, desk calender turned, diary closed, computer, phone and in-trays always in precise, unchanging positions. I'm surprised to see that the phone has shifted marginally too.

As I collect Harold's jacket from behind his door, the sudden brilliance of police lighting draws me to the window. A uniformed officer keeps spectators to the footpath but, away from the bright lights, a figure moves along the middle foot-path, heading towards the station, the opposite way to the runner earlier. There is nothing fleet about the man I watch now. A squat figure, slow and plodding, bowed down with heavy clothing. He is the only person who seems to be unaware of the activity going on around him.

Harold is with a police officer on the footpath, standing in the hazy glow of a streetlight that shows his height and bulk and close-cropped silver hair. I hurry back out with his coat, and he pauses in mid-sentence to slip it on, not really registering.

'I heard him call out . . .'

'Leave it for now,' the officer says, kindly enough. 'You can tell us at the station.'

After the chill of the park, the Police Centre in Flinders Street, is infinitely warm and inviting. I have been involved once before in a police investigation and give myself up to the procedures of it. I give my statement to a uniformed officer, going over what I saw, what I heard and what I knew of the dead man, but none of it amounts to much. I had never actually met Bill Diamond but Harold had told me about their recent conversations and I had seen them from my office window occasionally, sitting together in the park on sunny days. Bill was an old man with an air of watchfulness that showed in the constant moving of his head. But that is all I know of him – just a few impressions. It is my mention of the runner that arouses most interest.

'Can you describe them?'

I think back, remembering the speed and the awkwardness of that dark blur of clothing, but can recall nothing more.

'Anyone else you saw in the park?'

I tell her of the later sighting. The slow man with the heavy clothing, moving towards the station. But this was a comparatively long time after the death.

Next she asks for details of our work routine. We usually finish at half past five, but tonight we were held up by a missing document and a couple of last-minute phone calls. Harold had waited on the street for the courier and I had handled the phone calls, impatient with the delay, especially as I had to consult documents and files that had already been consulted many times before.

The officer has no more questions for me and I wait for Harold, drinking tea that I don't want, holding the cup for warmth, and aware of a vague hunger that has as much to do with cold and nerves as lack of food. As I sit there my thoughts go more to Harold than to the dead man. It is Harold who spent his lunch hours with him, who heard him cry out tonight and held his hand while life slipped through his fingers. I wonder how Harold is coping.

Eventually he comes out and I see with some surprise that his clothes are different. The jacket is the same but the trousers are not the usual luxurious fabric or stylish cut that I associate with Harold. What worries me most is the paleness of his face and the bruised look to the skin under his eyes. For the first time since I have known him, he looks his age.

City Road. Bay Road. Beaconsfield Parade. We take a taxi and are heading to Harold's house in Port Melbourne, with his offer of left-overs from last night's meal and, I suspect, the need for company. Harold's house is a conversion, like many others on this stretch. It has undergone extensive remodelling, which involved changing rooms around and replacing small front windows with huge unbroken sheets of glass. The front rooms of the upstairs section – the lounge, dining room and Harold's bedroom – all have uninterrupted views of the bay. Harold switches on the lights and turns the heater up to full blast, then hesitates as if suddenly unsure of what to do.

'You go and change, Harold, I'll find dinner.' He doesn't argue but plods off as if on autopilot. I hear drawers opening in the bedroom on the first floor and, in the bathroom next to it, the sound of the shower running.

There is a casserole dish in the fridge that looks promising. I take it out and heat the contents in the microwave, setting out plates and cutlery on a tray to take upstairs to the dining room. I don't think about wine – we need warmth and we need it now. I make coffee and add generous amounts of Harold's brandy to it. The warmth is instant, spreading out in a fiery, welcome glow.

When Harold emerges from the bedroom, he has changed into jeans and a thick jumper, and has put slippers on his feet. He looks warmer but not much better. He takes up the coffee with both hands, warming himself as I had done at the police station. I serve the food but he shows little enthusiasm for it.

'How were the police?' I ask tentatively, not sure if he wants to talk about the evening's events or not. I have no idea what to say to comfort him.

A silence before he answers. 'They went on and on, Marlo, going over the same details...I had his blood on my clothes.' He waves his hand vaguely over his body. 'I didn't realise...it was everywhere...'

I put my hand on his arm, understanding that this is an immense thing. This is what he will see tonight when he closes his eyes.

I look out at the view, giving him time. Usually I enjoy taking in the distinct structures along the coast – the double spiral of lighting on the Westgate Bridge, the string of yellow lights along the coast that jut out in glittering oblongs along the piers. But tonight I merely stare at the black sweep of sea, my mood heavy.

Harold adds more brandy to his empty cup. 'Bill Diamond

6

the derro,' he says musingly. 'It's funny how we have so many names for them . . . derro, tramp, vagrant. It's as though they don't count . . . no one bothers to find out their real names. Sorry, Marlo, I'm rambling.'

'Not at all.' After the shock and cold I am strangely languid, boneless, as though I could sit here for ever. Harold is silent again but looks deep in thought, turning some idea over in his mind.

'You know Marlo, at times I had the strangest feeling about Bill. Have you ever experienced déjà vu?'

Déjà vu. That compelling sense of familiarity when encountering the unfamiliar. A surreal experience and one I have read about just recently. Some unscientific theory to do with alcohol and the slowing down of the brain that gives a small discrepancy in time. The moment lived, is relived.

'Perhaps you *had* met him,' I say, preferring the practical approach.

'I asked him once but he said no.' He moves his glass in little circles on the tablecloth, his eyes following the track. 'I feel for you, Marlo, you know . . . so soon after Jenny. I'm sorry.'

'Yes, I know.' I put my hand on his and the movement stops. Harold is apologising for breaching the barrier of silence we have set up between us. I'm not sure how or when the barrier was instated exactly but, some time in the last year, both of us stopped referring to the death of my aunt and, as a consequence, to almost any death. I don't know if it's healthy, but at the time it seemed necessary. Too much of my life had been given over to it. Too many of my thoughts. Yet it is not to Jenny that my thoughts turn now but to this recent death and the memory of blood on a pale face and a single staring eye. I stand up, suddenly restless, disconcerted by it all. This is something I learnt with Jenny's death – how unwieldy it is, the horror of it sneaking up on you time and time again. I turn away from Harold and start stacking the plates together on the tray. A knife clatters to the floor.

'Will you sleep?' I ask, briskly. Harold looks at me for a moment. His face is not quite so ashen now.

'With enough brandy I sleep through anything. Would you like to stay over, Marlo?' His tone is very even, careful about appearing needy.

'I've got the dog to see to.' I pick up the knife and my voice is muffled. 'Why don't you come back with me.'

He hesitates a moment. 'No. I'm better on my own, but thanks.'

He insists on calling a taxi to take me home and we wait for it together, looking out from his first-floor windows.

'You know, Marlo, I have the feeling that with Bill's death, there is more to come.'

I turn to him surprised.

'In what way?'

'With Bill, there was something... that wasn't quite right. I've talked to enough homeless people in my life. Working where we do, you can hardly avoid them.'

Harold wouldn't do so anyway. He is the most sociable of men, finding pleasure in the conversations he strikes up with a wide variety of people. Until recently, the Flagstaff Gardens had been used by lots of homeless men, residents of a nearby hostel, who used to sit out in the park on sunny days. The hostel is closed now and the tide of residents has dried up. Harold is one of the few who has missed them.

'There is always the stamp of homelessness, that evidence of living rough that you can't avoid, but with Bill it wasn't quite there. He was scruffy enough but somehow... I don't think it was long term.'

'I never really noticed.' But this was something I couldn't possibly have seen from my office window. All I had seen were the obvious, outward things – the man in grey clothing, his hat pulled down, his collar pulled up and the rash of thin grey stubble. And that odd air of watchfulness.

'I wondered, at times, if he was playing some sort of role.'

'It's not a role many people would want to take on, especially in winter. What did the police say?'

He hesitates before answering. 'I didn't say much, Marlo,

8

because it's just speculation, nothing I know for a fact.'

The taxi arrives in a little rush of light and I feel a pang of guilt at leaving Harold. But he nods at me and I gather my things, anxious for silence and my own space.

Ebony meets me at the door with her customary delight, her paws scrabbling on the polished floor boards as she dances around me. She has been on her own for too long. I feed her and let her out into the back garden while I make tea and wander through the house.

It is a small place but in Jenny's day there was a spacious feel to it, a simplicity that was engaging. I haven't changed anything since moving in, save to bring a few pieces of my own — a photo of Mum's, a desk squashed into the lounge room, an extra, unused TV. Nothing much, but enough to clutter things up and add a discordant, jarring note.

I hadn't intended going on my normal nightly run — it is late and I am tired — but it is the wrong kind of tiredness for sleep. That earlier listlessness has evaporated and now I am restless and unsettled. If Harold's sleeping potion is brandy, mine is exercise. Every night, I run kilometres, welcoming the fatigue that exercise brings, the physical tiredness that allows me to sleep.

But tonight the run does only half its work. I wake in the early hours with images of the previous day flickering through my mind, like stills from an unsequenced film. Bill Diamond's staring, sightless eye. The trail of blood on his face. And, with this new death, my mind springs inevitably to those other, older deaths. Jenny's face on the pillow. Cate. The thoughts and emotions that have spun through my mind relentlessly over the past year come rolling back in like a dense, cold fog.

I spend some unproductive hours consoling myself with the thought that Bill Diamond's death has nothing to do with me. The death of a stranger is a long way from the death of a much loved aunt. In a few days, I tell myself, it will have faded into the past, lodged somewhere in my mind as a difficult but remote incident. Good advice perhaps, but sleep remains elusive and when daylight rims the curtains, the images of death are with me still.

Chapter 3

I take Ebony for our usual morning walk, feeling dry-eyed and tired through lack of sleep. The day is cold but clear and my breath escapes in little clouds of vapour, while out to sea, behind the breakwater, a tanker slides silently towards the city. Even this early, the running track is busy with people walking, running or skating. Ebony runs ahead of me on mysterious missions of her own but circles back constantly, keeping me in view.

As I walk, my thoughts linger with a grim inevitability on the events of the past year. Jenny's death and my cousin Cate's. The inheritance of Jenny's house. The distance that I have put between myself, my family and most of my friends in that time. Even my cricket career seems to be on hold.

As an antidote to depression I muster up a mental inventory of the people I have kept up with, or who have kept up with me, over these difficult months. Harold, of course. Alicia, friend and neighbour, with her steady supply of comedies on video and general good sense. My cousin Lucy's regular weekly visits that I look forward to more and more. Lee's frequent but random appearancess that always seem like a gust of invigorating air. The difficulty with Lee, I tell myself, is that she always says what she thinks.

On one of her recent visits, wandering through the house as I did last night, her heels tapping on the floor boards, she turned to me impatiently and said, 'What is this, Marlo, some kind of shrine to Jenny?'

It took me a moment to catch her drift.

'The house.' Her voice softened slightly. 'You haven't changed anything. This house is still much more Jenny's than yours.'

'Yes, I suppose so. I haven't decided . . .'

'Do you think that's what Jenny would want?'

'No. Of course not. I just haven't got round to it yet.' To change things you need purpose and energy and both these qualities have been sadly lacking in recent times.

'Move in with me again, Marlo.' Her tone was light. 'I could do with some company and you could do with a change of scene.'

I had already tried that with Tony – a disaster for both of us. To live with people you need some degree of sociability and consideration. When I refused, Lee turned away, brittle and brisk. Somewhere beneath the layers of self-preoccupation, I realised that I had hurt her.

'Self-pity, Marlo. It doesn't suit you.'

When we reach the life-saving club at Middle Park, my thoughts are still gloomy. I stop and call Ebony and she bounds towards me, pushing her head against my hand. I hug her for a moment, glad of the contact. Ebony is another one I should add to my list of safeguards. We retrace our steps. Out to sea, the tanker has cleared the breakwater and, along the running track, the people that make up the morning procession have changed and moved on.

At work I am the first one in and, after last night, the office is comfortingly normal. The phone is ringing on Irene's desk and I let it go through to voice mail.

My office is next door to Harold's and shares the same view

that I had looked out on the previous evening. A partition used to separate our desks but six months ago it was replaced by solid walls. This was Harold's idea, citing reasons of privacy. His privacy or mine, I'm not sure, but now you have to consciously listen in to hear the other person's conversations, whereas before, you had to tune them out. Anyway, he was right – the new walls are more private.

Across the road, in the Flagstaff Gardens, the police cordon is still in place and so is some of the activity. No ambulances now, but plenty of police. A group of cars is parked in the main entrance to the park, some marked, some not. Despite all this, there is a different, lighter feel to the park in sunshine.

I check the day's appointments and the documents that go with them and hear Harold and Irene on the staircase from the street. Harold's voice is a low monologue, broken here and there by Irene's questions. It is not hard to guess the topic of conversation. Harold walks in first. Behind him Irene is small and light with stiff grey hair above subdued clothing and sturdy shoes. I look at Harold curiously, wondering how he slept. His face is paler than usual, his eyes are tired, and the usual pink glow to his skin hasn't returned. I'm not surprised. I know all about waking up in the night, wide-eyed and staring.

Harold looks relieved to see me and breaks off his conversation with Irene. 'I'm glad you're here, Marlo. I've got something I wanted to run past you.'

He doesn't see the change in Irene's expression. Her mouth tightens suddenly and her eyes lose interest and animation. She turns away.

'Morning, Irene,' I say.

'Marlo.' She puts her bag in the bottom drawer of her desk and slides into her chair.

I follow Harold into his office. He closes the door and crosses to the window, looking out at the park momentarily as I had done earlier.

'I know who Bill Diamond is, at least I think I do.' His words are slightly rushed. 'Remember the sense of déjà vu we

13

spoke about? I couldn't remember last night but I guess there's nothing like a murder to galvanise the thought process.'

He moves from window to desk and back again, restless and uneasy.

'Go on,' I say, torn between curiousity and concern. In my experience Harold is rarely restless.

'I never realised in all the time we talked together in the park but I think I actually knew him thirty years ago. I should have remembered because people talked about him enough. When I lived in Burrdan Street, he lived a couple of houses down but his name was Bill Stone then.'

'Bill Stone.' I repeat. Stone is a long way from Diamond, but the same general idea. 'Have you told the police?'

He hesitates. 'Not yet. I wanted to see what you thought.'

'About remembering?' I am surprised. The problem doesn't seem a large one. In the front office I can hear Irene typing, the patter of the keyboard as comforting as the sound of rain on a roof.

I move to the window. Across the road, the police are still there, a little group of suits and uniforms, heads bent together, consulting.

Harold hesitates. 'I thought it might look suspicious, suddenly remembering like that. I spent a lot of last night thinking about being the one who finds a murder victim, and not just anyone, but someone I knew in the past.'

'Suspicious?' I echo, amazed at where his thoughts have taken him. He must see the incredulity on my face because he stops pacing suddenly and put his hand on my shoulder. 'Well thank you, Marlo, for that.'

'Harold, you are the last person anyone would think capable of murder. And anyway, you can hardly be expected to remember everyone who lived near you in the past.'

'Think so? Well, let's hope the police see it that way.'

'They'd be mad to see it any other way.' I say it so crisply that he smiles.

'Tell me about Bill Stone. Why did people talk about him?'

It is hard to shift perspective and see that grey and distant man as young, with an interesting life.

'As I remember, the rumours were different depending on who you talked to. Some people said he had another woman and went off with her. Others said he kept one step in front of the police, either because he was involved in minor crime or because he'd lost his temper and put someone in hospital.'

'Interesting choice,' I comment. 'What did you think?'

He shrugs. 'I know he was involved in some sort of minor crime because one night in the pub he offered me a cheap TV. I also know that he left a wife and four children.'

A tram passes in front of us, blocking our view of the park, and when it moves on, the police activity has shifted. Two men in suits stand together on the footpath looking across the road towards us, and a woman in overalls moves towards one of the cars.

'They always come back in daylight, in case they've missed something.'

'How do you know that?' I ask.

'I'm not sure really. Just something I picked up along the way.'

In the front office Irene has stopped typing and the patter of the keyboard is replaced by the whirr of the printer and the scrape of a chair. I think about Bill Stone and that air of watchfulness. The derro who, according to Harold, wasn't one at all.

The two officers cross the road and disappear into the office stairs below us. Beside me, Harold tenses and draws in his breath. 'Well . . . if you wait long enough, it seems they come to you.'

'Harold, I can't see the problem. Last night, when you found Bill Diamond, we were together.'

'Not quite,' he says with the relentless air of someone stripping away all possible comfort. 'You weren't with me when I found him. You were on the footpath, remember? What's to stop the police thinking I had an apoplectic fit and

15

clobbered him when your back was turned?'

'You,' I say firmly, 'and reality. What did Irene say about it?'

'I didn't tell her about knowing who he was. I wanted to talk to you first.'

The outside door opens and closes. Voices sound in the front office, a man's voice followed by Irene's. I am aware of Harold's tension and my own as a response. When Irene opens the office door, her eyes shift from Harold to me and she holds my gaze for a fraction too long. She is curious and I suspect not just about the murder.

'The police are here to see you, Harold,' she announces.

Irene and I have come a long way in recent months but she still has her prickly moments. I understand her better now, having realised belatedly what I should have seen clearly from the start. Irene is in love with Harold and her more acerbic comments are due to her annoyance with the ease of my friendship with him. A complex set of cause and effect that is not without irony because the reason my relationship with Harold is so easy is precisely because there is no possible chance of any complicating, sexual element.

'Thanks, Irene,' Harold says smoothly. 'Show them in.'

I pat his arm as I leave, stepping around the little crush in the door. One of the officers is an older man, obviously suffering from a severe cold. There are heavy bags under his eyes and he smells of cough sweets and peppermint. Behind him is a younger man, tall, with light brown eyes and pale skin, dressed in a dark grey suit. The older man steps forward and I hear his words before he closes the office door.

'Mr Underwood? We want to talk to you about last night.'

Harold's voice in reply is a low rumble that sounds easy enough but, for all that, I take a deep breath, as though the room is suddenly airless.

'Ms Shaw.' The younger man in the grey suit has not followed his colleague but is standing just behind me.

'Yes.'

'My name is Detective Senior Constable Peter Denton. I

need to talk to you about the statement you made last night.'
He smiles and looks friendly enough. His hair is short and
light brown, almost the same colour as his eyes, and his smile
reveals long, white teeth. Late twenties, perhaps early thirties.

'Come through,' I say. Irene is at her desk, watching us, not
bothering to pretend otherwise.

I offer him a seat at my desk but he moves to the window.
In the park, two uniformed officers remain. One of them is
taking down the blue tape lying like a long ribbon on the
grass. I look up into Peter Denton's assessing gaze. 'You
said in your statement that you heard someone running from
the scene?'

'Yes, and I saw them, but just the briefest glimpse.'

I show him through the window where I had seen the
runner – the dark grey trail of the central footpath that
cuts diagonally through the park from La Trobe Street to
Dudley Street.

'Could they have been running for a train?'

'No.' This is definite. 'They were heading up the hill, away
from the station.'

He is still and very watchful. Below us there is the usual
flow of cars but a couple of trucks build up speed from the
lights and a tram rumbles past, its trolley poles in line with the
window. Denton looks dubious and I guess that he is assessing
the possibility of hearing footsteps against the solid noise of
traffic. If I couldn't possibly hear someone running, how
reliable is my sighting? He doesn't say it, but he doesn't have
to. I answer the unspoken comment.

'I know what I saw.'

There is a small moment of consideration before he speaks.
'When did you meet Bill Stone?'

'I didn't meet him. I first noticed him just over a week
ago in the park, talking with Harold.' I told the police this
last night.

'And did Harold talk about him much?'

'Not really. Nothing of interest, save that he'd met him.'

17

'Do you know if Bill carried a wallet?'

I stifle a sigh. If I hadn't known him, how could I possibly know about his belongings? 'No idea. Is it important?'

'We're not sure. There are a few things that don't fit the image of a homeless person.'

I don't tell him about this morning's conversation as this is probably what Harold will be going through now.

'He had a wallet with him that contained a driver's licence and some money but the wallet was in a pouch under his arm. We wondered if he had another wallet, a dummy to cover daily expenses,' Denton explains.

'I have no idea.'

He changes tack. 'We have a few witnesses to an argument in the park last night.'

'Really? I didn't hear an argument. When we were there, it was very quiet.' I remember the sense of isolation as almost a physical thing. Voices, even voices raised in argument, would have been welcome.

'You didn't hear Bill Stone call out?'

'No,' I say, but feel the need to explain that Harold had been talking, and he was the one on the park side of the footpath.

He nods slightly. 'Fair enough, but if you think of anything else, please let me know.' He closes his notebook with a little snap and passes me a card.

I take it from him and he closes my door. In the front office, Irene asks him a question, her tone bright with interest. I tune her out and listen in to Harold. His voice is evenly paced and sounds easy enough but the police officer's voice is a brief grunt in reply.

Eventually, in Harold's office, chairs scrape and I hear the policemen leaving, then see them emerge in the street below. The older man who had talked to Harold heads to the unmarked car and sits in the passenger seat. Peter Denton exchanges some comment with a female officer, laughing at something she has said, his face lit up. She touches him lightly on the arm before the police car drives away.

18

I watch for a moment, wondering about the exchange they had made. There was a light friendliness about them that seemed out of place in the circumstances but, I remind myself, this investigation is all routine to them.

Harold comes into my office and we spend a few minutes with a 'he said, I said', type of conversation, going through our separate police interviews – not that mine amounts to much. Harold's went further, back to the old days, to the street in Ashburton, to Bill Stone, the married man with four children and an interesting selection of rumours.

'I wonder where he went at night?' I say. 'Hard to see him booking into a hotel.'

'He didn't sleep in the park,' Harold says, 'because he wasn't there in the early mornings.'

'No,' I agree. 'And why Diamond?' I ask, picking up an earlier thought. 'If his name was Stone, why call himself Diamond?' This part of the puzzle is appealing, focusing in on the academic, rather than the reality of a death. Harold doesn't comment.

'What did you talk about in the park?'

'Not much really. Politics and sport and the places he'd been. Perth and Broome and up and down the west coast. He hadn't been back in Victoria all that long – not that he said so – but he talked about the gardens here and how he'd forgotten how green things were in Victoria.'

If the gardens are green, it is not the result of natural rainfall but a sustained programme of artificial watering. This winter is a continuation of a protracted dry spell, the fourth year in a row of below average rainfall. These statistics and the threat of impending water restrictions are being referred to more and more often in the media.

'Anyway,' Harold's face gives little away, 'I got the strong impression that the Detective Sergeant doesn't much like coincidences.'

'They happen all the time. Life isn't all that tidy.'

'Like a homeless man with a stack of money?'

19

'Well . . . you said there'd be more to come.'

'The things I say, Marlo,' he says, with a welcome return to lightness. 'The more things you predict, the more chance you have of being right – the secret is to spread your net widely.'

My door opens and Harold and I turn at the same time. Irene's pale eyes flick between us, interested, curious.

'Harold, there's a call about the Dawson settlement this afternoon. I'm not sure of the details.' Her voice is brisk, no nonsense.

'Thanks, Irene. I'll take it in my office.'

Irene follows him out and I turn back to the window.

Chapter 4

Across the road, the park assumes an everyday normality. The sun shines benignly on the bare branches of ancient elm and oak, softening tree trunks and glinting on the sweep of grass. Already people are drifting in, unaware of last night's drama and the recent departure of the police. A woman with a pram. An office worker with a briefcase. A young couple, settling on to a distant park bench. A gardener in dark blue overalls standing with his back towards me. A jogger dressed in shorts and t-shirt.

I think about the runner from last night that Peter Denton dismissed so readily. The jogger I watch now is making heavy work of the uphill stretch towards Dudley Street, a long way from the fleeting moment of speed I glimpsed yesterday.

Despite the appearance of normality, some echo of disquiet remains in the park. Inspired by the desire to capture this atmosphere of doubt and unease, I get my camera out and take a series of photos. Perhaps I even hope that in some way I may be able to capture serenity in the simple process of framing shots and deciding on angle and focus.

My phone rings and I get caught up in a series of demands that take all my time and attention. In between phone calls, the morning is spent on work for a nearby accountant, tracking down details of property ownership in Victoria and arranging for agents in other states and territories to do the same for a bankrupt estate with regard to a Peter Norman Jenkins. After lunch, I keep my list of appointments in the city. A property settlement at the Stock Exchange Building followed by transfers at the Titles Office and a collection of writs to be lodged at different courts.

I used to enjoy my job but now, as with other things, I am not sure. The routines and variety that I liked in the past strike me now as tedious and predictable. The sense of purpose I felt moving around the city has slid into lethargy, as has the fun of socialising with people along the way. Now I find it hard to take an interest in lives that seem so different from mine, engrossed as they are with varying mixes of romance and children, holidays and football.

It's not the job that has changed but me. I'm in a rut and I am aware from time to time of the need to move on. I have even explored a couple of options in the form of a legal practice course at university and the offer to coach in a 'Cricket-in-Schools' programme a friend administers. Part-time study. Part-time work. Both options appeal to me but too distantly to muster enough energy and clarity to do anything about them.

When I catch up with Harold in the afternoon, his mood is different. More resolute somehow, as though this morning's fears have evaporated. He is at his desk, looking comfortable and relaxed.

'I've tracked down Bill Stone's daughter. She was the first number I tried in the phone book and she's coming in to see me.' He sounds pleased, like a child with a present. 'And I've been to see Shane Black.'

Shane Black is a legal executive who, when I began working

22

with Harold, worked for a large legal firm in La Trobe Street. He moved state a few years ago but has returned recently and now works in the Committal Advocacy area of the Office of Public Prosecutions in Lonsdale Street. Harold meets up with him from time to time in legal and social circles — various courts along the way, the pub at lunch times.

In another life I used to enjoy clever exchanges with Shane Black — a kind of running commentary of flippant remarks that was more like a verbal sparring match than a conversation. Not something I feel up to in my present state of mind.

'And you caught up with him because . . . ?'

'Just a chat really. We focused on motivation and how, without it, the police are reluctant to bring a case.'

'Against who?'

'Me, of course,' Harold replies.

'Harold . . .' I begin, but he must read my thoughts because his expression takes on a slightly sheepish look.

'I know.' He holds his hands up in protest and leans back in his chair, casting his eyes towards the ceiling. 'All I can say is that it's different when it's you.'

'Yes, I know. And I guess, with Bill Stone, at least the police can rule out greed as a motive.'

'Can they?' He leans forward. 'He had money, Marlo, lots of money tucked away.'

'But the money was still on him,' I argue. 'On the surface he was homeless and broke.'

'Yes, he was. Puzzling isn't it? The derro with money in his wallet . . .' He shrugs and trails off. 'He asked after you, Marlo.'

'Who?' My mind is still with Bill Stone.

Harold waits for me to look up. 'Shane Black.' He says the name slowly and with emphasis.

'He was pleased to see me, Marlo, but he was more interested in you. He said he'd rung you when he first got back, a few months ago now.'

'Yes,' I say, vaguely remembering a phone message that I hadn't bothered to return.

'He wanted to know how you are.'

I am surprised at his interest. In the months since the phone call, I don't think I've given him a thought. But Harold ploughs on against my lack of enthusiasm.

'He asked how the cricket was going. He said he would like to come and watch you play.'

Shane Black was one of the people in my working circle who had always shown an interest in my sporting career. I remember his delight when I made State level. It was translated into drinks and celebrations, and now I feel slightly guilty at my lack of effort in his regard. I pick up a pen and fiddle with it.

'What did you say?'

'That it is winter now, that you still play for Victoria and that last season wasn't your best.'

A kind way of putting it.

'I said you'd been busy and I'd let you know that we had spoken.'

I look at Harold for a long moment. 'Do you do this often Harold?'

'What exactly?' He meets the challenge face on.

'Make excuses for me. Try to organise my social life.'

Harold hesitates momentarily, his eyes watchful. 'It's no big deal, Marlo. I thought it might be fun for you to meet up with him. You used to get on well as I remember.'

'Yes, we did,' I admit. Past tense. 'A long time ago.'

'Ring him, Marlo. What harm can it do? And right now, he could use a friend.'

I drift back to my office and pick up the photo of the State team that has been sitting on my desk for years now. I hardly notice it any more. It is a conventional team photo, the players graded by height. I am in the back row. I stare curiously at my own image, aware that in the photo I look different – younger and happier. I know that my original dream to achieve national status is still in me somewhere. I am aware of it as a subterranean stream that will surface randomly at unexpected moments before slowly fading again. But for the dream to have survived the recent upheaval shows its strength.

The State games begin in October and are both competitive games and trials for the national team. Two months away. I have two months in which to gather the necessary energy and direction to apply myself to the selection process. Fitness, at least, is no trouble. I am as fit now as I have ever been – those nightly runs have seen to that. But mentally I am sadly lacking. I push the thought away as I have done so many times.

The noise of the fax machine springing into life breaks my reverie. The fax is from the agent we use in New South Wales, with details of property ownership for Peter Norman Jenkins. That means I now have information in from two states, with four states and two territories still to come. I add the information to the file I have started and get caught up in the demands of the working day.

'By the way,' Harold says, as we are getting ready to leave. 'I'm having dinner with Shane tonight, just a quick bite on the way home, if you'd like to come? The usual place.'

I laugh. Harold is obviously very determined.

'Count me out, Harold. I've got cricket practice.'

'How's it going?' Harold asks.

I tidy some documents away into the out-tray and consider my answer. 'The same as usual.' I don't add to this that it is like playing through a layer of plastic sheeting, like being dragged down by heavy weights. The feeling is so strong that at times it seems physical. I go through the motions but, more often than not, my feet seem leaden and my timing is stuffed to hell and back.

'It'll come back, Marlo, give it time.' His tone is very even, careful of my reaction.

'Yes. Of course.'

At least there is no sting of tears to blink away, as there was a year ago, and I am obscurely pleased at this. Lack of tears must surely indicate progress, must show that I am at last beginning to come to terms with everything.

'Harold, when you see Shane, tell him he can come and watch me play if he wants to.'

He raises a eyebrow. 'Those words exactly, Marlo? That level of enthusiasm?'

I smile, realising how it must sound. 'No, of course not. I'll ring him myself.'

The weekly winter indoor training session. Batters pitted against the bowlers in the nets. The full-on flurry of attack from different bowling styles. Lately I have been put up against the spinners as much as possible, a consequence of some perceived area of weakness in my game. I don't agree but don't argue the point. It is not just the spin bowlers I have trouble with and I might as well work on spin as anything else.

Tonight I am not as leaden as I have been at other times but I am still a long way from fluid, and nowhere near where I would like to be. The buzz of conversation of the players sweeps over me after the session but I make myself participate, smile and engage. As I linger in the changing room after the others have gone, too lethargic and dispirited to go home, I can hear a voice in the corridor outside. It is instantly recognisable – a selector who has always shown an interest in my career. Their disappointment is articulate.

'Is it nerves, do you think, or lack of fitness? It was like watching a different player, and a dull one at that.'

Another voice, in response, that I don't recognise, lower, but not so low that I don't catch her words.

'Not fitness, no. I heard there was a death in her family and she hasn't quite . . .' The footsteps move on and the voices fade.

Not physical fitness. A dull mind translating into dull strokes. A grim hanging in that shows little flair and absolutely no pleasure. Whatever I do, I have to shake myself out of this.

Chapter 5

I wake before dawn but not, thankfully, in the dead, early hours. I shower and make tea and toast, and listen to the news that gives way to a police appeal for witnesses to an 'incident' in the Flagstaff Gardens. I stop chewing and listen intently, the toast suspended in my hand. There is a brief listing of times and places and a description of the dead man, but no name, which surprises me. Afterwards I put my plate in the sink and head out with Ebony on our usual morning walk, taking the camera with me.

No sunshine today but a low raft of cloud and a muted glare off the sea. The day is cold and still, and I am pleased by the unusual light. Photography is the one area of my life that I have improved on since Jenny's death. It offers both an artistic challenge and the pleasures of isolation. It was a passion of Mum's too, and also a means of escape from a difficult marriage. The pleasure I feel now helps me to understand her more, and makes me feel closer to her somehow.

Lately I have been concentrating increasingly on line and the effects of light, experimenting with shutter speeds and apertures, trying to capture and enhance a mood. These are images I can see more and more clearly in my mind's eye, before the film is developed. At weekends sometimes I search out places further afield, usually around Port Phillip Bay, the sea baths at Brighton, with their extensive rusting poles or the red cliffs at Mentone. Today, I take photos of St Kilda pier stretching out into a pale grey sea. The only movement in the scene before me is a solitary gull and someone checking out the rubbish bins. Not Bill Stone, or Bill Diamond, but for a sudden jarring moment, I thought it was. I spare a sympathetic thought for Harold. Déjà vu and all that.

I take a surreptitious photo and think about clothing in terms of camouflage and disguise. There is not much of any individual that is apparent beneath the shapeless garments of a vagrant. But there is more to it than this. Most people, save for the Harolds of this world, are uncomfortable in the presence of difference. They avert their eyes and keep their distance. Adopting vagrant clothing, as Bill Stone had done, gives a person a kind of invisibility.

I think about the things I have learned in the last two days about Bill Stone. A man with money in his wallet and a daughter that Harold has made contact with. I imagine him visiting various second-hand shops, buying clothes for the part, and wonder what it was in his life that had made him want to disappear.

I am first in at work. There is a faint fragrance to the place that I hadn't expected but remember from the other night – the spring-like scent of jonquils. There are no flowers though. We all buy them from time to time but there are long periods of time when no one does. Someone's perfume perhaps. Not mine, because I never wear it. Irene wears something occasionally, but it's not something I associate with jonquils or spring. For that matter Harold's habitual aftershave is always the same. My phone rings and I get caught up with work.

For most of the morning I am out attending settlements,

lodging documents at the Supreme Court and Titles Office. More faxes have come through from agents in other states on the bankruptcy matter I am working on and I add the details to the file. Later I catch up on some phone calls, Shane Black's among them, and accept, in a moment of inattention and surprise, an invitation for lunch.

Before I leave, Bill Stone's daughter arrives in the office. She is slim with hair in various shades of blonde shaped around her face. The only bright colour about her is the green scarf that she wears around her neck, the same green as her eyes. She looks both affluent and self-assured. Her scent is a strong one, not jonquils though, but something more complex.

'My name is Rosalyn Stone,' she says in a cool, controlled voice. 'I'm looking for Harold Underwood.'

Harold must hear her because he comes out of his office, hands outstretched, smiling.

'Rosalyn. I would have known you anywhere.' The smile sounds in his voice.

'And you.' They link hands and look at each other for a long time.

Harold speaks first. 'I'm sorry that we have to meet again under such circumstances.'

'Yes.' She nods briskly as if to shake the circumstances away. 'But thank you for ringing. It was a pleasure to get a friendly call. You've hardly changed, Harold.'

'In thirty years? Thank you, but I think I have! You're the one who's hardly changed.'

I move away, feeling like an intruder. Good manners are very much part of Harold's make up but this greeting is gushing and, to me at least, slightly sickening.

'Marlo.' Harold's voice is light with pleasure. 'This is Rosalyn Stone. Rosalyn, this is my partner, Marlo Shaw. She was with me ... when I found your father.'

'I'm pleased to meet you.' Rosalyn keeps the smile despite the oblique reference to her father's death. Her eyes are appraising and her hand in my own is soft and warm and faintly clinging. I have the sudden desire to wipe my fingers down my trousers.

Irene arrives back with a bag of shopping and a rush of cold air. She too must sense the warmth because she hesitates and looks at me, as if out of her depth. I haven't seen her today and notice that her eyes are slightly pink as though she has been crying, and her skin is dull and grey. For a fleeting moment I feel complete sympathy with her.

'Irene, I don't think you ever met Rosalyn Stone in the old days. Rosalyn lived in Burrdan Street, a few doors away from me, but back then she wasn't much more than a child.'

'I don't think we've met,' Irene says hesitantly, taking Rosalyn in with a careful glance and moving forward to shake her hand.

There is no obvious hesitation or shrinking away and the conversation sweeps back to the past that Harold and Rosalyn and, to some unknown extent, Irene, shared in Ashburton.

I listen in because my knowledge of Harold's past has been mainly gleaned through other people: Jenny before she died and Alicia, my friend and neighbour, who invites him over sometimes for traditional Polish meals. I know nothing of Harold from Irene and have no idea how far they go back. They have never told me about the past – Harold because he's like that, Irene because she hardly talks to me at all.

Rosalyn is both animated and charming, sparkling in Harold's company. For someone whose father has just died, she looks amazingly unconcerned. I know Harold is attractive to women. I have seen enough evidence of it from the older women in my life and understand it all too well. Even in my own life, there have been odd moments, especially in the last year, when I have wished him thirty years younger.

Harold has had enough of introductions and small talk. 'Would you like some morning tea Rosalyn? There's a little café down the road that makes good coffee.'

Harold makes good coffee in the small kitchen at the back and I assume it is privacy rather than coffee that he desires. He picks up his folders for the afternoon settlements he has booked in and I suspect we won't see him for some time.

Shane Black is both similar and different from how I remember him. His features and build are the same – a slim man marginally shorter than me, with dark hair and pale skin. He has always been slight but there is a new wispiness about him, as though he has lost weight. His eyes are the same clear blue but there is a fan of lines around each one that either wasn't there the last time we met or wasn't quite so deeply etched. I revise my estimate of his age. I had thought twenties; now I think thirties. There is a comfort in the thought that he never actually knew Jenny, so it is possible he will not ask about the events of last year.

He orders calamari and a glass of red and I order chicken focaccia and orange juice because drinking wine at lunch time makes me fall asleep.

'So, you've been away?' I ask, directing the conversation to his travels.

He tells me something of his time in Perth but is much quieter than I remember. I sense more interest in me than before and perhaps less in himself. Not so much of the challenge of earlier times, and no tendency to spar.

Lunch is easier than I expected, simply because Shane keeps it going with anecdotes of his time away and some of the bizarre things that happened to him. There is a wry humour in his stories and his delivery, but his face is very still. I remember both the humour and the stillness from past meetings, and the lack of fidgeting that always struck me as admirable.

'How's Harold?' He asks after a while.

My thoughts turn to Harold and I wonder how his coffee with Rosalyn is going. 'Better after seeing you. He was shaken by the murder but finding a dying man is not an easy thing for anyone.'

'No.' He sips his wine. 'I know this is a slightly batty thing to say, but Harold is his own walking innocence.'

'Yes,' I agree, warming to Shane as a consequence and realising just how much Harold must have opened up.

'It's interesting that he is still befriending the homeless. I remember, before I left, that he used to have a little band of them.'

'There's not many around any more. They closed the hostel last year.'

'Yes, I heard that.'

We drift on to the mystery of Bill Stone: the things that don't make sense, the vagrant who wasn't.

'Harold said you were interested in it.'

'Only because it's intriguing. Things that don't quite add up are always intriguing.' I change the subject. 'Harold says you're interested in watching a cricket match.'

'Yes, I'd like to.'

'There's not much on for the moment,' I say. 'Only a couple of practice games before the State games in October.'

My mouth dries at the thought. Two months, I had told myself. It suddenly seems like no time at all and, more to the point, I have no idea how to overcome the general areas of lack I am painfully aware of.

I check my watch. An hour has passed and I have appointments to keep.

'Nice to see you, Marlo.' Shane says, standing up with me.

'And you,' I reply, meaning it, and vaguely surprised about the pleasantness of the meeting.

For an entire hour my thoughts have stayed on the moment at hand. I turn to watch him walk away. A slight figure in well cut clothing, darting across at the lights.

When I get back to the office, Harold is still out and Irene is reading the morning paper, her attention somewhere in the middle pages. She doesn't look up when I pass, but comes to my office later with a complicated query she needs help with. She is her brisk efficient self but her eyes are still pink. She hesitates when arrangements have been discussed and agreed upon.

'Harold's friend is a charming woman.'

I'm not sure about Irene's emotional state or what she wants me to say, but there is no point in evading it. 'Harold seemed to think so.'

'Yes, he did.' She nods agreement. Her voice is brisker and tighter but nothing more than this. 'Well, it can be pleasant to meet up with old friends.'

I look after her, momentarily distracted by her acceptance of Harold's visitor, and compare it to my own reaction earlier – that instant springing dislike.

I am packing up for the night when Harold gets back. It is almost half past five.

'Marlo, I'm glad I caught you. Rosalyn has invited us both to tea tomorrow night as a thank you for helping out when we did. Will you come?' He sounds both doubtful and hopeful. In the last year I have rejected most of the invitations that have come my way, not wanting to bother or, conversely, not wanting to inflict myself on others. I voice the obvious opposition. 'I'm sure having people over for dinner is the last thing they feel like doing.'

'On the contrary, Rosalyn likes entertaining. She said having us for dinner would do them all good.' The hopeful expectation on his face is enough. In the light of what I owe Harold in terms of support over the past year, it would be churlish to refuse.

'Well then, if she's sure, I'd like to.'

'Good. Six-thirty tomorrow night.'

He shows me her card – a pale lemon linen with ornate green lettering that looks both stylish and professional. It is not a business card, though, because the address is a home address and there is nothing to indicate her line of work. *Rosalyn Stone. 7 Blair Street, Brighton.*

The flush of pleasure on Harold's face has intensified. It is surprising what an attractive woman and a decent lunch can do. He must notice my dubious look.

'I told her what happened on the night. My part and yours.'

'Was she OK with it all?' I ask. Surely this must have been a difficult conversation but, knowing Harold, he will have carried it off as well as anyone could.

'I think so. It's always better to know than to wonder.' And remember, her father abandoned her so she didn't really know him.

'Yes, of course.'

There is something in his voice that makes me hesitate. 'Are you sure you want me there tomorrow night?'

He looks puzzled. 'I've said so, haven't I?'

'Yes, but it's you Rosalyn's interested in. I'm sure if I didn't go, Rosalyn would be delighted.'

'Marlo, Marlo.' Harold shakes his head in mock disapproval and slides his arm through mine. 'You sell yourself short every time. They will be lucky to have you as a guest.'

'It's not that, Harold,' I say, smiling. 'I don't want to cramp your style.'

We head down the stairs to the street, both of us on our way to Flagstaff Station and on to Melbourne Central. Me to a number sixteen tram down Swanston Street to St Kilda. Home to the dog, something quick and easy to cook, and a long, exhausting run. Harold to a restaurant in the centre of the city to meet a friend for dinner.

It occurs to me, on my run, that whatever negative thoughts I have about Rosalyn and her invitation, meeting up with Bill Stone's family will be interesting, if nothing else. I wonder which of the four children he left thirty years ago will be there and what light his family will throw on the mystery of their father.

Chapter 6

Harold picks me up on the way, as my house is in between his and Rosalyn's. It makes sense, he says, and I can't argue, but I have a feeling that he is also making sure I get there. He knows nothing of my change of heart, that strong thread of curiosity that has changed my clothes, styled my hair, and dug out appropriate shoes.

My outfit is the same as when Lee and I last had dinner together. I also wore it when Alicia had insisted that I come out with her, two opera tickets bought especially for the occasion. It is simple enough but stylish and more frivolous than the regulation suits and jackets or shapeless running gear that Harold has been treated to in the past year.

'Marlo, you look great.' He stares at me in such open surprise that I laugh.

Harold has dressed up too, in soft pale grey fabrics, offset with that particular shade of blue that brings out the colour in his eyes. He looks expensive and well dressed, and the pink glow from yesterday is still in his cheeks, his expression cherubic as usual. Between us there is a pleasant buzz of anticipation.

The first sight of Rosalyn's house doesn't surprise me. It is a large, double-storeyed house that occupies almost the entire block of land and incorporates a carport at the side. There are two cars in the carport – a dull gold Mazda and an old sky-blue station wagon. No cars at the front. The garden is small and neat, edged with dark, low-growing conifers that form a precise, even hedge.

Rosalyn greets us at the front door, and the light from the porch gleams in her streaky blonde hair. She is wearing a close-fitting dress in soft cream with a fold of brilliant orange-red silk around the neckline. She looks both welcoming and stylish. 'Harold. Marlo,' she says in her cool, controlled voice. 'Come through. You can leave your coats in the spare room.'

We walk down a long hallway that opens onto a living area at the back of the house. 'This part is the only modern bit,' Rosalyn explains, more to Harold than to me. 'We renovated it just before my husband died, three years ago now. I haven't had the money to spare or the inclination since.'

'I didn't know about your husband,' Harold says. 'I'm sorry.'

'There's a whole lifetime to catch up with, Harold. I'm looking forward to it.'

Harold's reaction to this invitation is obvious. His face is very still but the flush of pleasure intensifies and his cheeks are glowing.

The back section of the house is a large open space, divided into a lounge, dining room and long galley-style kitchen. A wall of windows looks out onto a small garden filled with ferns, glossy leafed creepers and camellias, all enclosed by a high wall. There is no sign of any other houses and I suspect that beyond the wall is the sea. I suspect that the upstairs windows have spectacular bay views. I suspect that the house is worth a fortune.

The lounge part of this vast room has a glassed-in wood fire and deep armchairs. A man and a woman break off their conversation and stand up to greet us. The man's face is familiar but I'm not sure where from. There is a sense that we are interrupting something important. Their smiles are too bright, too welcoming, masking something else entirely. It's impossible to tell exactly what. Strain perhaps, or grief.

'This is my sister, Kristin,' Rosalyn says.

Kristin is a large woman, tall and solidly built. Her hair is a tumble of long curls like wood shavings that shine a dark auburn in the firelight. Her face is lined but her clothes give an impression of youth – leggings beneath a wispy skirt, and a colourful bolero jacket made up of odd patches of silk over a black t-shirt. On her feet are solid, heavy boots with silver toe caps. I wonder what Rosalyn makes of her sister's style of dress.

'Ros was very excited to meet up with you again, Harold, but I'm not sure I remember you. It was before my time.' A joke against the oldies and everyone smiles. Kristin's face is slightly flushed, but whether it is from the warmth of the room or the empty wine glass that she puts down to shake Harold's hand, I'm not sure.

'It was a long time ago,' Harold agrees and his glance crosses Rosalyn's in a look of intimacy that for a brief dazzling second excludes everyone else in the room. I think of Irene's long-term interest in Harold and know, in one of those jarring moments of complete certainty, that her cause, if she ever had one, is completely lost.

I take a steadying breath, aware of things rushing past.

It was only yesterday Harold met up with Rosalyn again. Only yesterday they shared a meal. Can people fall in love so quickly? My own love affairs have been almost invariably slow, torturous things. One step forward, two steps back.

'My brother, Samuel Stone,' says Rosalyn. 'Sam is a neighbour of yours, Marlo.' I focus on Sam belatedly, confused by where my thoughts have taken me. Harold must have told Rosalyn where I live. Usually Harold is more discreet with other people's business. But then I have never known Harold in love before and people in love tend to be garrulous.

'Pleased to meet you.' Sam is stocky and powerful looking but slightly wooden. He has the same long, oval face and

37

green eyes as his sisters' but his features are more irregular, his face weathered. His grip in my own is firm but rasping, like fine sandpaper.

I am distracted by a figure outside on the paved area. Behind glass the woman seems shadowy and ghost like. I notice her because her hands are constantly moving, making small gestures with the occasional flourish. Suddenly she bows and I realise that she is using a portion of darkened glass as a mirror, studying her movements closely. I can't see her face but I can imagine the concentration that keeps her so involved. The movements start again, the same fluid flow, over and over.

Sam taps at the window and she stops and comes into the lounge room, bringing with her a breeze of evening air. The darkness and the glass have mislead me. She is not a woman, at least not yet, but a child. She is as tall as me but her face and body are very much that of a girl in transition, caught somewhere between childhood and adulthood. The difficult years.

'My niece, Amy,' Rosalyn introduces her. 'You might not remember, Harold, but Amy is Justine's daughter. Justine died six years ago.'

'Pleased to meet you,' says Amy. Her hand in my own is thin and cool. Her brown wavy hair is tied back, and there is a pale scatter of freckles across her nose. She is dressed in faded jeans, worn at the knees and an old loose jumper. She speaks to Harold next. I don't hear what he says but she laughs and relaxes.

We have pre-dinner drinks by the fire and I watch the flames leaping around a log in even spurts, too even for reality, while Rosalyn organises the dinner, designating different jobs to each family member. She is charming and friendly and I find myself wondering about that surge of dislike I felt for her yesterday in the office. How much of my response, I wonder, was to Harold's obvious pleasure in the meeting and to the threat it posed to my relationship with him? Something that feels suspiciously like jealousy. A disturbing thought because it aligns me with Irene and makes me step back from my initial assessment of Rosalyn.

The dining table takes up the entire end section of the room and looks like something out of a magazine with its full complement of dinner ware, crystal glasses, shining cutlery, stiff white serviettes and candle light. A vase of jonquils in the centre gives off a heavy, heady scent. I take my place at the table next to Amy and help myself to a series of dishes – an intricate spinach roulade, crumbed fish, scalloped potatoes and salad. Rosalyn starts the conversational ball rolling.

'Marlo is a cricketer, Amy. She plays for Victoria.'

'*Fantastic.*' Amy's eyes are bright with interest, but her tone changes suddenly as though a disturbing thought has occurred to her. 'I suppose that means you have good hand-eye coordination?'

'Yes, I suppose it does.'

Amy bites her lip and looks down at her plate. I'm not sure what worry I have inadvertently set up. Rosalyn smiles at me and the smile is both friendly and complicit, inviting me to join in her mild exasperation with Amy.

'You're well informed.' I say to Rosalyn, not wanting to take sides against Amy. She lifts her shoulders slightly. Not a shrug exactly but something studied and attractive.

'Your fame follows you.' This remark means nothing and evades the question.

'In what way?' She can either evade again or answer. There is a little glittering to her eyes as she meets my challenge. Annoyance? Amusement? I watch Harold out of the corner of my eye but he looks as relaxed as ever.

'Irene told me yesterday after lunch. I came back with Harold but you were out.'

Rosalyn is the last person I would have thought Irene would give out details of my life to. But she is also charming and I suspect expert in drawing information. She turns to Harold and changes the subject.

'Do you still cook, Harold?'

'Yes, of course.'

She sighs with pleasure. 'I thought you would. It was you I

got my love of cooking from. Even now I can still remember the smells that used to come from your house. To a child who lived on little more than a chop and three veg, your meals always smelled exotic.'

'As I remember, back then, it was all experimentation.'

'Then it was well worth it. I remember coming to your restaurant one night, not just me of course, but the whole family. Do you remember, Harold? It was called The Wooden Spoon and you came out from the kitchen to say hello.'

'The Wooden Spoon,' he says slowly. 'Imagine you remembering that.' He looks disconcerted for a moment but moves on smoothly. 'It wasn't my restaurant, Rosalyn, or my choice of name, just one I managed for a brief time. It was a deliberately down-market affair.' He smiles at me and I smile back. I didn't know Harold had run a restaurant.

The conversation sweeps on to old events, shifting readily enough, but mainly between Harold and Rosalyn. The rest of us are silent. Amy eats her food as though she is starving. Kristin plays with hers and drinks more wine than the rest of us, while Sam eats his food slowly and doggedly. No one makes any reference to Bill Stone, and there are no expressions of grief or glimpses of sorrow. After Jenny's death and in the weeks following Cate's, the various members of my family were awash with it. And on Rosalyn's part there seems to be a kind of pointed avoidance of mentioning her father, almost a touch of rudeness in her domination of subject matter. But, at a guess, I'd say Rosalyn is pretty good at keeping conversations where she wants them.

We are up to dessert when Sam proposes a toast, taking advantage of a lull as dishes are exchanged. 'To Kristin and her recent success.' He looks suddenly much more alive and there is a little stirring of interest around the table. The animation on Sam's face makes me realise where I know him from — he's a stall holder at the Sunday market on the Esplanade, selling bowls and toys and assorted wooden objects. His stall is not far from Alicia's, with her knitted jackets and jumpers.

'Sam . . .' Kristin looks fixedly at him, her face very still, her tone determined. 'This isn't the time.'

He shakes his head. 'I disagree. We need to celebrate what should be celebrated.'

'What is it exactly?' Harold asks, ending the debate.

Sam's face is slightly flushed, a grin hovering. 'It's the big breakthrough. Kristin has just signed a contract for work with a leading theatre company.'

Kristin draws lightly on the table cloth with her fork, watching the faint tracks the tines make in the linen. It is clear she wants no part in the discussion.

Sam falters, but only slightly. 'Kristin makes costumes and props for different productions. She was in Sydney on Monday for a couple of days, signing contracts for a new production.' Rosalyn drops her spoon against her bowl with a little clatter. The sound is unexpectedly loud in the still room and Kristin jumps.

'Congratulations,' Harold says.

Kristin looks up briefly. 'Thank you.' But she shows no pleasure or enjoyment in the attention and the conversation dries up for lack of fuel.

'One thing I did wonder,' I begin, wading into the silence in the room, 'is why your father called himself Bill Diamond?'

Harold's face goes carefully blank as it does when he is surprised – I don't usually blunder in on sensitive topics. Sam's eyes flicker but I can't read with what. Amy looks interested and alert while Kristin doesn't seem to have registered. But Rosalyn looks at me with a flash of pure annoyance that makes me wonder if I have miscalculated how much grief she is feeling. After all, who knows what behaviours people might adopt to hide their feelings. Her determination to keep the conversation firmly in the past, the people and events of Burrdon Street, could be cover for something deeper. Yet even as the thought registers, the hard flash of her eyes and the downward turn of her mouth give me cause to doubt it.

'We don't know, Marlo, but there is a lot about our father

41

we don't know.' She stacks the dishes with an abrupt clatter that sounds final, closing that avenue of thought. Amy looks down but I see her gaze sliding around the table and I'd say she doesn't miss much.

We carry dishes through to the kitchen and, following Sam, I realise that he walks with a pronounced limp, as though one leg is shorter than the other. Kristin disposes of the empties, scrapes food off the plates and heads out of the room. There is something jangling about her, something suppressed that makes me want to follow her through the door. But it is clear that the last thing that Kristin wants to do is to socialise.

While Sam makes coffee, Harold and Rosalyn move to the fire and stand with their backs against the flame. Rosalyn laughs often, the sound rising up in a gentle tinkling sound, like scales on the piano. Harold, by her side, seems utterly content.

Sam passes me a cup of coffee and I take it belatedly, noticing the curious look he gives me.

'I'm sorry about your father,' I say.

'Yes. Thank you.' He looks away pointedly and I sip my coffee. That's twice now that I have been warned off the subject of their father. This time I only seek to express sympathy but the result is the same. I feel ungainly, embarrassed at my lack of tact. Sam seems to sense this and changes the subject.

'I hope you won't mind but Amy has something to show us. I thought it was a good idea for her to go on with it. She's been practicing for ages and it seems a shame to call it off.' There is a faint air of defiance in his tone that suggests opposition from someone.

'I agree,' I say simply. 'Why should I mind?' At the moment, a performance of any kind seems welcome.

We make conversation for a while about the Sunday market in general and his stall in particular. We talk about Amy, who helps him out sometimes, and his son Jason, who couldn't come tonight. I tell him that Alicia, his near neighbour at the market, is also my neighbour and the fact that we have a mutual friend speeds the conversation along. He stops suddenly in mid-sentence. 'Here she is now.' He exchanges a look with Amy and nods slightly, then taps his spoon against his coffee cup and steps forward with a wave of his hand. 'Ladies and gentlemen, may I present the St Kilda Harlequin.'

Amy stands in the doorway and it is like looking at an older version of the child at dinner. Not quite a woman but no longer a child. She has put on make-up and glitter and has swept her thick wavy hair on top of her head. Her lips are a dark, wine red and her eyes are defined with green eye-shadow and dark eye-liner. Yet it is not just make-up that has added a sparkle to her appearance but also excitement. The threadbare jeans are the same but the jumper is replaced with a black padded jacket stitched with patches of silk. Not harlequin black and white but black and green. Deep green ribbons run down the sleeves, and at the wrists the silk extends into scallops of looser material. When Amy moves her hands the colours at her wrists shift between mid-green and black-green. Shot silk, I realise, one colour shot through with another.

I hear a sharp intake of breath from Kristin, and Rosalyn moves quickly towards us from the fire. Her expression falters, the ready smile she has shown Harold sliding into stony disapproval.

If Amy is aware of any reaction, it doesn't show in her performance. She seems confident and assured, keeping up a theatrical patter as she conjures coins and different coloured scarves from people's clothing. She threads coloured silks into a clear tube, first red, then blue, then orange, and taps the tube lightly with her wand. Some more theatre and patter and a gentle breath into the tube. The three fabrics float out, light as gossamer, tied together, like a long colourful flame. I feel a little rush of elation on her behalf, not so much at the trick, because I had done it myself as a child, but at her presentation. Amy takes a deep flourishing bow and looks around the little gathering, soaking up the applause.

Harold looks delighted and Sam's face is flushed with pride.

It is hard to work out Kristin's expression as her face is set and unmoving, almost as if she hasn't registered the performance. Rosalyn's expression is, if anything, too easy to read. Her mouth is tight, her eyes cold, and the shifting wash of dislike I have felt on and off since yesterday sets like stone.

Amy finally sees and falters, then rushes outside with her head bowed.

'That was wonderful,' I say in protest as Amy closes the garden door with an abrupt click. The intensity of my championing of Amy surprises me. A couple of hours ago, I hadn't even met her. I look at Rosalyn but there is no complicit glance now. Her face is fixed in an expressionless mask but I suspect that beneath the mask a heady anger churns.

I excuse myself and follow Amy through the garden door.

Chapter 7

It is cold outside, but the garden is sheltered from the sea breeze. I can hear the rustle of wind through the leaves and the gentle lapping of water on the sand – restful sounds, like a background whisper. In the air, there is the smell of salt and the faintest tang of ash, as though someone has been burning paper. The house lights cast great squares of light on the garden wall, against which Amy's shadow is immense.

'Amy, that was really good.' I sit down at the table next to her.

'Was it?' she says very evenly.

'Mm. Very skilful.'

'Aunty Ros didn't like it though.' Her head is down and a tremble has crept into her voice.

'No.' I agree. 'But I don't know why. I thought it was terrific.'

'She doesn't approve of amateur theatrics. She wants me to get a good job and not get sidetracked into something that takes up all my time and doesn't pay well.' I can hear Rosalyn's speech in the delivery. 'It's a whole load of crap but she doesn't seem to like a lot of things lately.'

'Well, it can be like that sometimes.'

'Two adults and one child is horrible,' she bursts out with conviction. This is something she has obviously thought about a lot.

'I'm an only child too,' I reply. 'It's not quite the same I know, but similar I guess. All the focus is on the one child.'

'Did you like it when you were growing up?' Her hands are very still. When I was growing up, being an only child was not really the problem. She has long fingers with the deftness needed to perform magical tricks.

'It was okay. When I was growing up, being an only child was not really the problem. I suspect at times it would have been easier to have had a brother or sister, but then, I didn't know any different. Have you been practising magic for long?'

'A few weeks.'

'Is that all? I thought it would have taken longer.'

'What I did tonight was simple. There's a lot more difficult things that I want to learn – tarot cards and fortune telling and some more serious magic. I'd like to build up an act, I think it would go down well at the market.'

Part of a camellia bush is lit up in the square of light coming from the dining room window. The leaves go from near black in the shadows to a glossy incandescent green, almost the same colour as the silk ribbons at Amy's wrists.

'I like your jacket,' I say. 'Was it made specially for tonight?'

She looks down at it, as if seeing it for the first time. 'I made it with my aunt out of bits and pieces.' She is dismissive and changes the subject. 'Are you having fun tonight or is this just something you have to do for some reason?'

'Parts of it are fun,' I say carefully.

'Really? Most adults pretend everything's all right all of the time. They've forgotten how to be honest.'

She sounds very sure and grown up. 'That's interesting.'

She looks at me with sudden intensity, as if interesting is something she hasn't considered herself to be. Leaning forward in her chair she takes on a conspiritorial air. 'Take Aunty Ros.

She was crying the other day but when I asked her what was wrong, she sniffed and said nothing. She didn't like me to see her crying.'

'Why not, do you think?'

She pauses and considers. 'She's had some trouble at work but it's a control thing. It's like she thinks I don't understand stuff like crying.'

'She probably doesn't want to worry you.'

'But that's just crap. Crying worries people a lot less than trying to cover it up.'

'Yes. I guess so, but there's been a lot for people to cry over lately.'

She hesitates, as if unsure of my meaning. 'You mean with my grandfather? I don't think so, Marlo. No one here had a good word for him, except maybe Kristin and she never said much.' She looks at me shrewdly for a moment and picks up my question of earlier. 'Why do you think he called himself Diamond?'

'I have no idea.'

'Aunty Rosalyn shouldn't have given you that look. I mean why shouldn't I know? He is related to me too.'

'Yes, but more distantly.' Grandparent rather than parent. Only parents have the power to hurt so much.

'Did you know him?' Amy asks. She is watchful, expectant.

'I never met him but Harold did – they used to talk together in the park sometimes.'

'I *should* know about him,' she says, her voice fierce.

'Maybe it's just more of the same. People not wanting to burden you with unpleasantness. Maybe they think you've had enough.'

She shifts position and her shadow moves, immense against the wall. 'With Mum you mean?'

'Yes.'

'I can't remember much about her you know. I was eight when she died.'

'And how old are you now?'

47

'I'm almost fourteen.' She changes the subject again. 'What's it like playing cricket?'

'Fine.' I reply. And with just one word I realise I have evaded her question in the same way that Rosalyn did. 'Well, no, that's not quite true. It used to be fine but just lately it hasn't been.'

'Why not?'

'Because I haven't been as good at it as I could be. I've had other things to think about.'

'What sort of things?'

I hesitate, amused despite myself. This is what I keep away from, the way one question leads to another. Jenny's death is something I haven't talked about for months now but there is something about the avid interest on Amy's face that makes me want to answer her question honestly, or as honestly as I can. I think it through for a moment, wondering how she would handle this particular truth. Perhaps in the circumstances it might even be a kindness. Perhaps, with the murder of her grandfather, it would help her to know that other people have had to face something similar. But for all that, the words seem too brutal and Amy far too young. I modify it, as I almost always modify it.

'Someone close to me died.'

'Oh, I see. I know about that; that's really hard.'

'People tell me just to keep going and things will get better.'

'Will they, do you think?'

'Of course. But it is taking longer than I thought.' My turn to change the subject. 'Do you play sport?'

'Hockey.'

'Are you any good?'

'So-so.' She smiles. 'Are you Rosalyn's friend?'

'I'm Harold's friend. Harold is Rosalyn's friend.'

'She likes him, doesn't she?'

'Can you tell?'

'Yes. She has that look on her face. I don't know what it is exactly; she looks . . . calculating.'

I laugh at the description. This is exactly how she looks. 'I think you see too much.'

She grins but suddenly it fades. 'They don't think that. They think I'm dumb but I'm not. I know a lot of stuff they don't think I know. Stuff they…' She trails away and gives a nervous little laugh as though realising she has stepped outside the limits of polite conversation.

Inside the house, someone switches off the dining-room light. Amy's shadow on the wall disappears and the leaves of the camellia lose their incandescent brilliance.

'Would you like to see my room?' The invitation is impulsive and straight from childhood. Born, I suspect, of the need to change the subject and loneliness.

'Great house.' I say as Amy leads me upstairs. 'Have you lived here long?'

'Since I was eight. This is the gym.' She throws open a door onto a vast room that, as I guessed, looks out over the sea. It has a mirror along the side wall and an impressive range of equipment.

'Wow,' I say and she grins.

'It looks flash, I know, but most of the stuff is pretty old.'

'Who uses it?'

'Rosalyn mostly. She wants to keep fit but she says she doesn't want the "indignity of the running track".' Her voice drops into perfect mimicry of Rosalyn's clipped tones.

Voices sound below us and we both stop to listen. I recognise Rosalyn's, low and hushed and very angry. '…inappropriate Sam, you shouldn't have encouraged…childish.'

'Bullshit. It's exactly what the girl needs.' Much louder than Rosalyn.

'Children need discipline, and between you and Kristin…' A little pause before she changes direction. 'Why do I get the sense that it's all up to me, that the only guidance Amy has comes…'

Somewhere in the house, a door slams and the voices fall silent.

'Me again,' Amy says and pulls a face. She shrugs it off and moves on. 'This is Kristin's room.' She taps the door as we pass. 'This one,' she indicates the room next to it, 'is Aunty Ros's. This one is where she sews. That's the bathroom at the end. And this is mine.'

Amy's room is large and surprisingly neat and tidy. On one side is a sleeping area with the bed made and clothes put away. In the corner there is a storage area with Amy's school bag, hockey stick and collection of CDs. The only mess is a clutter of objects on a table in the far corner.

'This is where I make my props.' She waves her hand across piles of fabrics and scissors, pens and papers, linseed oil and match boxes, and a bottle of turpentine. A saucer contains the pale grey ash of burned paper and a few stray matches.

Amy takes the tube and silks from her performance earlier and places them on the table. 'This is something else that Ros doesn't like,' she murmurs, her eyes on the clutter. 'She says that if I want to be creative I should do it in the sewing room. I tried it once but she didn't like it because I interfered with her precious fabrics.'

'Sewing must run in the family.' I comment, not wanting to take her part against Rosalyn too much.

'I guess. Aunty Ros doesn't make props or anything theatrical like Kristin, she just makes clothes for work.'

Now Amy has got me here, she seems unclear about her duties as host. We talk for a few minutes about boys and school and her hopes to make the finals of the school hockey competition coming up soon. She talks about a boy from a nearby school she walks home with occasionally. The family don't know about him and she says they wouldn't approve if they did. School doesn't muster up much enthusiasm but the hockey games and the boy do.

Time has passed since I left the others. I have been away too long for politeness but in reality I gave that away when I sided with Amy against Rosalyn.

I head downstairs and find Harold in the kitchen on his own.

'Where is everyone?' I ask.

'Kristin went to bed with a headache. Rosalyn and Sam have had a fight, and Sam has gone home. Amy was with you.' He gives a small sigh and says, 'Maybe you were right, Marlo. Maybe it is too soon to socialise. Are you ready to go?'

'Yes,' I say, not bothering to keep the pleasure from my voice. 'I'll find Rosalyn.'

I collect our coats from the study and hear a whisper from the stairs. It is Amy.

'Marlo, what's going on?'

'Ros and Sam have had a row.'

'I know that.' She sounds, disappointed. 'We heard them, remember?'

Rosalyn's voice floats up, followed by the sound of her laughter. Amy pulls another face and presses a note into my hand. 'Read it later.'

I wait for Harold for over ten minutes in which I check out the books in the bookcase, read the diplomas on the wall, and take in the photos of costumes that are grouped together. Some are of ornate and stylish clothing, others are more like sculpted costumes, flower and bird shapes in pale shimmering colours. All the photos are labelled – the production, the year. At the bottom of each one Kristin's signature, clear and distinct, almost childlike.

When Harold eventually arrives, he has a smile on his face and a jonquil in his buttonhole – one of the pale-centred jonquils that had formed part of the centrepiece on the dining-room table. This must have been what he was laughing at with Rosalyn. The winding of the flower into the buttonhole would have been a close business, tactile and heady. The romance is obviously in full swing.

From the car I look back at the house. I remember from Amy's guided tour that these front rooms are the bedrooms – Amy's, Kristin's and Rosalyn's. The windows are colonial style, divided into small, even grids, and two of the bedrooms are lit up. In Kristin's room a shadow moves across the window and back again. For a person with a headache she is curiously mobile. I remember her disinclination to talk about her success and her jangling exit after dinner and suspect that out of the three adult children I met tonight, she is the only one remotely cut up about her father's death.

Chapter 8

It occurs to me somewhere in the little maze of streets that lead out on to the Esplanade, that for someone intent on finding out about Bill Stone from his family, I have probably missed a lot by spending too much time with Amy. I have learnt next to nothing about the man.

'So, what did I miss?' I rouse myself to ask Harold.

His face is lit up sufficiently by the wash of street lighting and the sweep of headlights coming towards us for me to see the little gleam of interest in his eyes and the small smile on his lips.

'Bill had a house, Marlo. He came to see Rosalyn a week ago because he wanted to tell her about it.'

'Where was it?'

'South Yarra.'

'South Yarra,' I repeat. I was expecting Harold to say Perth or Broome or Fremantle, or somewhere unheard of in the distant west. South Yarra is only a few kilometres away and it is an affluent suburb. A house in South Yarra would be worth a fortune.

'But why did he want to tell Rosalyn about it?'

Harold hesitates. 'He wanted to tell her about the house because the family are going to inherit it.'

I look at Harold for a long time. His face is in profile, curiously clear against the scattered lights and moving scenery.

'An inheritance,' I say and the jolt of shock is echoed in my tone. A little chill settles on the back of my neck, as though some of the sea air has found its way into the car. Could Bill Stone have known about his impending death?

'Rosalyn has been in touch with the solicitor. The house is divided between all of them, with equal shares for the grand-children.' He lists the beneficiaries, most of them at the dinner tonight. 'Rosalyn, Sam, Amy, Kristin, and Sam's son, Jason.

'And what did Rosalyn have to say about it? About Bill coming to tell her about the house?'

He doesn't answer for a moment and I think that this is the first time he has thought about it at all. 'Bill was in his late sixties, Marlo. It's a time when a lot people think about what they have to leave to their families. And it wasn't just the house he talked about. He also wanted a photo of the family.'

This, at least, is understandable. He must have been curious about his own family.

'Rosalyn's asked me to check a few things at work and to take a look at the house in South Yarra.'

'Why doesn't she go herself?' I say, too bluntly.

'The funeral is on Monday apparently. She has a meeting at the weekend and after the funeral she is off to Adelaide for the week.'

'And at work?' I ask, knowing what his answer will be.

'The usual. Any other assets that might be in the wind. I said I'd see what I could do and gave her my usual spiel.'

I have heard Harold's usual spiel, and the patient tone he uses when explaining to outsiders what we do and the limits of our powers. Some people think that we have magical access to confidential information but the only information we can find out is information that anyone with time and money could access. This is a spiel he gives often, because to most people law is law, and not divided up into sections. Most people assume a legal search company can do anything and go anywhere.

Harold's expression hasn't changed and I suspect his mind is on the woman who wound the jonquil into his buttonhole. I think of her too but my thoughts are vastly different from his. I am struck by the coldness of her request. Her father has just died and her mind is already focused on the possibilities of inheritance. But why shouldn't she know? And I suspect that Rosalyn's request has as much to do with bringing Harold into her life as financial considerations. A little touch of manipulation.

We turn a bend in the road and the beam of the headlights juts out over the dark water momentarily before swinging back. 'How's Irene?' I ask, remembering her red eyes yesterday. She must have known even then about Rosalyn's effect on Harold.

'Good. Why?' There is no understanding in his voice.

'Just wondered.' I change tack. 'Did you remember them? Well, you must do.'

'Yes, but it was always Rosalyn who stood out for me. She was just a teenager when I knew them, not much older than Amy, but very beautiful.'

'What was she like?'

'Oh, you know,' he says, vaguely and I look at him closely. Harold is rarely vague and I suspect that even back then he had a crush on her. 'She was a pretty determined character as I remember. The others were too small to bother with. Kristin was around seven and Sam not much older. Justine was the youngest.'

'So it was always Rosalyn,' I say.

'She was sixteen, Marlo, and I was twenty-three. She was still at school.'

I do a quick mental calculation. If Harold is fifty-four, then Rosalyn is forty-seven. She looks younger.

At the traffic lights he pats his stomach. 'Great meal.'

'Yes.' And whatever I feel about Rosalyn, I have to admit that she is a terrific host. A lot of work and planning had gone into that meal.

'Mind you, I need to cut down,' Harold says, surprising me. 'I might even join you on the running track sometime. Not running of course, but a sedate walk of an evening wouldn't do me any harm.'

In all the time I have known him, Harold has never once considered cutting down on food and he has always maintained a lofty distance from the walkers and joggers on the track between our houses. I don't answer. Walking is a good idea. But in Harold's case, the thought is as disconcerting as sunshine at midnight.

'At least we know where Bill went at night,' Harold continues.

'The house in South Yarra,' I say, pleased that at least part of the mystery has been explained.

'You know, Marlo, I'm still having trouble with Bill as the homeless man in the park. It's a hard image to make any sense of.'

'Yes,' I agree. 'And we are still no closer to finding out what he was doing hanging around there, when he owned a house.'

He smiles at me. 'Intriguing isn't it?'

'It's fun,' I say thoughtlessly. 'I mean, not the death . . . but the puzzle of it.'

Harold looks at me and grins. 'Not quite your night for tactful remarks. Want to come with me to check out Bill's house?'

Yes and no. Part of me would rather have nothing to do with Rosalyn Stone and her life-changing capabilities. But, if anything, tonight has added to my curiosity.

'Of course. When?'

'No point in hanging around. I have something on tomorrow night but Saturday is good and at least we could go in daylight. How is Saturday for you?'

'Fine,' I say, feeling pleased at the prospect. A bit of snooping sounds like fun. Much better than my normal Saturday routine of shopping, cleaning and doing the washing.

We turn into Gilmore Street.

'What does Rosalyn do?' I ask.

He shifts in his seat. 'She runs a school.'

'A school?' I repeat and he must hear the note of surprise in my tone. I hadn't thought of her as a teacher.

'I think they call it a modelling school. They used to call them finishing schools in my day.'

I think about the snobby connotations of finishing schools that have survived over the years – the wealthy sending their daughters to be made more marketable for marriage. Surely they are an anachronism today? I remember Rosalyn's critical eyes on the first day I met her, the feeling that I was being assessed for some unknown agenda. I laugh and wonder if I passed.

Harold pulls up outside the house and I recall another surprise the evening has thrown up. 'I didn't know you ran a restaurant, Harold. Why did you leave?'

Voices are interesting in what they tell and what they give away. I hear in Harold's voice two things: concern for me and something underlying it, something evasive.

'It was time to try something new, Marlo. Sometimes it happens and when it does, you don't have a choice.'

I don't answer but I know that his words are shorthand. Harold understands my position and is giving me his blessing to move on, if that's what I decide to do. But right now I don't know what I want to do. If I knew, it would be easy.

I let Ebony out into the back garden and read Amy's note. It is simple, written in large roundish letters. '*Marlo. Can you ring me tomorrow between 5 and 6? Amy.*'

The choice of times is interesting – after school and, I assume, before the family arrive home. Privacy guaranteed. I wonder what it is that Amy wants to discuss with me and why she wants to keep it private.

Chapter 9

Friday is our busiest day at work. When I arrive the scent is there again, mixed faintly with the aroma of coffee. Tegan is already at the spare desk in the front office, her oversized bag propped up against the wall in front of her. She works every Friday, and on other days when and if we need her.

'You're early,' I comment, realising that for the last few Fridays Tegan has been in before me, opening up.

'I like being early.' She smiles and switches on the computer, her movements slow and unhurried. Tegan is a large-boned woman in her late twenties, with a round plumpish face. She wears business jackets and long slimming skirts, slit at the knee for ease of movement. She is a quiet person and in the year since she first began with us even Harold hasn't broken through her reserve. Her conversations with all of us are polite and friendly with none of Irene's curt briskness, but curiously restrained. I have learnt very little about her, except that she is very good at changing conversations when they look like getting personal.

Even with Tegan's help, there is no chance of sloping off for a long lunch on a Friday. This is the day when most property settlements are booked in and the usually quiet banking chambers in which they take place feel more like hectic street markets.

Harold spends his lunch time running searches on William Bradley Stone, courtesy of Index Searches in Victoria and the agent we use in Perth. William Stone is confirmed as the owner of a single property in South Yarra, Victoria – a property bought five years ago.

'Did you think there'd be more?' I ask when he shows me the results.

'Who knows? If the rumours are right about his criminal past, he could have houses and assets all over the country. I would hate to think of Rosalyn and her family missing out on something they're entitled to.'

In my break, I shop at the Queen Victoria Market, buying chicken pieces, salad and cakes in honour of my cousin Lucy coming for tea. She spends every Friday night with me, sleeping in the upstairs bedroom with Ebony on her mat beside Lucy's bed. The rest of the week Lucy spends at Kiah, a kind of halfway house for people with intellectual disabilities. Next year she is due to move out to a place of her own.

At five o'clock I ring Amy. She picks up the phone instantly as if she were standing next to it.

'Marlo. Thanks for ringing.' She sounds very young and a bit too grateful. 'I wanted to ask you something but you can say no if you like.'

'Ask away.'

She hesitates. 'We've got school sports next week. I wondered if you would like to come? Rosalyn will be away and Kristin is working.'

'Is this the hockey match?' I ask, giving myself time.

'Yes. Please come, Marlo.' There is something plaintive in her voice that stops me saying no.

'I'd like to. When is it?'

'On Wednesday. The game starts at three.' She gives me

directions to a school in Prahran, not far from the city.

'Three o'clock sounds fine. I can stay for half an hour or so.'

'Great.' She pauses.

'What is it, Amy?'

'Could you wear your tracksuit?'

I laugh, understanding belatedly the reason for my attraction. 'My State one? Why not?'

We leave work late. Harold, too, has spent time at the market, and is loaded down with shopping bags full of interestingly shaped packages that suggest cheeses and pâtés, mixed in with the frothy tops and bulging shapes of vegetables. Harold's dedication to good cooking is in full swing and I suspect his weekend menu will be vastly superior to chicken fillets and a salad.

I have just pushed myself onto a crowded tram in Swanston Street when I see someone on the street that I know, and I almost call out in surprise. Tony, ex-lover and ex-cricket coach crossing the road at Flinders Street station. The familiarity of his face is momentarily shocking. The broad forehead, the long jaw, the blond wiry hair.

Seeing him now, images of the few months we lived together flash up in my mind, as though superimposed on the window of the tram. A time of lurching between hostility, need and confusion. Most of it was my fault. All of it? After Jenny's death I had no room for anyone at all, no time or patience. For sanity's sake, both his and mine, the relationship had to end.

I blink the memories away and concentrate on the man through the glass, trying to glean how the world has dealt with him since we parted. He does look different. His hair is shorter, cut closer to the scalp, probably to combat the springy frizz of hair that I always liked. Tonight, his clothes are formal – a snowy ruffled shirt, a black jacket and thin bow tie. Tony never liked formal wear and in the past, his discomfort would have shown. But tonight he looks easy and relaxed and I have to remind myself that it is eight months since I last saw him. Not surprising, then, that he has moved on.

I am so engrossed in the unexpected sighting that it takes me a moment to notice the woman at his side. She is dressed in a long formal gown with a matching bolero jacket trimmed with fur. Her dark hair is swept up and held with a sparkling clip. They are not touching but look happy, striding along purposefully together. Outside Young and Jacksons, he slows down as if to listen better to what she is saying, his whole attention focused on her. He laughs suddenly and his face lights up. They look good together. Close and comfortable and contented. A better match than we ever were.

The tram clatters off and I stare unseeingly all they way to St Kilda, sifting through a complex web of thoughts and feelings. How, after all that has happened, can I even begin to explain that rush of longing that sits uncomfortably among more rational thoughts. Realistically, I have nothing to complain about. After all, he is only doing what I told him to do, eight long and weary months ago. Finding someone else to love.

Lucy is already at home watching some TV program that she drifts away from when she hears my key in the lock. Ebony follows her closely, pleased to see me but attached to Lucy like a limpet.

'Lucy. How are you?' I put my arm around her and breathe in her warmth and heavy perfume. For once she seems content to stay in the embrace, at least momentarily. Beneath her loose jumper she is too thin but I remind myself that this is nothing new. Lucy has always been too thin.

I show her my shopping and she grins happily at the display of cream cakes. We prepare dinner together, Lucy making the salad and pouring the wine while I take care of the chicken, slicing it into strips and cooking them in olive oil.

Lucy is a charmer. Her conversations are simple and engaging, although at times they can be infuriating in their vagueness. But right now her small talk is my intellectual equal and for once my thoughts don't dart away to other things. It occurs to me, listening to Lucy, that in the past year our situations have reversed. I used to think that I was doing Lucy a favour, making sure, as Jenny wanted me to, that she had a happy place to visit regularly. Now I look forward to Lucy's visits as a break from my depression, planning little surprises and unexpected things for her to eat. Her visits give me a purpose in the week outside of work and sport.

As usual the conversation moves quickly from one subject to another: Lucy's current boyfriend, the new shoes she found on special, what her boss said, a visit to her mother.

'How is your Mum?' I ask. I haven't seen my Aunt Emma for over a year. Cowardice and guilt keep me away and the longer I leave it, the harder it gets.

'Good,' she says simply. I decide not to pursue the subject.

I watch Lucy eat, hungrily as ever. She is dressed in her usual winter uniform of dark jeans and jumper, with polished Blundstone boots. Today, she has pinned a bright pink flower behind her ear that gives her a tropical look, incongruous given the temperature outside. After dinner she curls up in front of the TV, Ebony asleep at her feet. Technically, Ebony is her dog and they are always content in each other's company. I watch TV with her for a while and then prepare for my run to Port Melbourne.

On the way, I consider calling in on Harold briefly, as I feel the need for some company and conversation. This is something I have done on a semi-regular basis over the last year and Harold is always welcoming, offering a good dose of sanity whenever I turn up. But when I reach the house I see that the great first-floor windows are lit up and I remember the shopping bags, full of cheeses and pâtés, and Harold's pleased air at work today. I had put this down to the general state of play with Rosalyn but had not made the obvious connection. I do so now with a touch of scorn at my slowness.

Two figures in the dining room, sitting roughly where we sat on Monday night, looking out over the great sweep of Port

Phillip Bay. I can't see the food but the candlelight and flowers are articulate enough. Rosalyn's hair shines as a blur of gold, and candlelight catches in the pale wine as though the glasses were lit from within. From where I stand watching, at street level in the cold darkness, the intimacy inside is almost tangible.

I head for home. Ahead of me now there are no clusters of lights picking out the familiar structures along the coast, only the predominant sweep of the sea. The wind has strengthened and the usually quiet waters of the bay heave and pound against the sand. By the time I turn into Gilmore Street I have slowed to a walk, feeling as though I have run forever, my sweat cold against my skin.

I soak in the bath, warming myself and seeking comfort. This has not been one of my better days but a salutary one in that I have had to face some components of my character that are less than worthy – the unbidden wash of longing for Tony and the sense of being shut out just now by Harold. My reasonable, rational voice tells me I should be happy for them both, and I am happy for them. It is good to see people you care about moving on, shaking off disappointments from the past. I try to ignore the more craven voice that has been my companion for much of the long run home – a voice from childhood that wobbles rebelliously on the fringes of more rational thought. What about me?

Chapter 10

I sleep uneasily, my night filled with strange little dreams of being closed in while outside there is sunshine and warmth, and all I have to do is open the door and step out. I don't though. Something dull and weightless is holding me back and, try as I might, I can't shift it. I wake early, expecting the sunshine, but the constant low cloud of the last few days is still there.

Lucy and I fill the morning with our usual activities – breakfast and taking Ebony for a walk. After that we shop together and Lucy tries on endless quantities of shoes and scarves and winter hats. It is the scarves she likes most, the brightness of them against her dark hair and clothing. I watch her reflection in the mirror as she chooses between hot pink and a bright, dazzling orange. She may be too thin but her face is undoubtedly beautiful.

'Which one, Marlo?'

'I like the pink.'

'Yeah. Me too.'

At the cash desk we have a little tussle about paying. This is pretty much how it always goes when we shop together and I don't always win.

'What about you, Marlo?' She asks, looking worried momentarily as the well drummed lessons in money management strike home. 'You never buy anything for yourself. Can't you afford it?'

I tuck my arm through hers as we head for the street. 'It's not the money, Lucy. I'm just not in the mood.'

The concern on her face changes to puzzlement as though not being in the mood for shopping is something she can't possibly imagine. I laugh out loud and Lucy joins in. I'm not sure if she knows exactly what I'm laughing at but Lucy has always been good at following other people's moods.

After she goes back to Kiah, I dress in old jeans and runners and wait for Harold. After Lucy's visits, the house always seems very quiet. Today I fill the time by collecting things which will be useful for the afternoon's trip – torches, snack food, my mobile phone. When he arrives, Harold is dressed in jeans, a winter-weight shirt, and a beige reversible jacket. He looks well, I decide, settling into the car beside him, the glow of love still on his face.

We head across town to South Yarra, down Punt Road, then turning right at Toorak Road. On the drive we discuss déjà vu and the reason for Harold's sense of it on this occasion.

'I think as much as anything I remembered Bill through gesture,' Harold says. 'He had this way of moving his hands that seemed out of place. He came across as confident but his hands were always restless.'

'That's observant of you.'

'And his eyes are the same colour as Rosalyn's but I didn't remember that until I saw her again.'

Crowded roads give way to streets lined with old established trees which hang over the road, bare branched. In spring and summer the trees make a green tunnel but now they look stark and rather bleak. I tell Harold about my recent thoughts on Bill's clothing and we puzzle over why a relatively affluent man

65

would be in disguise. A spy checking out an enemy agent in the park. A hit man waiting for his target. A journalist doing a cover story. A drug runner checking out the competition. We laugh. This is the sort of nonsense I used to exchange with Shane Black in the old days – a delight in silly conversation. Harold looks at me and smiles at the lightness of my mood. He's right – I do feel better, lighter.

'What about this for a possibility?' Harold suggests. 'A family man checking up on his kids and grandkids, making sure they are doing alright. The wad of notes in his pocket could have been there in case they needed money.'

'And he did ask for a photo of everyone,' I add. 'But if it were true he would have visited them all and not just Rosalyn.'

'Sam certainly didn't volunteer that information but I think he's the sort of bloke that would keep things to himself pretty much.'

I am glad to realise that Harold noticed something else on Thursday night, apart from Rosalyn.

'I don't know about Kristin,' he continues. 'I didn't get much of a sense of her.'

'No. Me neither.' I consider Kristin. The successful business woman with a new lucrative contract. The pacing shadow at the window as we drove away. She obviously had not wanted to bother with company when her life was in such a state of upheaval. I, for one, can hardly blame her.

We are silent for a while. The most logical, acceptable spin on the situation – the family man looking out for his children – doesn't explain the need for disguise. Why not just come back into their lives.

Bill Stone's house is set behind a high front fence. I use one of the keys that Harold gives me to open the gate and we park in the driveway. The house is in much the same style as the others in this street – affluent and solid looking. I dislike it on sight. For all its lofty grandeur, the proportions and colours are wrong. The windows are too small for the tall expanse of brick work, the colours too dark and brooding. The garage is in the corner of the garden, in keeping with the house, but separate from it. The garden is overhung with trees, and away from the gate it is like stepping into dusk, a dark day made darker by the great tangled canopy of leaves.

The first key that Harold tries opens the front door and we look into a gloomy hallway with closed doors on either side and a flight of stairs at the back. I find the light switch but the power is off at the mains and we have to use torches to negotiate our way, opening doors and blinds as we go. The ceilings are high with ornate cornices and plaster roses, but the house is dark and has that bone-numbing chill of a home closed up for winter.

Downstairs there is a kitchen, lounge, study and laundry area. The kitchen is old with painted cupboard doors, lino on the floor, a pantry with a louvre door and a pull-down blind covering the small window that over looks the driveway. I open it to see the interior more clearly but light doesn't improve things. It's still gloomy and old-fashioned.

Upstairs there are four bedrooms and two bathrooms, all of which are bare. No beds. No mattresses. No bedding. No indication that this might be where Bill Stone slept at night. Harold looks at me, our thoughts the same.

'The mystery goes on,' he groans.

What I had expected I'm not sure. A key to the dead man's house had seemed so promising but these cold empty rooms tell us nothing at all.

'I'll check the garage, Marlo. I imagine that's what the other key is for. What will you do?'

'I'll catch you up. There must be something here.'

I take my time, lingering in the bedrooms, thinking about the man in question, trying and failing to get a sense of him. It is annoying never to have met him. According to Harold's property search, this house was bought five years ago and I wonder if he originally bought it for himself or for his children.

Footsteps below me. Harold must be coming back. I head

down the stairs to meet him, wondering if he has had more luck in the garage than I have had in the house.

'Hello.' An unknown voice greets me as I turn the bend in the stairs. I have never met the person before but there is something familiar about him. It's his eyes, I think. The family green. A young man, deeply tanned despite winter, with dark untidy hair. He is wearing black cargoes and a puffy cobalt blue vest with purple trims.

'I'm sorry,' he says slowly, as though suddenly unsure of himself. 'I thought someone called Harold would be here.'

'He's in the garage. And you are?'

'My name is Jason Stone. My father, Sam, told me about this place and that someone was checking it out today. I thought I'd come and see it for myself.'

There are similarities in appearance between father and son, but none in movement. Jason is all restless and fluid while Sam is solid and heavy. Jason looks about sixteen.

'My name is Marlo Shaw,' I say. 'I'm a friend of Harold's. I came to help.'

He looks around with interest, shifting from foot to foot. 'What's it like?'

I make a face.

'Pretty grim, eh? Oh well, an inheritance is an inheritance.' He sounds immensely pleased and seemingly spares no thought for the man who's death made it possible. I counter the thought. Why should he? As far as I know they never met.

'Typical of Ros, getting someone to do what it would take her half an hour to do.' He grins and I smile back. 'You know this is going to sound corny but I know you, don't I?' There is an appraising glint to his eye that is attractive.

'If you live with your father, then I live in your area.'

'I know,' he says, as enlightenment dawns. 'I've seen you on the running track. You have a black dog with you sometimes and you're amazingly fit.'

Now that Jason has said it, I remember seeing him,

fleetingly, at different times – a young man skating fluidly on the bike track.

'I work at it.'

'You were at dinner at Ros's the other night. How was it?' There is something careful in his tone.

In a word, chaotic. People reeling between emotions – grief, anger, resentment. 'Very nice,' I say and he chuckles, his grin inviting me to join in some joke against the family. I revise my estimate of his age. There is something knowing about his smile and the length of his gaze that is vastly older than sixteen.

'Why weren't you there?' I ask.

'I was working,' he replies. 'Do you mind if I look around?'

We both smile at the request and I answer as though the host and not the intruder, 'Help yourself.'

I hear him moving around in the bedrooms overhead and give a fleeting thought to Harold. For my part, I check every drawer in the bathroom, every drawer in the kitchen, every shelf of every cupboard. There is no crockery, no food, no rubbish. Nothing. If Bill Stone did sleep here, he has tidied all the evidence away.

The footsteps above me move then clatter down the stairs. Jason puts his head around the kitchen door.

'Bye, Marlo. My car was playing up before and I didn't realise the time. I've got to get to work.'

'What do you think of the house?'

'Not much. A good place to sell, I'd say. Listen, I was wondering . . . if you ever need a running partner, I'd be happy to go with you. It gets lonely on the track sometimes.'

He has his phone number ready, written on a piece of paper, and hands it to me. I don't find it lonely on the running track and I don't think I'll be ringing his number, despite his green eyes and friendly grin.

The front door closes behind him and seconds later I hear a car door slam and an engine roar lustily into life. If there was a problem earlier, the car sounds healthy enough now. As I examine the dusty louvres of the pantry door, a fleeting shadow slides across the driveway as though the sun has slipped instantly in and out of cloud or someone has passed the window. Harold, I expect, coming back. I climb the pantry shelves and on the top shelf is a single sheet of paper. I don't have great expectations but it is the only thing I have found at all.

A sudden distant crash from somewhere, a noise I can't quite place. The paper is still out of reach, just slightly beyond my grasp. I can feel it, but can't quite grab it. I make one last effort and the paper slides towards me.

Thought and realisation come together. A shadow in the driveway. A crashing noise in the garage. I call his name, already running, my heart hammering like a piston in my chest, 'Harold.'

Chapter 11

The garage is almost dark. Harold's torch has rolled away from his body and lies as a tiny pool of light on the grey concrete floor. So great is my fear that my senses seem to shut down. There is no sound and for a moment I am unable to take in what I am seeing – Harold's body crumpled on the floor, one arm stretched out, his face side on, as if he turned at the moment of impact. As my eyes adjust, I see that his shirt has a smear of oil on it from the garage floor. His glasses have spun off and lie some distance away, one of the lenses shattered.

Two thoughts: concern for Harold and an awareness of danger. Whoever did this could still be here. I pick up Harold's torch and hold it like a weapon, listening, searching. There is no sound save for the rush of breathing. My own is rapid and shallow; Harold's is snuffly, laboured. His blood has run in a little stream along his forehead and gathered in a crack in the concrete. The world spins. For one sickening moment I am back to the incident in the park. A man dying while I call the ambulance. I sink to my knees.

'Harold.' I take his hand. There is flowing blood and a pulse, and I come instantly to my senses. I use my mobile phone to ring for help and cover him with my jacket.

Stay alive, Harold. Who did this to you? I don't leave him, although part of me longs to do so, to pull the place apart searching for the person who has attacked my friend. I keep myself attached to him, my fingers on his pulse as if by touch alone I can will it to stay strong. All the time I crouch beside him, facing out with my torch raised, ready to spring.

Harold's eyes flicker open and close again and my thoughts leap. Like that evening in the park, I must have missed the attacker by minutes. I must have been metres away, seconds away. Waiting there, I understand the noise I heard from the kitchen. Harold's outstretched arm and the torch must have collided with some paint tins on a ledge above me, as one of them has been knocked over and another lies dented on the floor, wedged into a corner.

I wait, alert for the sound of sirens but hearing only Harold's breath, deep, ragged and guttural sounding. Every now and then it changes becoming lighter and easier. At the obvious change I hope he will wake and say something reassuring but, instead, his breath changes back again and there is a clicking sound in this throat.

I speak in the end, reassuring words to cover my own fear and the worrying sound of his breath. Odd little sentences that I repeat over and over – 'Everything's fine, Harold. You're going to be fine.' And then, thankfully, the sound of sirens in the distance, a tuneless wail of noise but as welcome as the most intricate aria. The hairs on my arms lift to its tune and the back of my neck prickles.

The ambulance backs into the driveway, followed by professional reassuring voices. The paramedics quickly check Harold and then lift him smoothly onto a stretcher. I pick up his broken glasses and follow him into the ambulance. For a fleeting moment the driver touches the brakes and the dense bushes along the driveway glow momentarily red. Through the glass my eyes lock onto something in the glow, but I am unsure of what I am seeing. And then suddenly I know and my skin crawls. Unclear features, a blur of white skin, washed with pink. Small pink eyes that disappear as the ambulance speeds away. I look out through the darkened glass for a long time as we speed through the streets, trying to make sense of that momentary glimpse. Brake lights turning white eyes to pink, white skin to pink skin, underneath the great structure of a jutting, sideways branch. No hair colour. No distinguishing clothing. Just a unifying darkness. Branches. Dark clouds. Dark clothing. Nothing distinguishable at all.

The journey feels immensely long and yet in reality is over very quickly, the road passing in a confusion of speed and light, the siren our accompaniment. I'm not sure if I am coherent at all. The only thing I remember is Harold squeezing my hand. I squeeze back and a little bubble of hope swells in my chest.

At the hospital I sit in the waiting room staring at the square patterned lino on the floor, hopeful and fearful in turns. My thoughts go round and round. A death on Monday. An attack on Saturday. Coincidence or not? The hope is there still, but so too is rage.

'Ms Shaw.' A voice at my side. Black polished shoes. A long, blue trouser leg. A young, fresh-faced police officer introduces himself – something I don't catch, so he shows me his ID. I have been sitting in one hunched position for so long that I am rigid, my muscles taut. I stand up now, unclench my jaw and fists, and take a deep, steadying breath.

'Are you OK? Can I get you something?' he asks, concern in his voice.

'No. Thanks.' The only hot drinks here are from machines and my stomach feels queasy enough.

I tell him what I saw but again it isn't much, arriving as I did after the damage had been done.

'No reason for the attack?'

I tell him about Monday night and the reason we were there today – Rosalyn's request that we check out the house the family were inheriting – and the link to Bill Stone's death. The officer makes notes in a racing, unclear hand.

I have Peter Denton's card in my wallet from Tuesday and I hand it over. 'He was one of the officers dealing with the case.'

'With this attack tonight, was anything stolen?'

'Stolen?' I say, as if the word is unfamiliar. I hadn't even remotely considered the possibility of theft.

'His wallet?' he prompts. 'Do you know where it is?' He must be used to dealing with people who are in shock because he says the sentence evenly and slowly.

'No,' I say dazed. 'I didn't think. Wait. His coat is missing. He had it on when he went to the garage.'

The young man nods. 'I'll be back. Try not to worry.'

'Ms Shaw?' No long, blue trousered leg this time, but the thick white shoes of the nursing staff.

I stand up quickly, and immediately feel dizzy and light-headed. The woman standing in front of me has large-framed glasses and short white-grey hair and she is smiling. Her smile is telling and the fear that has been gnawing inside me slides into relief.

'He's asking for you. Can you come?'

The walk along the beige wards to the bed is long, and my shoes squeak on the shiny surface of the floor, like an odd little musical accompaniment to hope rising. 'Don't stay too long, and don't let him talk too much, but he was anxious to talk to you. Seeing you will settle him down.'

Harold is in a ward of six. In the hospital bed he looks smaller than usual and infinitely more vulnerable. The things from his pockets are on the cupboard next to him – his mobile phone and a little pile of keys. I realise with a sudden stab of guilt that I have left the door to the house wide open. Not that it matters. There wasn't anything to steal.

Harold smiles and I take his hand in my own. His face is pale, and in his eyes I can see both pain and fuzziness. His skin is almost the same colour as the bandage wound around his temple.

'Pretty rough, eh?' I say, squeezing his hand.

'For you probably more than me. If I have one more person asking me what day it is or who the prime minister is I'll get up and leave.' There is a touch of querulousness in his voice but it is strong enough. Relief coasts through me again, fresher now, like a gust of cold wind.

'Don't talk,' I say. 'They said not to talk too much.'

'I want to. I'm feeling pretty peaceful now, save for my head. They've drugged me up with something and told me that I've got to stay in overnight for observation.'

'After that you're coming to my house.'

He pauses before answering. 'Yes, I'd like that. I don't know what happened really. One minute I was standing there, the next... you were beside me I think, and I was warmer and it was easier to go back to sleep than to stay awake.'

'Did you see who it was?' I ask the question expecting he did. He had turned, I think, in the moment before the blow. He would have seen the person who attacked him.

He looks confused for a moment. 'I heard someone behind me but I thought it was you. I remember turning round to say something to you... and then... I didn't see anyone, Marlo, I lost my glasses.'

'You knocked some paint tins over when you fell. I heard the noise. That's when I realised...'

'Saved by the paint tins.' He closes his eyes and I squeeze his hand again, thinking about the faultiness of memory and wondering if, in time, he will remember the face of his attacker.

The young constable is back again. 'No coat at the property,' he says turning to me.

'My jacket,' Harold says with ready clarity. 'I took it off before I went into the garage. It's a pale one you see. I remember hanging it on the wing mirror of the car.'

'And your wallet?'

'In the pocket I think, or maybe my trousers.'

Harold's clothes have been bundled into a locker. I take them out, and between us we check the pockets, but everything that was in them is on the bedside cabinet. There is no wallet.

'You can't think of any other reason for the attack?'

Harold looks at me. 'I told him about Bill Stone,' I say, bundling the clothes back into the cupboard.

'You haven't made any enemies recently?' the police officer asks.

Harold smiles thinly. 'None that I can think of.'

'Did you meet anyone at the house?'

'No. No one.'

'Wait,' I say, looking up. 'There was someone, Harold, but he'd gone.'

'Who?'

'Jason Stone – Sam's son.' I hadn't remembered Jason, hadn't thought of him at all in the last few hours. 'He called in to check out the house.'

'Did you see him leave?' the officer asks.

'I didn't see the car leave,' I say thinking back. 'I heard it though.' I must have finished the sentence doubtfully, because he picks up on it straight away.

'*His* car?'

'No. You're right. I don't know.' All I heard was the roar of a healthy engine, and Jason had already told me that he had car trouble. It could have been anyone. An assumption rather than clear knowledge. I know from the past how dangerous assumptions can be.

'He didn't come to see me,' Harold says quietly now, the drugs taking effect.

'He was late for work. He said he was in a hurry.'

Jason Stone. I see the words form beneath the constable's hand. 'Do you know where he lives?'

'Not exactly. Somewhere in the St Kilda area.'

'How do you know that?' Harold asks groggily.

'He mentioned it, and Rosalyn told me at dinner the other night,' I explain. 'She told me that Sam lived near me. I assume Jason still lives at home.' Another assumption. They are everywhere.

'His description?'

'My height. Dark hair. Very slim. Very fit looking. Green eyes and colourful clothes.' He writes it down and I wait for him to finish before I go on.

'One thing I do know...someone was there in the front yard. I saw them from the ambulance as it pulled away.' By sheer will power and worry, I have kept this nagging fear at bay. Now I know that Harold is OK, it comes crowding in with the velocity of an express train. A person standing in the dark driveway of Bill Stone's house. The sense of threat as I stood standing guard over Harold. The thought of someone out there, watching, waiting.

'And?'

As with the runner in the park, there is nothing to describe, only a fleeting, unclear image in my mind. 'I saw them for a moment in the brake lights but they were just a blur of skin and eyes.'

'Hair colour?' he asks.

'I didn't see. I don't know.'

He looks at me doubtfully. I'm not sure where his doubt lies – the possibility of seeing someone hiding in the shadows from a moving, turning ambulance or the opposite. If I had seen skin and eyes, couldn't I give a better description? It is frustrating, all these half-hidden sightings. All the damage that someone has done. All I can do is hope that next time I will be close enough to see clearly, close enough to do something about it. I close my mind against this. I don't want there to be a next time. Harold is still awake, but only just.

'I'll let him sleep,' the officer says. 'Someone will be in touch.'

'Pretty hopeless, aren't I?' I say to Harold, who is lying with his eyes closed on the pillow. But he doesn't answer. He has succumbed to sleep at last, his head turned more comfortably into the pillow, his breath the even pattern of sleep. I stay with him until the nursing staff tell me to go home. Time has passed and a different shift has taken over. Harold hasn't moved since he first fell asleep and he looks as if he will sleep for years. I scoop up his keys and my mobile phone and head for home.

It is just on midnight, ten hours since Harold picked me up. The weather has changed and the longed for rain has finally arrived. No ordinary rain but a torrential, almost tropical downpour. Water rushes off concrete and baked earth and flows swiftly along gutters. On the roads, the traffic has slowed to a crawl, barely visible behind the heavy, blurring curtain of rain.

Harold's car is in South Yarra; home and Ebony are in St Kilda. I could either take a taxi to South Yarra or a taxi home. If there was a choice, the deluge has put paid to it. I am too tired to negotiate the rain, and at the moment, I never want to see the house in South Yarra again. Tomorrow is soon enough.

When I get back, Ebony has been on her own for too long. She scrambles around me, her feet sliding on the polished floor, sniffing at my legs and dancing around the back door, asking to be let out. I feel a pang of guilt – I should have rung Alicia and asked her to take care of her, as she has at other times. Ebony rushes out into the wet garden and then I feed her, heating up some packaged pasta for myself.

I would like very much to talk to someone. I would like someone to be here with me. The emptiness of the house seems oppressive and I ring Lee's number but her answering machine clicks on. I leave a brief message, feeling oddly disappointed. It is not just anyone I want to talk to but Lee, with her heavy doses of honesty and clarity. I reflect on these qualities briefly, aware of how they can shift from being annoying to desirable. It is Saturday night and I guess that Lee will be out somewhere with her latest love. Last time we went out to dinner, she talked about him a lot and it was impossible not to be warmed by her glow. I was glad of the warmth, the feeling of coming back to life, no matter how briefly or vicariously. But the mood had faded with her departing car lights as the quietness of the house settled around me.

I head to bed now, stepping out of my clothes where I am. It is when I take off my jeans that I feel the crackle of paper in my pocket. Two pieces of paper – Jason's phone number and the sheet of paper I had come across in the kitchen cupboard, just before the attack on Harold. I take it out and turn it over and back again. On both sides the paper is blank. I crumple both sheets into a tight, angry ball and throw them in the bin.

Chapter 12

Despite the weight of tiredness, sleep is slow to come. I listen to the rain on the roof, heavy and relentless, and think of Harold in his hospital bed, wondering if he is still asleep or if he too is listening to the rain.

When I wake at first light, my mood is different. The rain has stopped and sunshine finds its way into the bedroom. It is like waking to another season. Outside, sunlight catches in raindrops dripping off branches, gutterings and gate posts, lighting up the individual drops, brilliant as diamonds. Despite the dramas and uncertainties of yesterday and the past week, I am buoyant. Harold is going to be OK.

Next door, Alicia is depositing bundles of clothing into her small yellow van. Even from here I can see the rich colours that she uses in her creations. Today is Sunday, market day, a break from her normal work at a chemist's shop. I head outside to tell her the news.

'Marlo.' She turns at the sound of my approach, surprised to see me up so early. 'Is something wrong?'

Alicia is grey haired and dark eyed, an intelligent woman

with a quick, clear brain. Briefly I give her the details and she listens with a gentle gravity. When she speaks her accent seems more pronounced than usual, her voice charged with feeling.

'Thank God he wasn't there on his own. The cold is very bad now.' Alicia is Polish and has a healthy dislike of cold weather. I asked her once why she didn't live further north and she laughed. 'I am inconsistent, Marlo. I like the seasons – when spring comes and the blossom starts on the trees – and for that you need a proper winter.' Now she looks concerned and asks, 'How can I help?'

'Come in later to say hello, and stay for tea. And if you're around in the week, that would be wonderful.'

'Of course. And the attack? Do they know who it was?'

'No.'

'I see,' she nods slowly. 'That must be hard.'

I pause before answering. The image of Harold, pale skinned and defenceless on that cold concrete floor is suddenly overwhelming. I clench my fists, pressing my fingernails into my palms.

'Yes. I don't like my friends being attacked. I don't like what I don't understand.'

'No, none of us do. I'll come over this afternoon.'

I head to Harold's house and use his keys to let myself in. It feels strange being here without Harold, as though I am intruding. The house is very neat, the dishes washed and put away, the furniture cleaned and polished. This is the same house I have been in a million times before, but now, without Harold's presence, the aromas of his cooking, or the sounds of his music, it no longer seems warm or welcoming.

I search out clothing – jumpers, pyjamas and a pair of jeans. His own soap that smells as he does – clean and faintly fragrant. Toothpaste and a brush, and a spare pair of glasses. At the last moment I take a handful of CDs from his extensive collection of classical music, with no idea of what he likes the most. On the way home I shop for an invalid – fruit, pasta, chicken, vegetables. Ingredients for soup and sauces. The soup is an old recipe of Mum's, something we used to cook together on cold winter Sundays. The image of me as nurse, providing sustenance to the injured, seems incongruous and makes me smile. It is not a role I have played very often in my life, or very convincingly when I did.

While the soup simmers, I change the sheets on both beds, giving mine up for Harold, as I don't want him to have to climb the steep stairs to the spare room. There is some salvia and westringia in flower in the garden – long purple spikes and tiny purple blooms that look like haze. I pick an armful and place them in a vase on the bedside table.

Next, I ring for a taxi to take me to South Yarra to pick up Harold's car. The sunshine is benign and sets off a feeling of ease and well-being that should be at odds with my thoughts after yesterday, especially considering where I am headed. But the current of gladness is back again and this morning, in sunshine, the house looks less forbidding. Harold's car is where we left it, parked in the driveway, and the garden gates are still open. The police seem to have locked the front door but it doesn't matter because I don't want to go into the house. I do, however, very much want to see the garage in daylight.

The garage door is open and the sunshine floods in. I see a lot of things I didn't notice yesterday – the cobwebs and dust and clutter that were invisible in the gloom. The garage is home to a lot of junk stored haphazardly around the walls – pieces of broken furniture, some old pipes, painting equipment, including the paint tins that were knocked over yesterday, a few bags of papers and rubbish and an assortment of old tools. Not much in the way of enticement for a stranger looking for easy pickings. The only sign of the attack yesterday is a small patch of dried blood on the concrete.

I check the driveway, thinking about that glimpse of red eyes as the ambulance backed out. I find the sideways branch, snaking out at right angles to the drive, and I stand under it, considering height, but whoever stood there could have been crouching. I check the ground for footprints. If there were any in this fourth year of drought, last night's downpour has wiped them out. I move away feeling increasingly uneasy. The only thing that this little experiment has achieved is to give me a case of the creeps. In all that time I waited for the ambulance, Harold injured at my feet, someone was there. Someone waiting and watching. Until now my interest in Bill Stone has been nothing more than academic, a puzzle to be solved. Now the mystery has come in close and a hovering sense of dread seems to settle in my spine.

I am at the hospital by eleven. Harold is waiting, his one-eyed glasses perched on his head. He looks like a pirate, benign and lovable and impatient to leave. 'I hate hospitals,' he says, summing up what I can read on his face, 'wonderful places that they are.'

On the way home I treat him as a fragile passenger, driving smoothly, trying to protect him from bumps and sudden stops and tram tracks. He is chirpy and uncomplaining, making light of things, but every now and then he closes his eyes against the bright sunshine.

I show him where he will be sleeping and he lies down on the bed with a little sigh of pleasure and relief. He accepts my offer of soup and I stay with him while he drinks it, feeling a strong sense of happiness and relief. Sitting up in bed with a cup of soup, Harold looks comfortable, almost well. When he has finished, I take both cups and wash them, looking out into the garden, curious about the pleasure generated by this isolated spot of domesticity. There is, I decide, something curiously pleasant about being needed.

By the time I have dried the dishes and put them away, I have modified the thought. Harold now, and Lucy, with her weekly visits are vastly different from the burdens of an intimate relationship. Both of these domestic times have clearly established limits while those few months I lived with Tony had no limits and no clarity. I find myself cleaning the benches in a little gust of energy, considering the virtues of clarity.

With Tony I hadn't known what I wanted or even who I was. On my part there were no limits or expectations, but nor was there much in the way of hope or joy. It's hardly surprising that the whole thing was a confused mess that did neither of us any good. It wasn't all my fault, given the timing and the circumstances, but it was no basis for any kind of working relationship. This is the first time I have begun to understand cause and effect in regard to my relationship with Tony and this new insight is suddenly very welcome. I wring out the cloth and hang it over the drainer to dry, wondering why it has taken me so long to work it out. For someone who seeks clarity in other things, it seems strange that with this particular relationship, I have been so unclear for so long.

I make a few phone calls about work, the first to Tegan, who without hesitation accepts the offer of work over the next few days, and the next to Irene. I give her a brief run down of the situation and she hesitates before speaking.

'Marlo...' Her voice sounds different, slightly muffled as though she has been crying.

'Are you OK?' I ask belatedly, my mind still on Harold and recent events.

'Yes, I think I'm coming down with something. Don't worry about me, you've got enough on your plate.'

'I'm sorry.' I am surprised because in all the time I have known her, Irene has never been sick.

We discuss arrangements and tactics for explaining Harold's absence. We don't want to sensationalise things but Harold is almost an institution in the city and a day away from work will be noted. We settle on a version of the truth – a fall at home.

In the afternoon I have a visitor. No double act this time because Peter Denton is on his own. His clothes are different from the day he interviewed me in the office, his shirt a winter-weight forest green that suits his colouring. He looks far better in casual gear than he did in the dark grey suit.

Harold is still asleep and I don't want to disturb him. Denton senses my hesitation.

'Bad time?'

'Come in. Harold is asleep.'

'I'm sorry that it's come to this, two attacks in the one week is pretty hard to take.'

I offer him some tea and we carry the cups into the lounge. The room is tidy and tastefully decorated but I have unbalanced it with my desk and the extra TV pushed into a corner. Peter Denton looks around with interest and for a moment I see the room through different eyes and wonder if he sees it as I do – stale and unchanging. No light touches as there were in Jenny's day – no flowers or piles of magazines, nothing to make it warm and cosy or lived in.

We sit looking out over the small front garden with the smudge of lavender bushes at the fence and the street beyond. I tell him what I told the officer at the hospital – the little I saw.

'Difficult for you,' Denton comments quietly.

I tell him what Harold and I have been mulling over with regard to Bill Stone's life. The theory of him hiding out in the park, the vagrant clothing a form of disguise, but for what reason we have no idea. Something from his past catching up with him. But that wouldn't explain the attack on Harold.

I haven't dealt with this yet. The attack on Harold seems to stop my brain working. My mind feels as sluggish as glue.

I hear Harold before I see him. His footsteps in the hallway sound slow and tentative and his face is very pale.

'I heard voices,' he says, extending his hand to Denton. 'I thought it might be you. They said at the hospital that you'd come.' He sits down on the couch next to me, his movements slower, stiffer than usual. Lack of mobility adds years to people and Harold looks much older and frailer than he did a few hours ago, tucked up in bed.

'I wondered if you've remembered anything about the attack?' Denton asks.

'Not a thing,' Harold says.

'The officer who filed the report says your wallet was stolen.'

'Yes.'

'And are you satisfied with that? Do you think that robbery was the motive for the attack?'

There is a silence as we wait for Harold's answer. He looks steadily out the window. 'I doubt it.'

Denton turns to me. 'Marlo?'

'No.' On this, at least, I am definite. 'Robbery doesn't explain the person who waited in the garden. If they'd come for a wallet they would have left when they'd got it. And last night, when I waited for the ambulance, robbery was the last thing that occurred to me.'

'So some other reason? Fine, but what?' He looks between us.

'I don't know,' Harold says. 'But there's a lot we don't know about all of this. Something to do with me befriending Bill perhaps? Who knows . . .' He goes quiet.

Denton takes over. 'The house in South Yarra has been vacant for about a month. Before that, there were a string of tenants. We've spoken to the neighbours, most of whom were watching footy yesterday. The only one who noticed anything remembered a young man who fits the description of Jason Stone. There were no other sightings. The lab has checked out the garage and we're waiting for the results.'

No one says anything and Denton continues. 'Who knew you'd be at the house yesterday?'

Harold stirs himself momentarily and shifts his gaze to Denton. 'The people at dinner on Thursday night – Bill Stone's family. I knew them from before, but you know that.'

'Marlo?'

'The same. I'm not sure about Kristin Stone because when Harold and Rosalyn were making arrangements, I think she'd already gone to bed. And Amy was with me. Not that it means much, because they could have talked about it afterwards.'

'Anyone else? Friends? Workmates?'

'There wasn't much time. We arranged it on Thursday and

I don't know if it came up much on Friday, although people are interested in Bill Stone's story. You know, a homeless man with a house in South Yarra. It's the contradiction that fascinates people.'

Harold, I know, has a poor memory for his own conversations. He remembers clearly what people tell him but not a lot of what he tells others. The kind of person who will tell you the same story a few times, as though each time it is fresh and new. Harold chats to lots of people but it's hard to see someone in his extensive network following him with an attack in mind. And whoever he told or didn't tell, he would never have given out the address, or details of the task.

Denton pushes it further. 'Suppose for a moment that the attack on you has nothing to do with Bill Stone. Is there anything else that could explain it? You haven't made any recent enemies?'

'No, I'm sure of that.' Harold's gaze has returned steadfastly to the view out the window, as though disinterested in all this. I put my hand on his arm, worried about him. Denton's tea must be cold by now, but he finishes the last of it.

'How are you getting on with Bill Stone's death?' I ask. 'Was there any response to the appeal for witnesses?'

'Some response,' he says guardedly. 'Nothing on the runner you mentioned but we're working on a couple of things.' This, I assume, is police speak for mind your own business, but he goes on. 'We have a few witnesses who overheard an argument in the park over some money. One of the men was Bill Stone. The other man went away but there's nothing to say he didn't come back.'

I look up surprised. I was so sure of the my theory. Bill Stone's past finally catching up with him – that an argument over money seems out of place. Denton must see the look on my face.

'It might not matter what he got up to in his life, Marlo. It is his death that counts.'

I don't answer.

'The other thing we're working on is Bill Stone himself. He arrived in Melbourne on the 21 July as a passenger on the Indian Pacific train. One of the cabin staff recognised his photo.'

I look up. This I can cope with.

'He wasn't quite so derelict then. He was described as being a quiet, clean-shaven, well-dressed man, but there's no doubt it was him.' He raises an eyebrow. 'Amazing what a bit of second-hand shopping can do.'

'Yes,' I agree. 'And ten days is plenty of time to grow stubble, if not a full beard.'

Beside me, Harold is very still, his gaze unshifting.

Denton picks up his earlier theme. 'But even if we accept the idea that Bill Stone was up to something or lying low for some reason, it doesn't change the fact that he could have been killed for the few dollars he had in his pocket.'

'No. Except that the few dollars in his pocket were still there?'

'That happens more than you'd think. It's the shock of what they've done that gets most muggers. Someone dying at their feet isn't easy to cope with.'

Again I don't answer. This is the first time I have involved myself with the murder as such. Up to now I have been concentrating on the man and the mystery of his life. I'm not sure I want to get involved with the mystery of his death. Somehow the question leaps out anyway.

'What was he killed with?'

'The rail of the park bench.'

'Sorry?'

'There were two blows. The first blow was struck through his hat – something curved, the lab says. It could have been something the attacker brought with them or something they picked up in the park, the nearest implement to hand. Whatever it was didn't kill Bill Stone. He fell and fractured his skull on the park bench.'

I stand up and pace the room, unable to sit still. The nearest implement to hand. There is something chilling about the words, and the lack of definite facts bothers me. There seem to be a lot of things about Bill Stone's murder that aren't definite. A fact would be nice. I like facts.

'There is something the pathologist has said that changes things.' Denton's tone seems ominous. I see Harold shift his head and notice the renewed interest on his face.

'According to the lab, it took Bill Stone some time to die.'

Silence for a minute. 'How much time?' Harold's voice.

'Ten minutes, give or take.'

We all contemplate it, the horror of a slow death. The blood draining from his body. Ten minutes. No murderer is going to hang around for ten minutes with a dead body. My knees feel weak and I have to sit down.

'So the argument was at least ten minutes before he died.'

'Yes.'

No wonder we didn't hear it. This is something, at least, that makes sense. Ten minutes before we found Bill in the park I was stuck on the phone, and Harold was waiting on the street for the courier. Beside me Harold is unmoving and I put my hand on his arm. He looks like he should go back to bed.

'Did you run a check on Bill Stone?' I ask.

'No criminal record either here or in the other states. We've been to see Jason Stone about the attack on you, Harold, but he wasn't home. Not surprising, I guess – it's the weekend and he's a young man. You met him, Marlo, what was he like?'

'He was friendly and pleasant.' An attractive sequence of images rises up – the bright clothing, the green eyes, the dark skin and wide smile. I dismiss them and concentrate on the question.

'He was curious about the house and his inheritance but that's all I can tell you.' Which is nothing at all. In the same situation we would all be curious.

Silence again. Denton stands up and we follow, Harold with more effort than I like to see.

Denton looks at him. 'I'd avoid dark places for the moment and I'd keep company with others, at least until things are clearer.'

'Yes, I intend to.' Harold looks grim.

'We'll be in touch.'

I go with Denton to the door and open it. He stands there a moment as if considering something. 'There's a whole lot of stuff on the blood evidence, Marlo. I didn't want to mention it in front of Harold, because he looks done in but if you're interested, it might help you to understand the reasons we think what we think. I can see you're interested.'

'Yes, I would like to know what it's all about. I don't like things that don't make sense.'

'I understand that. I had you down as the curious type when I first met you.'

'You had me down as the unreliable type,' I counter, smiling. 'You didn't believe me about the runner.'

He pauses before answering. 'Disbelief is too strong a word. It just seemed unlikely.'

I can hardly disagree.

He smiles, surprisingly friendly. 'Ring me if you want to talk.'

When I sit down, Harold looks as if he is coming out of some protracted reverie.

'Confusing, isn't it?' He says wearily. 'One good thing, Marlo, is that whatever remote thoughts I had about the police suspecting me have been well and truly blown out of the water. I guess there's nothing like a personal attack to shift suspicion.'

He almost seems pleased with the idea and this surprises me.

'Any other thoughts?' I ask.

'Only a couple. The first is that what happened to me is also what happened to Bill Stone. Am I alive simply because I have a harder head?'

'Probably.' I agree, thinking about the runner and the ten minutes it took Bill Stone to die. I think about Harold lying still on that cold concrete floor and anger stirs in me again.

'And the other thought?'

'Is that I'm very glad you were there.'

I hesitate, and for some reason feel like crying. Instead I try for lightness. 'I've always told you that I have my uses.' And am rewarded with a smile.

Harold goes back to bed and I prepare chicken casserole for tea. When Alicia arrives, cool and brisk after her day at the market, I take Ebony for a walk along the seafront. Not Port Melbourne this time, but the other way – to Elwood, Brighton and beyond. Palm trees, Norfolk pines, the silver green of salt bush. The sea stretching on and on in two distinct shades of blue – dark blue near the sea wall and rocky breakwaters; silvery blue in the distant, deeper sea channels.

Ebony runs ahead, enticed by new scents and places to explore. I am pleased to get out of the house and have the time and space to think. Not that my thoughts take me anywhere except the same inconclusive paths they have already travelled.

Just past the Elwood canal, the house I visited on Thursday night comes into view. It has that heavy solidity of houses built in the 1920s and, unlike the house in South Yarra, it has grace and style. In daylight the need for maintenance is more apparent than before. The house is clean enough but in need of attention and fresh paint. I think of Amy and wonder how she is. I wonder if she is nervous about the hockey match on Wednesday and if she has had the chance to practise any of the more serious magic she talked about.

It is impossible to tell if anyone is home as only the top floor is visible behind the garden wall. It occurs to me that since the attack on Harold, I haven't thought of Rosalyn at all. I didn't think to contact to let her know the news. But then, there is no need. Harold is up and moving around and he has his own phone. If he wants to tell her, there is absolutely nothing stopping him. I am pleased about this. I don't want to invest Rosalyn with more importance in Harold's life than is strictly necessary. And perhaps, along with the relief, I feel just a little bit smug.

Chapter 13

When I get back Harold is in the bath and Alicia is sitting at the kitchen bench working out her accounts from the market.

'How'd you go today?' I ask as I take the salad ingredients out and wash the spinach, mushrooms and tomatoes.

'It was a good day,' she says, looking up over her glasses. 'The weather helps but I don't want to talk about that. I want to hear the rest of what happened.'

I tell her the sequence of events and about meeting up with Sam Stone at the dinner on Thursday night, the conversation we had about the market and about Alicia in particular.

'Do you know his son, Jason?'

'Yes, of course. He often helps out with the stall.'

'What does he do?'

'Why this sudden thirst for knowledge about Jason?' Alicia asks, her use of idioms precise and attractive in her accented English.

I tell her about meeting him, the timing of it all, just minutes before Harold was attacked. Alicia shakes her head slightly. This is one thing I have always admired about her –

no matter what I say, she doesn't dismiss it out of hand.

'He's studying horticulture at the local college. I went along to their open day last week.'

'I didn't realise you knew him so well.'

She shrugs. 'I've been friends with Sam for years now and you get to hear about the kids. Can I help with dinner?'

'You can open the wine if you like.' I dig out the corkscrew and take a bottle of Tyrell's from the fridge.

'Harold told me some of what happened earlier,' she says.

I slice the mushrooms thinly, my knife making little chopping sounds as I go. 'What do you think?'

She looks at me for a long moment. 'Among other things, that for you, it is too soon after Jenny. Are you sure you're up to it?'

'Up to it?' I repeat. I haven't seriously considered doing any thing about it, save thinking about the puzzle of Bill Stone's life.

It is only now, after the attack on Harold, that Bill's death offers itself up to me as something that needs to be solved, with it's little flotilla of compelling reasons – concern for Harold, the need for resolution so that life can return to normal, and, more simply but just as compelling as the need to understand.

But I know what Alicia is driving at. After all, I was the one who solved Jenny's murder. I found out that the murderer was a member of my own family.

'I haven't done anything yet, Alicia, except go round in circles.'

'Harold said it was confusing.'

'The police think that Bill Stone was killed as the result of an argument over money. I'm not sure what they think about the attack on Harold but they seem to be considering it as a separate thing.'

'And you don't?'

'I don't think so, but I'm not sure. None of it makes much sense.' As I chop the tomatoes into thin segments, the knife cracking loudly against the board, I tell her my latest thoughts and fears.

'How do you think Harold is?' I ask.

'He's OK. A knock like that is not good for anyone but he is very strong and you were there to help.'

'Tomorrow I have to go to work and Harold is staying home. I wondered if you'd come in to keep him company.'

She pushes in the wings on the bottle opener and the cork slides out. 'Of course.'

I say my thoughts aloud as they come. 'If Harold's attack and Bill Stone's death are linked, as I guess they are, the answer *must* lie with Bill Stone. I want to know why he was hanging around Flagstaff. I want to know what it was in his past that sent him there in disguise. Until I know that, I can't accept that he was a victim of a random argument over money.'

Alicia finds two glasses and pours the dark red wine. I look up from my pile of chopped vegetables. 'That's what I'm going to do,' I say decisively, with the air of someone making a great announcement. It feels like one too, like direction and purpose.

Alicia sips her wine. 'Good luck to you, Marlo,' she says even toned.

After dinner, Alicia goes home. Harold sees her to the door while I do the washing up.

'I rang Rosalyn today,' Harold says, coming into the kitchen.

'How is she?'

He contemplates his answer. 'Upset about the attack on me, and, to make it worse, the funeral is tomorrow. After that she has to go to Adelaide.'

'So soon?' But not really so soon. It has been almost a week now. It just seems an eternity. 'Are you going to the funeral?'

'I said I would. I think Rosalyn needs support.'

'I'll take you. Tegan is coming in tomorrow anyway and I'm sure they can cover for us both for a few hours.'

Harold doesn't argue and I suspect he is glad of the offer.

'Aren't you running tonight?' he asks.

It is past eight o'clock and I am tired, drained of energy. I feel as if I could hardly climb the stairs to bed, let alone run the usual seven kilometres. 'Not tonight.'

We spend the rest of the evening discussing things like safety precautions. Only yesterday, personal safety was taken for granted, something guaranteed and immutable. Our safety strategy is simple enough, but hopefully effective – things like Harold keeping the dog with him, and programming all our numbers into his phone. Alicia has also agreed to keep an eye on him.

'Don't worry, Marlo,' Harold smiles. 'I have a very good sense of my own importance.'

He goes off to bed and I let the dog out. Between Bill's death and Harold's attack, something doesn't sit right. I have talked about it, thought about it, become preoccupied with it all, but I haven't got the balance right. I haven't given enough consideration to certain things and perhaps have given too much to others. Curiosity is as definite as hunger and I recognise the feeling with absolute clarity. I would very much like to know what it is that I have overlooked.

I head up to bed in Lucy's small upstairs room but before I go to sleep, I spend some time committing facts and impressions to paper. It is an interesting process and the pages fill up quickly. I reduce the bulk of words to key points. The muddle reduced to a concise list.

My mind full of it, I cross to the window and look out. Lucy's room offers distant glimpses of the sea and a good view of the street below. The night is clear and sharp and I breathe in the crisp air. Next door, Alicia's bedroom light is on and I feel comforted by her closeness. Below me, Harold is asleep in my room. Apart from Lucy, Harold is the first overnight guest I have had since Tony and I parted company. I lie in Lucy's narrow, warm bed and listen to Ebony's soft breathing from her mat on the floor. Gradually sleep overcomes me, a gentle sleep uninterrupted by dreams.

Chapter 14

I forgo my usual morning walk in deference to Harold's safety. It is no sacrifice because the weather has changed again. The dense cloud cover is back and cold gusts of air hurtle in from the Southern Ocean, rattling the kitchen windows. When the wind eases, the rain begins, pelting hard against the roof.

I look through my notes of last night and commit the facts as I know them to computer, storing them on the hard drive and on disk. I ring Alicia to let her know I am leaving and tell her about the safety precautions that Harold and I discussed last night. In deference to the weather and the need to take Harold to the funeral later, I drive in to work, parking in Harold's permanent spot behind the office. Irene is in before me, her rigid grey head bent down over Harold's appointment books and folders. Her clothes match her hair colour, the same iron grey in skirt and jacket. The only colour on her desk is the bunch of jonquils by her phone – the pale, early flowering variety with their heady, effusive scent.

'Morning, Irene.' I wait for her attention and when she does look up, her eyes are still pink and dry looking. She looks immensely tired. 'How are you feeling today?'

'Not too bad,' she says with a touch of martyrdom in her voice. 'I thought I'd come in early and sort things out.'

I tell her of my plans to take Harold to Bill Stone's funeral and for once she doesn't comment or change expression but instead picks up the jonquils.

'Can you give these to him for me?'

'Of course, but he'll probably be in tomorrow if you want to give them to him yourself.'

She shakes her head. 'Best to get them to him today.'

'Thanks for setting things up here.'

A small shake of her head, dismissing thanks. Her face is very still. 'I'm glad he's staying with you, Marlo. I'm pleased to know he's in good hands.'

I can tell that it's a hard thing for her to say but she does it anyway. This is one of the few positive comments we have shared recently. Despite various thaws in our relationship in the past, the wall between us is still immense.

'Thanks, Irene.' I head to my office and close the door.

The morning passes uneventfully. I have all the faxes in now for the Peter Jenkins case and I spend the first part of the morning completing my report. I hear Tegan and Irene from time to time but don't catch much of what they are saying. I don't think Tegan is any more forthcoming with Irene than she is with me. Sometimes I think I should make more of an effort with Tegan. Sometimes, I don't. It is her decision, after all.

At eleven I am out and about when my mobile phone rings. I check the display. It's not Harold. And I don't recognise the number.

'Marlo, this is Shane Black. I've just heard about Harold.' His tone is quiet but full of concern.

'He's OK. He's coming in tomorrow.' I say, as I have said to everyone who asks, but Shane doesn't seem to want to leave it there. I can hear another question building in the silence.

'Marlo, did he really just fall at home? Irene sounded strange this morning.'

I don't think Harold will mind Shane knowing the truth. 'He was attacked, Shane. Someone hit him over the head.' I hear him take a deep breath.

'What was it, a mugging?'

'We're not sure.'

He hesitates. 'I see. So what do you think?'

I almost smile at his pushiness. Here is someone used to finding things out. 'It's complicated.'

'I've got a spare hour at lunch time, you could tell me then.'

I hesitate. Adding another hour to my absence this afternoon is not going to make any difference to the office but this is the man who loves a good argument. This is the man who likes to tie people up in knots of their own making. But then I remember that this is an old image – the man I spent time with last week was nothing like this.

The prospect is tempting. I would very much like someone else's opinion and Shane Black seems like a good choice. He is an outsider, he should be impartial and he has a good analytical brain.

'I could meet you but I have to leave at one o'clock.'

'A coffee on the run then. Same place. And I have some news that you might be interested in. I'll tell you then.' A cryptic comment. I love cryptic.

The half hour in the café passes in a blur. Shane doesn't interrupt or comment save to ask a question or two.

'None of it seems to make any sense,' I say in frustration.

'Life is never quite as orderly as we would like.' Shane's face is still but for once his hands are restless. He runs his finger up and down the length of his thumb.

'I don't need orderly, I just want it to make sense. You said you have some news I might be interested in.'

'The police have made an arrest for Bill Stone's murder. It's on the grapevine at the moment but I have it on good authority.'

I put my coffee cup down with a little jolt. This is news.

Peter Denton seemed nowhere near making an arrest yesterday. But Shane Black, working where he does, would be in a position to know from the start. His office is the first port of call for documentation from the police, the first step in the legal process. Curiosity burns and he must see it on my face.

'I don't know the details yet, because we're waiting on the paper work. I could let you know when it comes through if you like.'

'Yes, I would like that very much.' It's five to one. Unless I leave now I will be late picking up Harold for the funeral. 'I've got to go.'

'Say hello to Harold for me.' Shane takes a card from his wallet and presses it into my hand. 'If you ever feel like talking, Marlo, about this or anything else, I'd be pleased to hear from you. I'll ring you soon.'

The drive home takes longer than usual, simply because the weather is so bad. The rain blows in hard against the windscreen, reducing visibility, and great gusts of wind buffet the side of the car. I find myself considering Shane Black again. The changes in him since he left Melbourne two years ago are immense. But then, I think, that he is probably thinking much the same about me. Between us both, I would hazard, there are a couple of stories to tell.

When I get home, Ebony greets me at the door with her usual bounding welcome. Inside there is a note on the kitchen bench from Alicia and under the note is a video. As usual it is a comedy, part of Alicia's stategy to cheer me up. I appreciate both the kindness of the thought and the contradiction of a chemist offering humour rather than chemistry to lift my mood.

In the kitchen there is also a great bouquet of flowers that Alicia has placed in a vase, along with a card from Rosalyn: *What can I say? Get better soon. With love, Rosalyn.* She hasn't spared any expense. The flowers are colourful a mix of tulips, jonquils and early daffodils, all blues and yellows, with feathery sprigs of pale green fern.

Harold is asleep and doesn't stir to my footsteps or when I quietly call his name. His breathing is deep and his face peaceful. Outside, the trees are bent hard against the torrent of the raging wind. I have no wish to drag Harold from a warm bed and healing sleep into such a bitter, cold day. Whatever I do, the funeral will go ahead without him. I make an executive decision and steal quietly from the room.

I pull up in the car park, next to Rosalyn's dull gold Mazda. I have decided to go to the funeral instead, so that I can explain Harold's absence to Rosalyn and make up somehow for the support he wanted to offer her. I want to pay Harold's respects to a man he had shared his lunch with and my own to a man I had never met but whom I have become inordinately interested in. The rain has stopped now and the wind is quieter than before but the sky is still leaden and the car park grey and waterlogged.

As I am late, I sit just inside the door and wait for the funeral to be over and for the family to come out. There are only two of them – Sam and Rosalyn, both dressed in dark clothing. No sign of the grandchildren or Kristin. No clusters of the family and friends that you would normally associate with funerals. Suddenly I feel unsure about being here. I am no good with other people's grief, but Sam has already seen me and nods acknowledgment. He looks like I feel – out of place and anxious to get away. He drops a hand lightly on Rosalyn's shoulder and heads off. Rosalyn hesitates, unsure of the reason for my presence.

'Harold couldn't come,' I say and explain the circumstances.

'I see,' she nods in a single large gesture as though to someone short-sighted. 'Thank you for coming to tell me. I appreciate it.'

In the dull foyer it is hard to read her expression. 'Come and have a coffee with me, Marlo. There's a café two doors down and I would like the company.'

Given the circumstances, I can hardly refuse and we walk, heads down, our pace slow against the wind. Rosalyn finds a seat and I order coffee and two blueberry muffins. When they arrive at the table Rosalyn looks at me briefly and nods her thanks but her mouth twitches faintly and I wonder what emotion she is suppressing.

I cut the muffins in half and spread them with butter. Rosalyn takes a miniature bottle of brandy from one of the compartments in her bag and adds some to her cup. She offers the same to me.

'No, thank you.'

'Funeral supply.' She smiles faintly. 'Did you meet my father, Marlo?'

'I wish I had.' This is true but not for the usual reasons. My curiousity seems slightly crass given the circumstances. 'What was he like?'

This is the same question I asked Harold at the beginning of all this, a question I have asked myself often over the past week. I am beginning to feel like Alice in Wonderland, constantly trying to make sense of some strange world, forever running after different people asking questions they don't really want to answer.

'He left us a long time ago, Marlo, and I think it was the best thing he could have done.' Her voice is closed and for a moment neither of us speak. Rosalyn crumbles her muffin into small pieces and picks at the crumbs, eating them in a succession of little attacks, like a bird eating seed. Curious table manners, I would have thought, for someone who runs a deportment school.

'Tell me, Marlo, do you believe in family characteristics?' Her voice is slightly slurred and I suspect that the brandy she has just added to her coffee isn't her first.

'What do you mean exactly?'

She waves her hand airily, flashing a great silver ring on her small finger. 'Oh, you know, little things, like a father being a suspected criminal or losing control enough to put someone in hospital. A savage gene or a criminal gene. Do you think the it shows up in the children?'

'No,' I say definitely. 'I think things like green eyes show up but not criminal tendencies.'

She licks a finger and wipes up the last of the crumbs from her plate.

'Just as well, eh? In the circumstances.' She finishes her coffee and stands up.

'Can I drive you home, Rosalyn?'

'Don't you think I'm capable?'

I don't, but I don't say so. 'Funerals are difficult.'

She smiles at me and the smile is simple and charming. 'Yes, they certainly are. Thanks for the drink and the thought, but I'll be fine.'

She heads out of the café and I follow her, a tall woman in high heels, ash-grey stockings and a dark winter coat. She swings her arms as she moves, and her heavy silver ring gleams in the dull light. A jaunty walk, and from behind she looks as if she hasn't got a care in the world. Perhaps, in the circumstances, you can't expect grief, but you can expect something, surely. Some sense of sadness or loss.

Another thought strikes me as I watch her, one that has nothing to do with death and family relationships but the well-being of a valued friend. Despite the reason I am here, she hasn't once asked about Harold. I watch her walk away, feeling colder than ever towards her. I remember the fleeting twitch of her mouth and it comes to me in a little flash of understanding what that was about. She was amused at my thoughtful inclusion of the muffins.

She picks her way across the sodden car park to her gold Mazda, sidestepping puddles as she goes, and there is no doubt about the spring in her step, the sense of satisfaction with her lot that her walk conveys.

Chapter 15

As I open my car door, a sky-blue station wagon pulls in next to me. Kristin gets out and looks around uncertainly before recognising me.

'Marlo, I've missed it, haven't I?'

'Yes, Rosalyn's just left.'

She looks paler than the last time I saw her, as though the headache on Thursday night has been with her ever since. Her eyes look tired, her hair less glossy and her skin dull.

'I couldn't get back in time. What . . . were there many people?'

'Sam and Rosalyn and me. Harold couldn't come.'

She closes her eyes as if the light is bright. 'Three people. Not much for a life time is it?' She blinks rapidly. 'I heard about Harold. How is he?'

At least she asks, I think. More marks for compassion than her sister. 'He's OK. Getting better.'

'Amy wanted to come but Ros said no.' She runs her hand through her hair, dragging at it with her nails. 'I'll just go in and say goodbye.'

'Yes, of course.'

I watch her walk across the car park, a heaviness to her tread and head for home, glad to be away from it all. I make another casserole, lamb this time, flavouring it with onions and rosemary. Still no news of the arrest.

Harold wakes in the late afternoon, looking rested and more comfortable. I make tea and give him the flowers from Irene, the small bunch of jonquils that look lost next to the huge bunch from Rosalyn. We sit in the kitchen with its aroma of slowly cooking food, watching the rain easing down the window panes, and I tell him about going to the funeral in his place.

'How was Rosalyn?'

'Fine,' I say but leave the rest of it silent – too fine, glowing with it.

We move on to the routine things of the day – work matters and the messages of goodwill from different people. I have the sense that Harold is almost enjoying himself.

I follow up with the real news, the arrest that Shane told me about. I am pleased to see the look of interest on his face sharpen – a look that is a long way from yesterday's detachment, because it shows me that Harold is coming back into the world.

'I've been doing some thinking today,' Harold announces. 'I remembered a conversation I had with Bill. We were discussing some crime or other that was making the news, and he said there were two reasons why most criminals get caught.'

'What are they?'

'The need to tell someone how clever they've been, and not being able to leave well enough alone – the criminal equivalent to thinking you've left the iron on. He said that if you don't get sucked into either of these things, then there's a good chance of getting away with it.'

'He didn't have a criminal record.'

'No, I know that, but I bet there was something personal in it.'

If Harold thinks so then it is quite likely to be true. He is a perceptive man in most things. For some reason I think of Irene's strained face at work today. If Harold lacks perception anywhere, it's to do with the strength of Irene's feeling towards him. I don't comment. His personal relationships are none of my business and Irene isn't usually high on my list for sympathy.

Alicia visits to see how Harold is, and I head out for an early run, leaving them with instructions to answer my phone in case Shane rings.

We have eaten and washed up and Alicia has gone home before the phone rings. Shane Black's voice is quiet but informative. 'I'm sorry to ring so late but I've been out. That information we talked about today has come through.' I hear the rustle of paper. 'The informing officer is Peter Denton and the arrested man is a Jamie Griggs. Apparently Griggs and Bill Stone had an argument in the park, shortly before the murder. Do you know him?'

'Jamie Griggs? No.'

In the lounge, Harold has put on some music, something that I don't recognise. It must be one of the CD's I picked up from his house. A single flute rises up, fragile and eerie.

'Griggs was a local apparently. He lived in the hostel for a long time and no one seems to know where he moved to. Harold might know him.'

'I'll ask, if you like.'

'Yes, do that.' His voice is hesitant, as if there is something else he wants to say.

'What is it, Shane?'

'No, it'll keep. I'll catch up with you soon, Marlo.'

I hang up and head to the lounge. Harold looks up when I come in.

'Jamie Griggs. He used to live in the hostel.' Harold's face, drops, his shock visible.

'I don't believe it,' he says, coolly, emphatically. 'Jamie Griggs wouldn't hurt anyone.'

'I don't know who he is.'

He shakes his head slightly. 'I think you met him, Marlo. He was the one who always had something in his hands — a stone

105

or a feather or a leaf. He was an older man, very stiff, as though he'd slept outside all his life.'

My memory leaps back to a time before Jenny's death. One lunch time in the park. I remember a man sharing Harold's park bench, almost warily, as though at any minute he might simply disappear. In his hand he held a parrot's feather, his fingers running down its length, the blues and greens of the feather, shifting with the movement. He had kept his eyes down, absorbed in the object, as if concentrating on something small and close would keep me and the outside world at bay.

I remember the night of the murder and the shuffling figure on the edge of the bright police lighting. Jamie Griggs. At least we have a name now.

'He was there, Harold, or someone very like him. When I went back for your coat I saw him from the office window.'

I put my hand on Harold's shoulder, not sure what he is thinking.

'I don't believe it,' he says again. 'He is much too gentle to attack someone and leave them for dead.'

I don't know that I agree. What I have learned in the past is that people are capable of extraordinary things and there is no way of judging an individual's capacity to kill. We are quiet for a moment, both of us concerned with our own areas of doubt.

'Jamie Griggs doesn't explain the runner. If Jamie Griggs murdered Bill Stone and headed off before we arrived, who was the runner? What were they doing hanging around? And if they were innocent, why haven't they been in touch with the police?'

Harold looks at me. 'The runner,' he repeats. 'I'd forgotten about that.'

'And why was Jamie Griggs still there when I went to work to get your coat. If it took Bill Stone ten minutes to die, why was he still there?'

He stands up and looks defeated. 'No idea, Marlo. Maybe it will look clearer in the morning.' He shuffles slightly as he walks. 'I'm off to bed.'

I let Ebony out, thinking it through. When she eventually wanders back I haven't made any headway. Ten minutes between the attack and the death. More time than that for the ambulance to arrive and for me to collect Harold's coat. Twenty minutes, maybe. Ten minutes for the runner. Twenty minutes for Jamie Griggs. Enough time to call the police or get help from someone. Neither of those people in the park had gone for help or made their escape. This is a fact. Why not? Why didn't at least one of them go for help?

Chapter 16

Another day of rain. Ebony looks mournfully at me – she hasn't had a walk since Sunday, so we head out anyway. When we get back, we are both drenched. Harold comes into the kitchen while I'm cooking breakfast.

'If I'm going to work, Marlo, I'll need some clothes.'

'Well, let's get some then.'

He smiles and doesn't argue. 'We. That's careful of you, Marlo.'

'Well, why not? You're too precious to lose and I'm not the only one who thinks so. Even Irene likes me now, because I'm taking care of you.'

He smiles. 'Ah, one of the benefits of being clobbered is peace in the office at last.'

I go with him to his house and wait in the hallway which overlooks the rainy street, bemused by the role of bodyguard that I have taken on. The house is silent and cold and I am glad to leave.

'Got everything?' I ask.

Harold pats the bulky sports bag. 'The important things,

Marlo. Jocks and socks and jumpers, and a couple of decent bottles of Brown Brothers. All set.'

At home he unpacks his clothing and I leaf through a library book while I wait. It is a collection of sporting photos from the sixties, blurred images of athletes straining at the tape.

'I've got something to tell you,' Harold says coming into the room and looking slightly puzzled. 'It might throw a bit more light on Bill Stone.'

'What is it?' I ask, changing focus easily.

'There was a letter in Bill Stone's pocket from someone called Derek. The police asked me about it last week and they asked Rosalyn. It's only now that I've realised it could mean something.'

'Go on,' I say, intrigued.

'The letter was written on the 17 July in Perth. It was short enough, so I can remember the gist of it if not the actual words. Apparently Derek, whoever he might be, was coming back to town on the 19 July, after a long absence. He said he was looking forward to catching up with Bill again.'

I look at him for a long time, working out the implications.

'Yes, you're right.' I say eventually. It is not so much the words in the letter but the timing that is important.

'The letter was hand delivered and if Derek wasn't already back in town, he must have had a friend deliver it.'

'And Bill Stone ups and leaves soon after. Not much of a welcoming committee.'

'Yes. Exactly what I thought.'

'Where's the letter now?'

'No doubt the police still have it in one of their innumerable evidence bags. They asked Rosalyn if she knew any Dereks but of course she didn't.'

Enigmatic words contained in a letter – words that seem to be from a friend, but could as easily be from an enemy. Bill Stone arrived in Melbourne on the 21 July and this letter was written and possibly delivered on 17. Four days between the delivery of the letter and Bill Stone's arrival in a distant city.

Whatever else it means, it shows that Bill Stone lost no time in getting away.

We look at each other for a moment. So the reason for him living rough is out there somewhere. Not just idle eccentricity as I have sometimes thought.

'Tricky, isn't it? Harold says, chewing over the problem. 'We could find out all we need to know about Bill Stone. He could be a criminal six times over. He could be anything on the planet, but the police have their case and they seem to believe it has nothing to do with the man himself.'

'If he was on the run from this Derek character, it doesn't explain the attack on you, at least not to me.'

Another pause for contemplation.

'Unless it was mistaken identity, Marlo. Heaven knows, it was dark enough in the garage. Perhaps whoever it was thought I was Bill.'

'But Bill was dead already,' I say. It seems obvious.

'Yes, I know that and you know that but perhaps whoever attacked me didn't.' A lift in his voice as he follows the thought. 'It makes a kind of sense. Bill Stone was attacked out of the blue, for no reason, save a few dollars in his pocket. But the person Bill Stone was hiding from might not know that. I mean why would he?'

'The death made the newspapers.' I suggest.

'It did. A small paragraph on page six that you wouldn't see unless you were looking out for it. And anyway, the article I read didn't name him. It said something about an unknown man being found dead in the Flagstaff gardens by some city workers. You and me mate.'

We look at each other for a long moment and I remember that the police appeal on the radio hadn't mentioned names either.

'It's possible,' Harold says, but his enthusiasm for the idea has already faded and his tone matches my thoughts. Possible but unlikely.

'But the rest holds,' I say. 'Bill Stone was hanging around in the park to keep out of the bloke from Perth's way.'

'And . . .' Harold finishes for me. 'The bloke from Perth arrived.'

It makes perfect sense. It is the only thing so far that has.

'What will you do?' Harold asks.

I check my watch. It seems as though we have done a lot this morning already, but if I drive we may still get to work on time.

'Tell the police when we get to work. What about you?' I ask.

He doesn't have to think about it. 'See what I can do to help Jamie. If anything.'

I nod, unsurprised. This is exactly what Harold would do.

Chapter 17

The rain eases as I drive, but the sky stays overcast and sullen.
At work I make a little list of things to think about. None of
the far travelling that I indulged in last night but a very short
list of all the things I know for certain about Bill Stone,
things that, so far, I have made no sense of but that should
mean something. Diamonds, for instance. Why tell Harold his
name was Diamond? A game player. I wonder what game
was he playing?

Sometimes when you reduce things to simple terms, you
see the uncluttered picture. I list four things. The criminal
world that Harold had told me about. Diamonds. Western
Australia. Game playing. Without the weight of language and
detail, it seems easy enough to put a hypothesis together, and
the one that comes sweeping in is obvious enough. From what
I've heard about the dead man's character, it is a possibility. I
do some rapid typing, adding to the file I have already begun
at home. It is a long document now, and growing. I date the
amendments and print out two copies. Next, I ring Peter
Denton. He is out somewhere so I leave a message.

The police input on the letter is a non-event. Peter Denton returns my call at half past ten and I tell him about the theory that Harold and I have put together regarding the letter in Bill Stone's coat pocket. I expect something. Instead there is a pause.

'We've made an arrest on that, Marlo.' He sounds dismissive.

'I heard about that but I thought the letter was significant.'

'I've seen the letter. I don't think there's much in it.'

'Except for timing and effect,' I counter.

The silence on the other end is articulate of doubt. This is similar to the episode with the runner. I don't push it, because to push it would do no good.

'You haven't come up with anything else?' he asks eventually.

'No.' I don't tell him my hypothesis that seemed so satisfactory an hour ago and was, in part at least, the reason for my call. Now, in the light of his scepticism, my theory feels audacious and far-fetched. Before I share it with anyone, let alone the police, I would like to check it out.

We end the call and I feel oddly deflated. The dismissal in his voice seems a long way from that reasonably pleasant half hour at home on Sunday. I feel like the game has shifted somehow, and I am stuck somewhere at the beginning, grounded by ignorance, not sure of the rules, but knowing that they've changed.

The State Library. I am here to test my hypothesis. The pendulum has swung back and my speculation seems to be logical rather than audacious. The frustration I have felt on and off since the start of all this kicks in hard – I still wish I had met the murdered man. I wish I had joined Harold in the park on the sunny days and talked with him, got some sense of him for myself.

I work in the newspaper room and type variations of my search criteria into the CD-ROM databases. Diamonds and Western Australia are unchanging, and although crime is not, there are only certain possibilities. Even so, I expect to be there for hours because, in my experience, research is invariably time consuming. This time though, I am in luck. Among a glut of articles on diamonds and Western Australia, there are one or two that match not only the components of my search but all my expectations. I read the blocks of text, transfixed, delighted that my hypothesis is sound.

The CD-ROM listing gives me both the date and the text of the article that made big news in the west. I find microfilms for various Western Australian newspapers of the time and read through a wealth of coverage on a prolonged conspiracy to steal diamonds from a mine in the north of the state. My eyes sweep the text, looking for names. Derek James Wilkins. Bingo! I stop reading, settle back against my chair and laugh out loud. The connection firms a little more.

According to the article, the bragging of Derek Wilkins was the most significant factor leading to his arrest. The whispers in Perth's social circles had become loud enough for the police to take an interest. This is what Bill had commented on to Harold – the criminal's need to tell someone how clever they are. The need to brag.

No mention of Bill Stone or William Diamond, but that is to be expected, because Bill Stone doesn't have a police record. From Harold's description of him, it is possible that he weaseled his way out of it all. And at least, if nothing else, I understand the choice of name. Stone to Diamond. A tongue-in-cheek flavour to it. The man who liked to play games.

I make notes of relevant dates. The three years of steady, clandestine theft. Derek James Wilkins was brought to trial five years ago and given a six-year prison sentence but not all prison sentences run their course. It is possible that the sentence will have ended. Next I print out relevant articles from various newspapers, replace the microfilms on the trolley and sit at one of the computers to update my notes and add my conclusions. Around me the great building is hushed, disturbed only by the faint sound of tapping keyboards and pages being turned.

I stare at the stone wall in front of me and my mind is filled with images of the distant, desert landscape. Someone close by shifts and coughs and I come back to the moment. I walk back to work, aware of my heels tapping jauntily on the wet pavement, like Rosalyn's yesterday.

At last I have something to run with. And if I learn that Derek James Wilkins has been released, then it might explain why Bill Stone was hiding out in the Flagstaff Gardens. Derek Wilkins had a motive to murder, and one that was far superior to an attack over a few dollars that weren't even taken. I think about Denton's scepticism earlier and wonder what he will make of this.

Harold is in his office, his chair swivelled towards the window. He doesn't look up at my approach or greet me with his customary smile. I suddenly remember what Harold was going to do this morning and the buzz of elation fades.

'How did it go?' I ask.

He takes a moment to answer and I wonder how long he has been sitting like this.

'The Defence were pleased for me to come and talk to Jamie. Shane suggested it to them and they contacted me. But I didn't help much. It took ages to get a word out of him. He's closed up more than ever.'

'What will you do?'

'Keep trying because that's all I can do. But it makes you feel so helpless.'

'Yes, I know.'

His eyes are suspiciously bright. I put my hand on his shoulder and follow his gaze to the park across the road. A gardener is working on a distant sweep of lawn, raking leaves into a pile.

'The Filing Hearing is scheduled for tomorrow at eleven o'clock. I thought I should be there.'

'Do you feel up to it?'

'Of course,' he says with a conviction that belies the rest of the sentence. 'Will you come?'

'Yes, if you want me to,' I say evenly, but the surprise must seep out. Signs of vulnerability in Harold are few and far between.

'I like having you with me, Marlo. I like the clarity of your mind.'

Clarity. The gardener scoops leaves into a green wheelie bin. He works fast, his movements a blur of green in the distance.

'And what about you, Marlo? You look like you have news.'

'I have. It's a bit like the letter you mentioned. I have found something, but I don't know what it's worth, if anything.'

I show him the printed articles from various Western Australian newspapers and the notes I made of my conclusions in the library. He looks up after a while, his eyes not exactly glittering with excitement but better than before.

'Does it ring true to you?' I ask.

'Yes, undoubtedly. Bigger fish than Bill normally played with but, from what I've heard, much the same style.'

'Enough money to buy a house in South Yarra?'

A hesitation. 'I don't know, Marlo, but we always hear about the allure of diamonds. You know, enough money to finance small countries hidden in the soles of people's shoes. Why not? And for someone with dubious contacts there would always be somewhere or someone to sell them on to.'

'Yes.'

'You don't look convinced.'

'I am. I'm just not sure if any of this matters. With Jamie arrested, it's all past tense, and, I don't know, something doesn't feel right. It's a long way from diamond smuggling to an old man murdered in a park . . . The police could be right. What does it matter what he got up to in his life? It is his death that counts.'

'All things are possible, Marlo.'

'Yes, and if my theory is true, at least the trip to Melbourne makes sense.'

'What next?'

'Back to the police. They need to know.' I am oddly discouraged. If we have found out about the whys and wherefores of Bill's sojourn in the Flagstaff Gardens, what good does it do us? The police are firmly rooted to their conviction that the attack was random, and I am not looking forward to going back to the them once again. I leave yet another message for Denton to call me and settle down to work.

I make a long-distance call to the agent we use in Perth. My query is an unusual one but he takes it in his stride. In this business you get used to things that are out of the norm. I could do it myself but it is easier for someone on the spot to access the right information.

Three significant phone calls late in the afternoon. The agent in Perth has done some digging with someone he knows in the legal fraternity. William Bradley Stone was known to be an associate of Derek James Wilkins. And, more to the point, Wilkins was let out of jail on the 19 July. The date that he would call on Bill Stone, after 'a long absence'. Despite my grey mood I smile at the confirmation of the innocuous letter as a possible threat.

Shane Black is the next caller. I am pleased to hear from him, as much as anything because he sounds so normal. He offers supper after cricket training tonight. Harold is cooking dinner and has invited Alicia so I know he won't be left alone. I accept Shane's invitation without the usual internal discussion. It feels suspiciously like a date and it is a long time since I've been out on anything as frivolous as a date.

I think about telling Harold but I don't, because to do so would be to give the outing more importance than it deserves. And besides, Harold is on the phone to someone. I can hear his voice going over some point of law, although the words are unclear.

Peter Denton returns my call late in the afternoon. I had expected coolness or annoyance or a rushed 'too busy to talk' but, surprisingly, he is affable and friendly. He sounds almost pleased to hear from me, as if the dismissive conversation this morning never happened. I tell him about the theory that I have backed up with printed articles and my own notes.

'I can't see you now,' he says, 'but I have a meeting in the city at nine-thirty tomorrow. I could meet you just before that if it's important.'

'Fine.'

We arrange a time and a place. Nine o'clock on the Spencer Street footbridge across the Yarra. Before I leave work I make photocopies of the documents I put together in the library and stow them in my bag. One for Denton and one to keep. Harold comes in to say goodbye. He has bought a new coat, I realise. Something long and dark grey, warmer than the one he left with Bill.

'Harold, I'm driving you,' I protest.

'No you're not. You've got cricket practice and I'm getting a taxi, but you can see me off if you insist.' A glimmer of a smile, the amusement showing in his eyes. He is feeling better, I realise, and is making fun of the tight rein we have agreed on.

We wait together on the footpath, under the roof awnings because it has started to rain again. The rain now is gentle and after the drought and downpours of recent days, it seems almost healing, soaking deep into the earth. I find myself telling Harold about the reason for my defection from the dinner table tonight.

'Good for you, Marlo.' The taxi arrives. 'Have fun.'

At cricket, I am in an unusual mood. I am more concentrated, as though the discipline needed to find out about Bill Stone has released something in me. Or perhaps it is grappling with something concrete rather than the nebulous grey sea of the last year. Whatever the reason, I find myself stepping out against the bowlers with more confidence, and time and again I have the satisfaction of hearing the ball strike against the bat truly and soundly, the ball spinning off with control and direction.

I write down the details of the upcoming practice match

between the A team and the B team, shower and change. The restaurant Shane and I are meeting in is in Middle Park, not far from home, and he is there before me. He stands up to greet me as I cross the room, and I notice that he is dressed in a particularly well-cut suit in a dark charcoal with a dark shirt underneath. The darkness of his clothes seems to accentuate the pale blue of his eyes. The rims of his irises are darker, an attractive contrast.

I order risotto and a glass of red while he orders something unpronounceable from the specials board. He directs the conversation my way often enough to keep the spotlight off himself, and I am happy enough to tell him the details of the situation so far – the fact-finding mission to the State Library and Harold's attempts to help Jamie Griggs. The conversation explores it all, digging deep into the small details. I find myself grinning, amused by the lack of anything personal in our exchanges. A long way from the idea of a date that I had entertained earlier. But now I am here, the lack of the personal seems like a good idea.

Over chocolate roulade with King Island cream, and the last of the wine, we drift on to the subject of cricket. Shane talks about his aunt, who use to play for Australia. As a child Shane had often gone to watch her, which explains, in part, his interest in my career. I hadn't exactly forgotten this in the two years since he left, just hadn't thought of it. Then, as now, he invested his aunt with the status of family hero, speaking of her with awe and enthusiasm. I see an echo of that animation now, odd in one so still.

'When we talked before, Marlo, you had the same dream of playing for Australia.'

I stifle a sigh. This particular subject just keeps on coming back. 'I'm not sure about that any more.' There must be something closed off in my voice, because he looks at me steadily.

'Why not?'

I have two choices. I can close up or I can tell him about the obstacle in my way. There are only a few people I have talked to about this – Harold, of course, and Lee and Alicia – but a long time ago now. And, to a lesser extent, on Thursday night, a fourteen-year-old with problems of her own.

But I don't want to go over this old ground again. I am warm and comfortable and pleasantly relaxed, and I have no desire to look at any of it right now.

'It's gloomy,' I say.

The pause before he speaks tells me he knows some of my story at least. 'So?' His single word is a challenge that surprises me. Across the table, he is very still, content to wait, unfazed by silence. In my experience, most people skirt away from gloom and fidget in the presence of silence. In general they get restless, their minds drifting off somewhere, or worse, they rush in to fill the gap. But not Shane.

'Some other time,' I say.

'Fair enough.' He checks the level in the wine bottle and changes the subject diplomatically.

'You're close to Harold aren't you?'

'Yes. He's a good friend.' I don't expand on all that he means to me – a father figure, patient and supportive. A long way from the reality of my own father.

Shane doesn't speak for a long time and again I get the feeling there is something he's not saying. Some area of disquiet in his life. Bearing in mind my own reluctance to open up, I don't push him.

'You're lucky,' he says lifting his wine glass but covering too late the fleeting twitch of his mouth. It doesn't matter anyway because I recognise the tone.

'Yes.' Lucky with some things, unlucky with others. Like most people.

Shane puts his glass down on the table and pats his pockets, hiding his feelings in a little flurry of activity. 'Thanks for tonight, Marlo. I must go, I didn't realise it was so late.'

I gather my belongings and walk with him to the car park, testing the quality of the silence as we walk. A few things come together. Harold had said Shane could do with a friend and I have often thought that there is a whole lot he isn't saying. I should have worked out that there was something wrong at our first meeting, but I have been preoccupied with other things, completely and obtusely blind. I think of his support recently, both of Harold and of me. I think of him in the past, when he was a kind of one-man cheer squad for my sporting career, and feel a stir both of compassion and guilt.

'Shane...' I begin.

'Some other time, Marlo.' I have the feeling that he knows what I am going to say, even if I'm not sure myself. He shrugs away my sympathy and bends to kiss me, his breath warm on my cheek.

'I'll see you,' he says, unlocking his car door and driving off in a little burst of speed.

Driving home, I consider Shane dispassionately. So far, he has done all the running, has set up our different meetings and done most of the talking. If I'm any judge of the possibilities and paths to romance, he won't ring again. If I want to see him again, I will have to do some of the running.

I think about both the ease and the disquiet of the evening. The fact that we had travelled wide in our conversation but kept ourselves hidden. Small things register. The lines around his eyes. The stillness of his hands and body. The warmth of his breath and lips.

I feel annoyed with myself for my constant self-preoccupation. I have no idea why Shane left Victoria or why he returned. Such ignorance is articulate of two things – a lack of interest on my part and privacy on his. I find myself wondering about him and, in a sudden moment of insight, face an unpleasant fact about myself – it seems a long time since I have thought of anyone else at all. Lee was right, self-pity really doesn't suit me.

Alicia and Harold are in the kitchen finishing the washing up.

'How did it go?' Harold turns to me, an expectant smile on his face.

I smile at the situation. This, believe it or not, is something, I had always wanted as a teenager. A father figure waiting up for me, interested in my evening, wanting to talk to me about the progress of any possible romance. It is a pleasant enough fantasy, I suppose, when you are fifteen.

'A good night?' Harold asks, misinterpreting my smile.

'An informative night.'

'You learnt something about Bill Stone?' Harold asks, understandably enough. We have talked about little else for days.

'No, this time I learnt something about myself.'

Chapter 18

I dress in the requested track suit for Amy's hockey match and drive in with Harold, parking my car in his space behind work. Peter Denton is waiting at our meeting spot, a single figure standing in the centre of the new footbridge across the Yarra. He smiles when he sees me coming. He seems open and friendly.

'How is Harold?'

'He's fine. He's back at work.' I hand him the documentation I put together in the library, together with the information from our agent in Perth, his contact details and my own notes. 'I've made photocopies.'

'Efficient,' he comments, taking it from me.

I don't explain any of it but let him read it for himself. I pass the time by looking out at the landscape and the swollen river at our feet. We stand beside thick glass panels that block the wind and reflect the city skyline and the wavy reflections of the river. It is a day of fitful cloud and brilliant sunshine, powerful enough to lift steam from the soggy grass verges along the river's edge and touch the distant high-rise windows with molten gold.

My mind is idle and studies the effects of light closer to home. I see it play on the delicate scroll work of Denton's ear, and the strands of mid-brown hair against his neck.

'Fascinating,' Denton comments, looking at me suddenly. I have to turn away and look fixedly at the river as if mesmerised by the heavy flow, oddly flustered at where my idle thoughts have taken me.

'I'll say one thing for you, Marlo, you don't give up.'

'No.' At least he sounds as though he doesn't begrudge me his time.

'You've done well to find this out.'

I realise he isn't patronising me, just commenting. 'It seemed logical,' I say.

'So you're saying that Derek Wilkins is the person who murdered Bill Stone?'

'It's a possibility. According to our agent in Perth, Derek Wilkins was released on the 19 July. I just thought it was something that should be checked out.'

'And what is it you want me to do?'

'Check if he came to Melbourne. Check if he was the man in the park, that Bill Stone was hiding from.'

'I'll talk with Perth about it.'

'Is there anything else you've found out?' I ask. 'About Bill Stone or Harold?'

'Nothing more than I've said.'

I tell him about our doubts, Harold's and mine. The different reasons we think what we do about the arrest of Jamie Griggs.

'It's not an exact science, Marlo. In my experience I have learned that it is impossible to know what people are capable of. Given the right triggers...' He trails off and I can't argue.

I know what he means all too well. What I have learnt about people in the past has shocked me rigid.

'I know his life was complicated, believe me, but it doesn't follow that his death was. We believe that it was an attack in the park over a few dollars that went too far. A simple death, Marlo. The stuff we deal in, day in and day out. End of story.'

I don't argue. Simplicity is appealing and it is my favoured option when things go wrong. I almost wish I could believe it, but it doesn't explain the things I know – the twenty-minute delay, the runner.

'And Jamie Griggs?'

'Is a law unto himself.'

I recognise this for what it is. Jamie is someone they can't pigeon hole, someone who doesn't fit into the categories that society ordains. He is a simple man, living rough, who plays with sticks and feathers and leaves.

'You mentioned the blood evidence last time we spoke.'

'Yes, I did. Griggs had Bill Stone's blood on his clothing.'

'I see.' That's it then. Blood on his clothes. It's hard to get past this.

'But in this case the blood evidence is inconclusive,' Denton continues. 'The death blow was the rail of a bench, and the dead man's body acted as a screen. Whoever hit him, Marlo, would almost certainly have got his blood on them but not in any conclusive patterns. Usually with an attack there are blood splatters and sprays to work with.'

'I see.'

'But it does prove that Griggs was there at the time.'

'Yes, I understand that.'

I look downstream towards the docks – the Exhibition Centre, the Polly Woodside at its permanent mooring, a few cranes, lots of vertical lines against the sky.

'Will you let me know what you find out about the Perth stuff?' I give him my card and he pockets it, smiling at the reversal.

A ferry swishes past below us, sending out a fan of ripples on the silver-blue surface.

'I'll be in touch.'

Harold is already in the Magistrates Court and I join him, sitting on the right-hand side behind the defence. At first the court is very hushed. Sometimes it is possible to hear the clock ticking, and sometimes background noises prevail – various conversations in whispered tones, someone coughing and clearing their throat.

There is a little stir of movement as Jamie Griggs is brought through the door to the dock, flanked both in front and behind by court security. He stands blinking as though dazed by the light, then they all sit, with Jamie in the middle. He keeps his eyes down, fixed on something in his hands that I can't see behind the partitioning, disengaged from the procedures that will determine his fate. He looks smaller than I remember and a lot more vulnerable. A long way from the image of a killer. Harold shifts beside me, an indication of restlessness that doesn't show in his face.

The Filing Hearing takes less than ten minutes, the magistrate moving between the prosecution and defence, seeking information as to mental state, crime and Griggs' criminal history. Mental state takes the longest because of the lack of success both the police and the defence have had in getting information from the accused man.

Jamie stands to listen to the magistrate's orders and for the first time I see what he has in his hands. No feather or stone, but a piece of green material that he spills repeatedly from hand to hand. The magistrate is speaking now, and I take my mind from the fabric and concentrate on what is being said – the order for psychological assessment, custody arrangements and the date of the next court appearance. The Committal Mention is set for Monday 4 October.

Jamie leaves the dock and there is a shuffling as various people depart the court. Harold looks shaken and I take his arm as we walk slowly back along William Street towards the office.

'How was he this morning?' I ask.

'Still mostly silent. He remembered me though.'

'Well, that's something,' I say.

He tells me what the defence had told him – something I learned just an hour ago from Peter Denton. The blood on Jamie's clothing.

There is a bench in the corner of the park, not Bill Stone's bench but one, hopefully, with fewer connotations. I sit down and Harold follows.

'The problem is he's not too good at defending himself and he can't or won't talk. I'm not sure he even remembers the night in question.'

I'm not surprised after witnessing the way he tuned out from his own fate in the courtroom, absorbed in a scrap of material.

'He's a kind man, Marlo. He could even have been trying to help.'

'There's eight weeks to the committal hearing,' I say, practically. 'That's enough time to put him through a whole range of psychiatric assessments and, with luck, enough time for things to change.'

After Harold has gone back to work, I linger in the gardens. This is the first time I have been here since Bill Stone's death and I register the persistent underlying hum of traffic. Again I wonder about the possibility of hearing footsteps – I can barely hear the faint trembling of birdsong. The thought dismays me and I begin to doubt the evidence of my own eyes and ears.

Back at work Tegan looks up from her phone call to smile at me and waggle her fingers. Irene must have taken over my appointments. I draw my breath in at the thought – Irene will have loved that.

I spend time on the phone and organise documents for the next few days into folders for various lodgements. I like this work. Making order out of things. I work through until after two and then pack up for the day.

Next door, I can hear Harold in his office, speaking quietly on the phone. There is something about the quality of his voice, something soft and confiding that makes me concentrate on the words. Rosalyn I guess, ringing in from Adelaide to see how he is. I am curious about the state of the relationship – that moment of dazzling certainty at the dinner party has, in the light of recent events, or recent absences, faded away.

'It's hard to tell, Emma. She seems better. I'd say she has a bit more purpose . . .'

His voice goes on but I have tuned out again and hear his voice as only a background murmur. Not Rosalyn but my aunt Emma. And worse, the topic of conversation is not any blossoming romance but me.

Harold hangs up and I head straight to his office, going in and closing his door with an abrupt little tap.

'Who was that you were talking to?' My voice, like the sound I made closing the door, is sharper than I intended.

He looks up at me, his expression guarded. 'I ring Emma from time to time. She asked how you were.'

This is too much. Shane. Emma. 'That's twice you've interfered in my life, Harold.' My voice is cold.

'Yes, I know.' His tone is calm.

'It's my life, Harold.' Anger dances in my eyes.

'I know that, but isn't it time you stopped making a mess of it.' He stands up and leans against his desk and I step back as though impaled. 'Don't you think it's time to face up to things. I've never taken you for a coward, Marlo.'

This is harsh yet I can't help but recognise the truth of the remark. It is something I have thought myself often enough in the past year. I turn away and look out of the window to the green serenity of the park. I haven't seen Emma for over a year now. Thirteen months ago. A day that is marked forever in my mind. The day Emma arrived home from her holiday overseas and I had to tell her the news. Her sister murdered; her daughter dead.

Behind me Harold's voice is very quiet. 'Marlo, you are not alone in coping with difficulties. We all have them but it's what we learn from them that counts. We can't ignore our relationships, Marlo; we can't pretend there are no difficulties. If I have learnt one thing, it's that we have to be honest.'

I can't deny it. I have thought it too. 'How is she?' I say slowly, carefully.

'She would like to see you.'

'I'll think about it.'

I have thought about it so often. Thirteen months ago Emma said to me, 'No blame, no guilt.' Such a simple sentence. One of those sentences that sound good but are impossible to keep. If she has no blame, then I have enough guilt for both of us. If I hadn't followed my suspicions, perhaps some of last year's grief could have been avoided.

There is a long silence between us.

'It's hard, Harold.'

'I don't doubt it for a moment but avoidance won't make the problem go away.'

'I didn't know you kept in touch with Emma.'

'Not just Emma, Marlo, but all of Jenny's family. I thought she would want me to.'

I sit down on the chair for visitors and swivel away, fighting the impulse to cry.

'So not just Emma?' I say.

'I ring everyone from time to time, save for Lucy.'

I turn back, curious. 'Why not Lucy?'

'A few reasons. Out of all of you, she has the most support. I also believe that she is less traumatised, although I admit it's hard to tell...' he trails off.

'And?'

'It seems... inappropriate. An older man with a young woman, and Lucy, as you know, can be dangerous. I didn't want to lay myself open to any... difficulty. There you are, Marlo. My own form of cowardice if you like.'

'Or common sense.' I stand up, remembering Lucy's past flirtations, 'Harold, you amaze me. So Simon, Steven, Laura...'

'Yes, all of them.'

A long silence that I finally break. 'And me the most.'

'Only because you're constantly...'

The anger flashes before the words are out. 'What, Harold? What word are you looking for?... Needy? Wanting? Hopeless?' Even as I say the words, I recognise the reaction for what it is – a shot of misplaced anger from that well I seem to have permanently inside me. Misplaced anger spilling up over those I love.

'That wasn't what I meant, Marlo. You are here with me every day. I know how you're faring.'

I close my eyes against the wash of tears.

'Marlo, whatever you do, don't deliberately misunderstand me. The situation is difficult enough.'

'Yes, I know.'

He passes his hand across his scalp and looks vulnerable. 'I think we should talk about this openly and have done with it.'

This sounds ominous. I turn to face him.

'I don't know if you're ready for this, because sometime over the last year we stopped talking.'

'Yes, I know.'

'You did nothing wrong save get caught up in an untenable situation.' He is very still, his voice quiet and reasoned, but his hands are clenched and his knuckles white. 'When I think of the grief and pain that one person caused through arrogance and greed ... well, if you must know, I'm glad she's dead. Otherwise I would want to tear her apart myself.'

I am surprised. I didn't realise that Harold felt quite so passionately about this. He has turned away slightly so that I cannot see his eyes, and his voice trembles slightly. 'That's where the guilt and the blame lies, Marlo, not with you ... never with you.'

For a shaky moment I see the whole unwieldy edifice of the past year through other eyes, see Jenny not just as my aunt but as Harold's close and long-term friend, and the shifting of perspective leaves me short of breath. I understand at some deeper level the despair of others, including the various members of my family – the all-consuming process of guilt and withdrawal we have all been caught up in, with Harold standing at the sidelines offering what little comfort he can. I must be getting soft because recognition of this thread of kindness makes the tears flow freely. Tears I have fought against, tears I thought I had done with.

I retreat to my office and cry again, this time in relative privacy. At some time I become aware that I am not just crying for myself but for other people. Harold, Emma, Lucy, the various members of my family who have been torn apart by it all. I dry my eyes eventually and look out over the gardens, pressing my hot face against the cool glass, aware of feeling both empty yet more peaceful, as though the process of crying has eased the pain and, in some small way, aided healing.

Chapter 19

I arrive at the hockey match in time to see the teams take up their positions. I have patched up my red eyes courtesy of Tegan's make-up and now look vaguely presentable. Amy waves at me from the pitch and I wave back. Her team is dressed in brilliant red in contrast to the opposition yellow. Against the bright day the colours are vivid, dazzling. I am among a group of parents and teachers. A solitary boy watches from the opposite line, walking up and down with the play.

The recent heavy rain has softened the pitch and the game is both wild and erratic, the mud working against the players. I remember my own hockey games at high school and the frustrations and pleasures of playing in mud. Amy is centre forward and attacks the game with gusto from the first blow of the whistle. The game is furious, with all the unleashed energy of teenage girls – all speed, grit and determination. As I watch them I realise that Amy was modest about her hockey ability. She is good – a thoughtful player, passing to others when there is need and not scared to run with the ball herself. A player who makes the most of opportunities that come her way. And, on a more basic level, she is strong in the wrists and very fast, surprising me with the ground she covers. In a moment of stoppage, she sends me a quick thumbs up gesture.

My mobile phone rings. Harold, I think, but it's Peter Denton.

'I made a few phone calls after I left you.' He pauses as if choosing his words carefully. 'I have something to knock your theory to pieces.'

'Go on.'

'I've been in touch with the Western Australian police and they've had a talk with Derek Wilkins.' There is something significant in his tone. 'All the background stuff you got is right. Wilkins was screaming about being robbed and talking revenge...'

'But?'

'Wilkins was let out on the 19 of July.'

'Yes, I know that.'

There is a little silence before he goes on. 'This is where it falls apart.' I'm not sure I read his tone properly. Sympathy? Pleasure at me slipping up? 'Wilkins hasn't moved from Perth since they let him out.'

I can hear the sense of satisfaction in his voice. You were wrong and we were right. We have the right man under lock and key. On the field Amy intercepts the ball neatly, strikes it sharply towards goal. Someone on the other team misjudges and her stick thuds against Amy's legs, the ball already moving away. I see Amy retaliate, her stick sweeping out in a sudden, savage blow that connects sharply with her opponent's legs. I feel short of breath as though someone has punched me.

'Are you sure?' I say, knowing that he is – he wouldn't have phoned me otherwise.

'Positive. His mother is seriously ill in the Royal Perth and he's been to see her every day since they let him out. He only goes home to sleep and by early morning she is fretful and looking out for him again. If he had missed a day, they would have noticed. According to the hospital staff, he is a good son.'

His tone is dry.

I sense an incapacity in him to soften the boundaries in his mind, an inability to see light and shade. A son who is a convicted thief cannot be a good son. Good is good. Bad is bad. Simple. I don't comment, unsure of what to say, feeling both breathless at the news and distracted by his rigid thinking.

'I've checked the flight times,' he goes on remorselessly. 'There's no possible way he could have got here and back in a day without being missed.'

'Yes, I know.' Perth is a three-hour flight away. Six hours there and back, let alone taking the time out to hit someone over the head. I know the flight times because I checked them out for myself last year when I went to visit Tony.

'I see. Well . . . thanks for telling me.'

The play has changed, moved towards the other goal, but I can't concentrate any more. My great theory has come to nothing and the comfort of it lies around me in ruins.

A player is down, a body crumpled in pain and the skin on my scalp tightens. I think of Harold lying on the cold concrete floor. If Wilkins was in Perth, then who attacked Harold? And why? I have no comfortable theories to hide behind any more. I cannot seek refuge in the thought of a stranger from the west. An outsider. The more acceptable explanation of the murder.

The shift of thought is sudden and compelling, and now I am here, it seems as obvious as a freight train bearing down on me. If I can't, for various reasons, accept the police version of events, there is another possibility that has always been on the edge of things, beckoning but hidden by the glare of an easier, more acceptable theory. Family.

The idea of family as evil runs like a well-worn groove in my mind. This has been my personal nightmare for over a year now, and the motivations for murder scream at me. Motivations I had dismissed. Simple, compelling motivations, like the price of a house in South Yarra. Who knew Harold was at the house on Saturday? The answer is obvious. Who stood to benefit from the terms of Bill Stone's will? Only family.

I blink and my vision clears. Despite the sun, I am suddenly cold as though the chill of my thoughts has seeped into my skin. The game has moved again and a cluster of red players gather against the goal like an invading army. The ball is hit with a healthy thwack and flies as straight as an arrow into the back of the net. The red players come together, dancing in a cluster like a spurt of leaping flame.

'Marlo.' Amy's voice at my shoulder. 'You're still here, I thought you had to leave.'

I haven't registered much of the second half; my thoughts have been elsewhere.

Her red sports uniform is skimpy and mud splattered, and her face is flushed with heat. Across her cheekbones is a fine spray of mud, the individual drops standing out bolder than her freckles. She looks very young and very happy. Just as I register the thought, she reaches up to slide the band from her hair, shaking it loose in one long flowing movement. It is the gesture that is disconcerting, the pure womanhood of it. She looks at me, her intelligent green eyes lit up with energy and interest.

'I changed my plans.' My voice is very steady. Very normal.

'We're through to the finals. Good, eh?' she says with simple enjoyment before her expression changes to curiosity. 'Are you OK, Marlo? You look different.'

'Yes. It's just the sun. It's brighter than I thought. Great game,' I manage. 'Do you all play sport in the family?' I continue, grasping for something to say, rather than out of genuine interest.

'Not sport exactly, but we all keep fit. Kristin runs, Jason skates, Sam plays bowls and Rosalyn plays tennis in a mid-week competition.' I hear the little list from behind too many thoughts and don't really engage with it.

'What are you doing now?' I ask.

'Showering and going home.'

'I'll drive you, if you like.' I make the offer without ulterior motive. It is only when the words are out and irretrievable that I realise the implications, the dilemma I am in. This girl/woman in front of me is part of the family that has suddenly consumed me.

She looks pleased but adds, 'You don't mind waiting while I shower.'

'That's fine, Amy. I've got plenty of time.'

She grins and darts off, turning to shout, 'Back soon.'

I watch her go. Don't hurry Amy, I need time to think.

My choices are simple. The police or me. The police have arrested someone. I'm fairly sure they have put the attack on Harold down to a random robbery, courtesy of his missing jacket and wallet. They haven't been there every step of the way as I have. I remember the mix of feelings in Denton's voice just an hour ago and his insistence on the simplicity of Bill Stone's death. I wonder what he would think of where my thoughts have taken me now.

With Amy I have the perfect opening. Someone young and trusting. Someone who likes to chat and who doesn't measure their words and reactions. Another part of my mind intervenes. Don't tell me, Amy. I can only use it against people you love. This, I realise, is a dilemma I need to talk through with someone I trust, someone I should have visited a long time ago.

Amy comes back in her school uniform, her heavy bag over her shoulder, weighing her down on one side. The tunic, blazer and long socks make her look young again. No flush of heat or mud sprays. No disconcerting glimpses of the emerging woman.

I am more resolved to the situation, less inclined to run away. I am cold though. I hadn't realised standing there watching the game, how cold I was. There is a café across the road from the school.

'Feel like a drink? I need something to warm me up.'

Amy looks pleased and then panic stricken. Not hard to see where her mind has gone. Not enough money in her pocket.

'My shout.'

She grins easily. 'Great.'

In the café, she orders a chocolate milkshake. I have hot chocolate, wishing I had some of Harold's brandy from last week for added warmth. There is a little silence while we drink. I feel alive with curiosity but the questions stick in my throat. There is something abhorrent about using Amy to find out about members of her own family. In the end, paradoxically, it is Amy who sets the ball rolling.

'Do you know if they've found anything out about Bill?'

'The police arrested someone,' I say, not following the thought.

'Rosalyn told me that.'

'How are they coping?'

'Don't know really.' She sounds vague. 'I don't see so much of Kristin any more because she has this big job on and spends a lot of time at her space.'

If she doesn't see much of Kristin and Rosalyn is in Adelaide, then she must be at home on her own.

'Her space?'

Amy looks at me as if I should know about this. 'She has a space in an old warehouse in Richmond. It's pretty crap really but she keeps all her things there – fabrics and stuff like that. Sometimes she even sleeps there.' She says it with an air of wonder, a touch of admiration at the prospect. 'I wouldn't like to, it's creepy.'

Perhaps this is the answer to the question that has puzzled Harold and I from the start – the answer to where Bill Stone slept at night.

'Why creepy?'

'You have to see it.' Her voice is heavy with emphasis. 'It's next to the old hat factory in Riley Street and that's creepy in itself.'

I finish my chocolate and listen to Amy slurping up the last of her milk. There is a question I would very much like to ask her.

'You asked me once if I had ever met Bill,' I say.

'Yes, I remember.' A stillness settles on her and for the first time she looks wary.

'Did *you*?'

'No.' There is something too quick about the answer and I sense the lie. I don't pursue it but it is Amy who continues this line of thought.

'I know that Rosalyn asked Harold to find out about Bill. Do you know if he did?'

I almost laugh, keeping it down to a smile and Amy smiles back, not sure as to the cause of my amusement. The situation is ludicrous. I went into this meeting with reservations about pumping a fourteen-year-old child for information and this is exactly what she is doing to me.

'He didn't find out much, Amy.' This is an evasion. I keep my knowledge of Bill Stone's criminal activity strictly to myself. 'I do know that Harold liked him. You can talk to Harold about him if you want.'

'Would he mind?'

'Talking is the last thing Harold minds,' I say. 'He could get a gold medal at the Olympic Games for talking.'

'You like Harold, don't you?'

'Harold. Yes, of course.' The last of my good intentions evaporate. The moral high ground is no contest for curiosity. 'Did you know that he was attacked on Saturday at your grandfather's house?'

'Sam told me. He's a bit like Harold: he likes to talk. I see him most Sundays at the market. Sam says Harold's OK.'

'He is now.'

'They told me about the house. Apparently my share is to be held in trust until I'm twenty-one.' There is little expression in her tone but she grins happily. I turn away, not sure I can cope with this.

'Come on, I'll take you home.'

★

I pull up in the driveway. It is almost half past five and the house is dark and closed looking, very different from the dinner party a week ago. It looked almost festive then but now it is forbidding and cold.

'Where is everyone?' I ask without thinking.

'Rosalyn's in Perth, Kristin's at work.'

I look at Amy beside me in the passenger seat. 'Perth? I thought Rosalyn was in Adelaide.'

'Adelaide. Perth. What's the difference?' Her tone is dismissive.

A lot. Almost three thousands kilometres. Perth is the site of the diamond thefts and her grandfather's criminal contacts. It seems to me that in the last couple of weeks the city of Perth has assumed a lot of different connotations.

I look at the dark house. 'Don't you find it lonely on your own?'

'I'm used to it. And anyway, even when Ros is home, she works most nights. Would you like to come in, Marlo, I could make you a drink.'

'No thanks. I must go.'

'Thanks for the lift and thanks for coming today.'

'Pleasure.' I give her my card. 'Amy, if you ever feel the need to talk to me about anything, ring me. I'm a bit like Harold: I like to chat.' It's a bit of a lie but I would very much like to chat about all of this.

'Thanks,' she says simply, but her eyes flick over me assessingly. The front door closes behind her and the lights go on inside.

Chapter 20

Emma lives in Hawthorn near the University, in a small house with a tiny garden that she tends carefully. When I knock, the outside light comes on and the door opens simultaneously. I look at Emma curiously in that moment before recognition and surprise shows on her face. She looks thinner than the last time I saw her, thirteen months ago – a day that has haunted me ever since.

'Marlo, I've been hoping you'd come.' She sounds both welcoming and wary. She has aged in the year but then haven't we all. Yet she doesn't look unhappy. There is a fine transparency to her skin that gives her an almost serene look. 'Did Harold tell you that he rang me today?'

'Yes,' I say. That lunchtime conversation seems a century ago.

'Come in. It's too cold to stand around outside. Can I get you something hot?'

'I should have come before,' I murmur while she busies herself with the kettle and cups.

'Yes . . . but I understand how hard it's been.' I can't pick up her tone, am not sure what she really thinks.

'Harold says I've been a coward.'

She smiles briefly. 'Shock tactics, Marlo. I think only Harold could get away with that.'

I don't answer, not knowing who could have got away with what a year ago. A year ago I was a very different person.

'But I understand that sometimes we have to hide away before we can face the world. I know I did.'

'Yes, well, I've been hiding.'

She moves the teapot in little circles to aid the brewing process. 'I've forgotten how you have your tea, Marlo.'

'Black and as it comes.'

She pours the tea into small china cups that I recognise as her good set.

'How is Simon?' I ask. Simon is my cousin, Emma's son. Another member of the family who is closed off to me now. Whereas Emma said no blame, Simon ranted and raged.

'Simon's way is to pretend that last year never happened, at least that's the face he presents to the world. With me, though, he doesn't pretend quite so much.'

'Well, that's something,' I say, feeling inadequate.

'He is sadder and quieter, but then aren't we all?'

'Yes.'

'Lucy enjoys her visits to you. She shows me the presents you buy her.' I'm not sure what I read here. Disapproval? Criticism?

'Little things, Emma.' I am a touch defensive. 'And not all the time. If you knew how much I look forward to Lucy's visits . . . a few presents are nothing.'

She smiles again but this time it seems both warmer and more natural. 'I understand, Marlo, because it's much the same for me. Without Lucy. . .' She trails off but I can follow the thought easily. Without Lucy, getting through the past thirteen months would have been unimaginable.

She looks at me curiously. 'Why have you come today?'

I take a swallow of tea before answering. It is hot and slightly strong. 'I came because I need your advice.'

141

She is puzzled. 'How can I advise you, Marlo?'

'I think you are the only person who can.'

'I see. You'd better come through to the warmth.' She leads the way to the lounge and indicates a sofa set up in front of the fire. We sit side by side and I tell her all about Bill Stone's death. It is a smooth telling because I know it so well.

'And the problem is?' She looks at the heater. The element is a series of five rectangles, only two of them on, giving out a soft and steady glow.

I take a deep breath and say the words. 'It's another family, Emma. I don't think I can face bringing that level of grief to another family.'

She doesn't answer for a long time and her gaze is fixed on the fire. 'Every criminal must have a family, Marlo.'

'Yes, of course.'

'That's the tragedy, isn't it? The murder, of course, but also the grief the criminal brings to their family. I think sometimes that is the hardest thing.' She stands up and presses a button on the heater panel, as if she is suddenly cold. A blue flame sparks for a moment and another grid glows.

'I wanted to know what you think . . . if you tell me not to interfere, then I won't.'

She hesitates. 'That's a big responsibility, Marlo. What do the police have to say?'

'They've arrested someone else,' I reply and tell her the circumstances – the man who hides in the dock engrossed in a scrap of fabric. The man who has the weight of the police case against him and can't or won't say a word to defend himself.

Again she is silent, her face closed, as if wondering where to begin, how to apply herself to the scope of my question. 'Do you remember when I first came home I said to you no blame and no guilt?'

'Yes, I've thought about that a lot.'

'I didn't know then how hard this year was going to be.'

I feel a wash of coldness sweep through me. These words

have often been a source of comfort to me but I understand the discrepancy between first thoughts and feelings and the hard, unrelenting reality of coming to terms with grief. I don't speak and after a while she goes on.

'What can I tell you? You probably don't want to hear about my life during the past year. You know yourself how complex it is.'

'Yes, I do know.'

She looks at me closely, as if by examining my face she can see the the past written there. 'I think you do. You've changed, Marlo. You're face is finer . . . older. And I can see in your eyes . . .' She sighs and looks into her empty cup as though consulting the tea leaves. 'In the past year I have gone through the whole gamut, Marlo. Anger with you so thick I could taste it . . . '

'I understand.' My hands are tight around my tea cup, too tight for comfort.

She shakes her head with sudden emphasis. 'No, you don't, not really. I have come to see, or perhaps I have always known, that any anger with you was not really with you.' She smiles at me with surprising friendliness. 'Sorry if that's confusing.'

'Not at all,' I say, putting my cup down on the coffee table and flexing the stiffness from my hands.

She nods. 'But the simple answer to your question is that there were times when I regretted your part in what happened, when I wished you hadn't . . . interfered.'

'Yes. There must have been.' So that's it then. An answer of sorts.

'But it doesn't end there, Marlo. I'm not sure yet where it does end, but not there. You did nothing wrong. You were brave and strong and, looking at it rationally, it had to be done. I don't think you had a choice.'

'Perhaps not, but this time I do. I can simply walk away and let things take their course.' The image of Jamie Griggs floods back in – that defenceless man.

Emma considers what I have said for a while.

'I don't think you can. You see, there are other times when

I have been very glad that you did what you did, and that's what I come to more and more.' She pauses for so long that I think she won't go on, but then, suddenly, she does so in a little rush. 'You see, we don't know where it might have led. We don't know who else might have got caught up in it all. It had begun, hadn't it – that thought of stopping others. I read her diary...'

'Yes, I read it too.'

I don't seem able to leave the subject there but need to worry at it, like a sore tooth. 'It's just that there are so many people who might be hurt.'

'There always are, Marlo, but I think in the end the truth must come out. And if you don't find out the truth then innocent people will be hurt. You see, the thing that has tipped it for me, the one thing that makes me know for certain that you did the right thing, is Lucy. Without you, who knows what would have happened to Lucy.' Her words are very quiet. I follow her thoughts. The chaos of lies and confusion against the simplicity of truth. 'That's it really, Marlo. Complexity in a nutshell.'

Silence for a long time. We don't talk of other things or seek to strike up neutral conversations and, after a while, I stand up and clear my throat. I want to tell her I'm sorry for not being there for her over the year but somehow I can't find the words.

'There is one thing,' she says forestalling me.

'What?'

'I need to talk to you about Cate but not now.' She says it so hastily that I wonder about the expression on my face. 'Some other time.'

I don't answer and she goes on. 'Thank you for coming, Marlo. I appreciate it.'

'Thank you,' I say, not really sure what I am thanking her for. Her insights. Her forgiveness.

We walk together to the front door and stand on the porch, unsure of how to end the meeting. I embrace her suddenly and the warmth of her body against mine is like a balm.

144

'Come again, won't you?' Her voice is soft and when she turns away, the night air strikes coldly against my body where her warmth has been.

Chapter 21

At home, Harold and Ebony are still at Alicia's. Before visiting Emma I called Harold and told him of my plans. Now I change quickly into my running gear, not sure if I can cope with any more conversation.

Around the bay, the lights are cold and clear, reflected sharply in the black sea at my side. I consider the members of the Stone family one by one. All the people that Harold had counted off on his fingers to explain the beneficiaries of Bill Stone's will – Sam, Kristin, Amy, Jason, Rosalyn. I think about motivation. About Shane Black reassuring Harold that without motivation there is nothing for the police to work with. Money and greed are common motivations, but who out of that little band would need money so much they would kill for it?

At least I have met them all. And with this family there is not the weight of years to undo – I have no preconceived ideas. But even as the thought strikes, I know that, in fact, I do. There are some that I like, some that I don't, and some that I hardly know. I think about Amy and Sam, people I have liked from the start, and then there is Rosalyn. My thoughts turn to Rosalyn time and again, with something of the inevitability of a collision that you can see happening but can do nothing to avoid. Rosalyn as murderer. Rosalyn as Harold's attacker. It is like breathing in icy air, almost painful, and the sense of dread I have felt on and off since the start of all this kicks in hard.

I consider her as dispassionately as I can. All the glimpses I have had of her in the last week layered like an intricate dessert. The dislike. The cloying sweetness. The touch of jealousy on my part. The disapproval over Amy. That jaunty walk after the funeral. Her lack of interest in Harold's health. I think of the intimacy between them, the glowing lights in Harold's house last week and the devastating effect on Harold if she is guilty. This both leads me on and appalls me. If Rosalyn is guilty – and right at this moment this is where my thoughts lie – what will it do to Harold?

I dredge up the counter arguments. If Rosalyn is the murderer, why would she have invited Harold into it all? Surely if she had killed her father, she would have left well alone. But the other side of this seems equally compelling. It would be comforting to have a friend in law on your side, and who knows what information she might have expected Harold to have about the criminal investigation.

I think about of the geography of the murder. All of the family live or work close to the city and could easily have commuted to the Flagstaff Gardens. All except for Kristin, I realise, who, on the night of Bill Stone's murder, was signing contracts in Sydney, a thousand kilometres to the north.

At Harold's house, I turn for home, thinking again of the runner. The speed was there but there was also an awkward-ness to their gait. Who among the family could run so fast? A couple of names spring immediately to mind – Amy is fast, I have seen this for myself, and Jason, fluid skater on the bike track, would also have a fair turn of speed. I picture it now, putting runners on his feet instead of skates, and sprinting with him along the running track. Kristin, according to Amy, trains regularly. I think about Sam, not sure of his speed. He is the wrong body shape and a limp is hardly promising, but I remember that touch of awkwardness and don't dismiss him out of hand. Perhaps this is exactly what it was, someone running with a limp.

By the time I get back home, I have decided on a few things. The first is the need to adopt the clean slate policy I used with Jenny's death. Then, I was forced to give up assumptions and consider each person objectively. The only exception I make is Amy. I remember the tremble that crept into her voice on the night of the dinner and refuse to believe a fourteen-year-old capable of murder. I also decide to tell Alicia where my latest thoughts have taken me. I need help and someone to discuss things with. At the moment Alicia is a better bet than Harold – she hasn't got anything riding on this and she has helped me out before.

Perhaps most importantly, I have decided to concentrate on two areas – the geographical and physical criteria that will hopefully eliminate innocent parties and point the way to the real murderer. These things are practical and give me something to work with. And, although I am not sure if this is relevant any longer, I would still very much like to know where Bill Stone slept at night.

Chapter 22

The next morning Alicia takes my suggestions in her stride. I have told her about my visit to Emma last night and my aunt's thoughts on finding out the truth. I spend quite some time explaining my suspicions and Alicia listens carefully without once changing her expression.

When I have finished she looks at me levelly. 'For what it's worth, I agree absolutely. Without truth, we might as well give up.'

'That is what I'm going to do, Alicia, try to find out what really happened. I wondered if you would help.'

'Yes, I understood that.' She doesn't hesitate. Perhaps this is part of being older. Perhaps you don't spend so much time agonising over things. Whatever the reason behind her acceptance, I am very glad to have her on my side.

'What are you doing today?'

'Working this morning.'

'If I can arrange it, could you come visiting with me in the afternoon?'

'Yes, of course.'

'I want to visit Sam,' I say. 'I'm trading on you knowing him.' I know how much I am asking of her. She likes Sam and Jason.

'It's important to find out the truth, Marlo. If it will help eliminate anyone, then that's what we have to do.'

I don't voice the obvious thought – it could incriminate, not eliminate. But Alicia is intelligent enough and I can see her registering the thought.

I ring Tegan and line her up for the afternoon then arrange to pick Alicia up at two o'clock.

Harold and I are very quiet on the drive in to work. On my part it seems safer not to speak; Harold is too astute at reading my mind and I'm not sure I can cope with telling him what I think. My mind scurries with the problem. Perhaps there will be no need to – perhaps something will happen quickly to change things. Perhaps it is all a false alarm. Perhaps my suspicions are wrong.

'Rosalyn rang last night,' he says, as if on cue. 'When you were at Emma's.'

'How is she?'

'OK. She's still in Adelaide, she gets back on Friday night.'

'Amy said she was in Perth,' I say.

'She rang me from Adelaide.'

As Amy would say, what's the difference?

'Sam has consulted a real estate agent about the house. They've valued it at around $500,000.'

'I thought it would be something like that.' I am careful to keep my voice neutral. A tidy sum between the five of them – $100,000 each. A bit more than the few dollars Jamie Griggs is accused of murdering Bill for.

'So things are moving on,' I say, concentrating on parking in the space behind the office. When I look at Harold, his face is as blank as mine.

In the office I ring Rosalyn's number. No reason behind the call, save curiosity and the chance to hear her voice, a link to where my thoughts have taken me. The phone rings precisely six times before the answering machine picks up and Rosalyn's voice sounds, soft and melodious. A voice that tells me nothing at all, save for the fact that she is careful in her speech and presentation. But I already know this. It was evident in her efforts with the dinner, the food and the flowers, her careful dress. I hang up at the end of her message, wondering what else she is careful of.

On the Australian Securities and Investment Commission register, I find that Rosalyn Stone is the director of the Advance Modelling School, the address listed as 110 Lonsdale Street, Melbourne. It might be interesting to pay a visit.

Tegan comes in at twelve o'clock as arranged and we go through the work for the afternoon. Irene looks at me, eyes cold, lips compressed, and I realise that I haven't told her about taking time off. At the moment I couldn't care less. I finish off some work and head out at one o'clock.

First I drive down Lonsdale Street to check out the Advance Modelling School. The building is nondescript and gives nothing much away, save for its age. This is the poorer end of town, an area not yet overtaken by developers. I don't stop because there are no available parking spaces, and this particular building is not far from work so I can visit more easily on foot. Next I make a detour to Riley Street in Richmond. Richmond is an inner city suburb that has, in recent years, gone through a slow and piecemeal process of change. New affluent buildings sit alongside others that are old and neglected. In some streets factories have been remodelled into apartments while some retain their original function. The houses are the same – some affluent and charming, others broken down and dilapidated. I like the muddle of styles, the melding of old and new, and the sense of not being able to define the area as one thing or another.

But when I drive down Riley Street, I have no difficulty in defining it. This particular part of Richmond has been overlooked in the haphazard process of change. No trendy apartments here; nothing but old brick buildings, smashed windows, graffiti and abandonment. The derelict hat factory takes up most of the street, the lettering above the door still vaguely visible through decades of grime. Amy was right, it is creepy, but I take more notice of the single warehouse that stands next to it. Inside there are a couple of lights on that speak of owners or tenants, and a small bank of letter boxes at the front, some of which are labelled, including Kristin Stone's.

I work out from the labels that Kristin's space is against the outside wall. The windows are thin, impregnated with mesh, and Kristin's are the only ones that seem to be open. I walk around the warehouse and find that it is a self-contained rectangle. Down the side alley the windows are barred with heavy steel but at the back, like the front, a couple of the higher ones stand open. Behind the building there is a space filled with weeds and a prolific scatter of rubbish, and the high embankment of the railway line. Standing half way up the embankment, I can see into Kristin's space, which is divided off from the rest of the building by high partitioning. Extensive sky-lighting throws light on the interior and I can make out a workbench, some bolts of material and a cluster of domestic things against the far wall. A bed, a cabinet, a kettle and some cups. If Bill Stone didn't sleep at the house in South Yarra, then this is the most likely answer to the question of where he stayed at night. I'm just not sure what it means or what relevance it has to other things.

I drive on to Alicia's. She is waiting in the garden and slides into the passenger seat next to me.

'Tell me about Sam,' I say as we pull away from the house.

'He's a nice man. He's taken an interest in Amy and encouraged her with her magic. He has a good sleight of hand himself.'

I'm not sure I want to hear about Sam being a nice man or that he takes an interest in his teenage niece. It would be far easier not to like him, not to like any of them.

Alicia is silent now apart from giving me directions, and I wonder what she is thinking.

'Do you mind doing this?' I ask out loud for the first time.

'Visiting my friends to find out whether they are capable of murder? Yes, I do. But we touched on that this morning. I think we need to find out the truth for everyone's sake and I guess if they're true friends, we'll sort it out.'

We drive on in silence and it occurs to me that we have been here before, with Jenny's death. Last year, I relied heavily on Alicia's common sense and her protection. She helped me unflinchingly and, driving to Sam's now, there is something of the same feeling. She must feel it too, because she comments, 'A bit like old times, Marlo, being with you like this, tracking people down.'

I shift in my seat. 'I never thanked you for what you did last year. I couldn't have done it without you. I couldn't do this now without you.'

She lets out a small puff of air. 'I never wanted thanks, Marlo. Last year, I would have done it myself if I'd been in a position to. It's the same now.' The enormity of it all goes unsaid and Alicia turns to practical matters. 'So, the agenda for the day is?'

'A gossipy chat, I think. One in which we find things out and they don't.'

'What sort of things exactly?'

I consider my criteria. Curiosity about Bill Stone. Geography. Physical ability. 'About Bill Stone in the main. What they know of him. Whether he stayed with them before he died. Where they were the night Bill died. How fast they can run.'

She looks at me with disbelief. 'You're joking.'

'Not entirely,' I say. 'Anything along those lines would be good.'

I know too that now I have decided on this course of action, part of me cringes from it. Interrogation lets people know what you know, confronts people with your knowledge.

Puts you out there among the disagreeable and the dangerous.

Alicia pats my arm. 'Piece of cake.'

'Half an hour max. If they get too chatty, make an excuse. If it's too hard, fall back on the social visit.'

The house, when we pull up, is very small and old, but very neat. The front windows are framed in leaded panels with different coloured glass. Red and blue and a corner square of green. There is a polish to the wooden front door and the path is swept. The garden beds along the path are a stunning drift of primulas and jonquils. There is a gardener in the front yard dressed in loose blue overalls, a rubbish bin full of garden clippings in front of him. It is only when we close the car doors and he looks up that I see the gardener is Jason. He looks different from the last time I saw him – heavier and more solid in his overalls. He smiles at Alicia, welcoming her, but his expression changes when he sees me, becomes more wary. But then a recent visit by the police over the attack on Harold would make him wary.

Alicia is bubbly and greets him warmly, and Sam comes out of the house at the sound of voices. When he sees Alicia, his face lights up with pleasure and surprise, and I feel a wash of unease. I had turned to Alicia instead of Harold, aware of the difficulty of suspecting those you love and not wanting romance to impede things. But despite the difference in ages, it is not hard to see what Sam thinks of Alicia.

'Alicia. How nice.' Genuine pleasure in his voice.

'You know Marlo?' Alicia asks him.

'Yes,' he smiles, but guardedly, and I have the feeling he is remembering my too obvious curiosity at dinner. His words are bland. 'Good to meet you again, Marlo.'

He seems easier here than he did at Rosalyn's, but then the whole evening had been something of an ordeal – the conversation at dinner, the strained air, the headaches and the fights. A difficult night, and my first impression of all of them save for Rosalyn and Jason. Who knows, I think with a rising sense of frustration, what was real and what was assumed? Who knows what behaviour was in character.

'Come in and have a drink of something. A wine or a beer?'

'Wine would be nice,' Alicia says. She looks at me for a moment, and I see her decision to leave me to my own devices.

'Not for me thank you.'

They drift inside and I stay where I am with Jason. The conversation takes a moment to get going, until Jason settles on something safe.

'You didn't get back to me about the run.'

'No. I thought about it though,' I reply, not saying in which context.

I go for the direct approach: 'You heard that Harold was attacked?'

'The police came to see me about it.' He looks guarded but I try not to read anything into it.

'I wondered if you saw anyone.' Then I tell him what I saw, the pink eyes in the darkness of the bushes.

'The police asked me that but I didn't see a thing. Is Harold OK now?'

'In body at least, but I think he's more affected by it than he lets on.'

'Yeah. Tough on him.' The wariness is still there.

'I wondered if you had met up with your grandfather before he died?'

Jason looks at me for a long time, his mind busy with the thoughts that my question has set up. It's a simple question but the situation is a complex one. When he does speak his voice is polite. 'What gives you the right to ask?'

'Curiosity. And the hope you might tell me.'

He smiles faintly. 'You're cool, I'll say that. I thought when I met you that you were a bit too interested in things.'

'I was interested in your grandfather,' I say, going back to the original puzzle.'

'And what have you made of things?'

'Not a lot,' I say honestly. 'But the police have arrested

someone. Did they tell you?'

'I heard about it.'

'So, out of curiosity, did he stay here with you?'

'No.' He looks puzzled at my persistence and I answer the expression rather than his words.

'He had to stay somewhere. Given the life that he led, I wouldn't have thought there was much chance of him having friends from thirty years ago who would invite him to stay. But then, you never know.'

He doesn't answer so I go on. 'I thought he would have come to see you.'

'And why did you think that?' His tone is uneasy.

'Because this house is easy to find. He only had to look in the phone book to find out where his son lived. He would have known about you and he would have been curious.'

'Well . . . if he was . . .' His voice trails away.

'What?'

He shrugs. 'There was this old bloke on one of the park benches along the track when I went running once or twice. I had the feeling it was me he was looking out for. You know what it's like, nothing you can explain very well, just a feeling you get.'

'Yeah. I know.'

This would explain the photo Bill had asked Rosalyn for, the need to know what his grandson looked like. I wonder fleetingly what approach, if any, he had made towards his granddaughter. I asked Amy the question and I'm pretty sure she lied to me. I dismiss the thought because right now I haven't time for thoughts of Amy. I wonder how Alicia is getting on with Sam.

'I like the garden,' I say, taking renewed note of the beautiful banks of primulas and jonquils. 'Alicia says you're doing a course.'

He looks more relaxed now and I suspect the change of subject is a welcome one.

'It's a bit dead at the moment. The next few weeks will see a difference.'

'What will you do when you finish your course?'

'Start a small nursery. I've already made some contacts, I just...' He breaks off, but the pleasure and determination in his words are articulate enough. Part of the different criteria I considered last night. Motivation. Nurseries, even small ones, must cost a fortune.

I can't think of any other questions to ask that don't sound enormous and intrusive, and Jason is not the sort to fill the silence with polite chitchat. Just as the silence begins to stretch on uncomfortably, even for me, Alicia and Sam drift out with wine glasses. I watch Sam descend the three front steps of his house and see the side-on turn he makes to complete the manoeuvre, the decided limp as he comes towards us.

'Are you sure you don't want one?' he says, lifting his wine glass.

'No, thanks.'

Sam invites Alicia to take a tour of his shed to see where he makes his toys and wooden items. I follow along, very much an afterthought. The back yard is compact and Sam's shed takes up most of one side. The rest of the yard is devoted to horticulture, rows and rows of plants in different-sized tubs that stretch from fence to path. Sam's shed is bigger than the house and devoted solely to his business, save for an area near the door for garden tools and overalls on a hook. The workbench is full of wooden objects in different stages of production, and his tools are lined up neatly on the shelf behind, along with oils and paints and stains.

There is a batch of finished bowls on the bench. I pick one up and feel the heavy sensuousness of the wood. I don't know how all this industry translates in terms of money, but Sam certainly seems to enjoy what he does. His face is relaxed as he explains to Alicia some of the processes behind the work. A basket on the workbench contains a pile of different fabrics in bright colours and I play with them as Sam talks, sliding the cool silk between my fingers.

'What are these?' I ask

He turns his attention from Alicia. 'Offcuts from a guy who makes up silk scarves to sell at the market. I thought Amy might use them in her magic, and what she doesn't want, I can turn into sails for my wooden boats.'

'Nice,' I say and let the fabrics fall back into the basket. Alicia looks at me and I nod slightly.

'We must go Sam. Marlo is driving me into town. Thanks for showing us around.'

He takes the wine glass from her hand. 'I'll see you Sunday then.'

We say goodbye to Jason and he nods without speaking, but when I drive away, I can see him in my rear-view mirror, following the progress of the car.

'I didn't realise about you and Sam,' I say to Alicia as we turn the corner.

'What's to realise?'

'He likes you.'

'Oh, that. Yes.' She doesn't comment further and her silence is articulate. This is not an area for open discussion.

'How d'you go?' I ask after a while.

She pulls a face. 'It's not easy is it? I asked him about his father and that was OK, I would have done anyway. Apparently Bill had contacted him but Sam wasn't too interested.' She shrugs and continues, 'I suspect Sam knows what we're up to – he's no fool.'

'No,' I agree uneasily, aware that Sam is a long way from being a fool. 'The only thing I came up with is that Jason could do with a decent amount of money, but that applies to them all.'

'I don't think Jason's in the running.' Alicia says quietly.

'Why not?'

'Jason has an aversion to blood and not just his own. I remember years ago when Sam nearly sliced the top of his finger off, Jason was the one who went white and almost vomited. He was much younger then of course.'

I digest this information. Hard to imagine anyone who gets

ill at the sight of blood bashing someone over the head for their inheritance. Hard to imagine but not impossible.

She smiles. 'Cheer up, Marlo, things can only get better.'

'Or clearer. What's wrong with Sam's leg?'

'He lost it in a motorbike accident years ago. He has an artificial leg.'

I don't know much about artificial limbs. 'Would it stop him running?'

She smiles. 'Absolutely. The disabled sprinters you see on TV have special legs. I'm pretty sure that Sam couldn't run to save his life and if he could, it would only be for a few steps.'

I look at her for a fleeting moment and smile. We have gone from a possible elimination to a definite one, from hopeless to hopeful in the space of a few seconds. No tortuous path to knowledge here, but something simple and easy. Amy is out. Sam is out. Kristin is out. Three down, I think almost happily. Only two to go and Jason has an aversion to blood. If this counts him out, we are four down and one to go. Rosalyn. Her face swims before me with a kind of grim inevitability. Rosalyn again and again.

Chapter 23

I drop Alicia off near Melbourne Central, park the car at work and set out for the offices of the Advance Modelling school.

Close up, the building is in a worse condition than it had appeared in the quick glimpse from the car. There is grime on the windows, dust in the corridor and footprints on the lino. Rosalyn's office, I see from the directory in the foyer, is on the first floor.

When I reach the reception desk, it is clear that the Advance Modelling School is in the process of closing down. There is a stack of empty cardboard boxes next to the reception desk and a feeling of disuse about the place that shows in the dust and the vase of dying flowers on the coffee table. The office is empty but in the hallway behind the front desk there are more boxes, taped and labelled. I am surprised. When Harold had told me about Rosalyn's work, it was always in the present tense.

The reception area remains reasonably intact as though leaving this room until last was deliberate. A few chairs surround a coffee table with some books on etiquette and fashion. I pick up one of the smaller books and see that it is about the symbolism of flowers. I flick through it with interest, intrigued by the illustrations and presentation, and stop when I get to the page that deals with jonquils. Jonquils had formed part of Rosalyn's centre piece on the dining table the night Harold and I went for dinner. She also wound a jonquil through his buttonhole. According to the text, the gift of jonquils means that the giver desires a return of affection. I laugh out loud. So even the flowers were planned. And if Rosalyn plans things down to flower type, what else is she capable of planning. But then another thought comes spinning in. If she is a planner, and I know she is, why would she do something as messy as attacking her father in the park with the first thing that came to hand?

My laughter brings footsteps from the corridor behind the office. A woman appears with some files in her hand. She is in her fifties, thick around the waist, dressed in a track suit and runners, with a pair of glasses on a cord around her neck. I adopt a suitable expression and hope to give the appearance of a potential customer.

'I didn't realise you were closing down.'

'The whole building's closing down. Can I help you with anything?' There is an abruptness to her tone that tells me she wants to get on with things.

'I'm looking for Rosalyn.'

'Not here this week.' Her words are clipped and uninformative. If she is the secretary, her manner is a long way from what I imagine is expected of employees of a finishing school.

'I need to get in touch with her fairly urgently. Do you know where she is?'

She looks at me properly for the first time and I show her my card and deliver the lie. 'We're sorting out probate on her father's estate. There are some questions that she can help with.'

The woman puts her glasses on and takes the card from my hand. The card is credible and necessary to obtain the information I am curious about, but I feel the first misgivings. This is something she will remember, something she will keep.

The whole thing feels too much like showing my hand. It is effective, though, because she consults a diary on the desk and writes down a number on a piece of paper. I read the neat printing. Hotel Elan in Perth. More and more interesting. Why tell Harold Adelaide when she is in Perth?

I turn to go. The woman has already turned away and is pulling out drawers and sifting through folders. There is a timetable on the notice board at the side of the desk and I check out the night classes at the bottom of each day's listing. They give subject, room number and teacher initials. RS is the teacher for three separate night classes. I had known this, though, courtesy of Amy. All night classes begin at seven o'clock. At the latest, the murder of Bill Stone took place just before six o'clock, less than a block away. If Rosalyn is guilty, then she had plenty of time for a little impromptu murder before her scheduled class.

It is later than I thought. Irene and Tegan have gone for the night but Harold is waiting for me.

'What's happening?' Harold looks at me directly. 'Don't hedge, Marlo, I know you too well.'

For a moment I consider not telling him. I don't know if I can bear the thought of any more discord between us. But the thought dies before it is full born and I know I can't hide my suspicions from him any longer. I tell him about the jolt of realisation when Denton phoned me at the hockey match – that the murderer was not some stranger from the west but family. Someone in that small, select group of people who would clearly benefit from Bill Stone's death.

Harold is very still, his expression unchanging. 'You've made a leap, Marlo.' His voice is cold. 'If not the derro or the diamond thief, then it has to be the family. A bit sweeping, isn't it?'

'Most murders are domestic,' I say, sounding far too much as though I am justifying my position rather than backing up my hypothesis.

'You sound like a crime buff.' His voice is distant.

'I've gone over it again and again. You said you didn't believe that Jamie Griggs was the murderer. I don't either. The family are the ones with motivation. Remember that talk on motivation that Shane had with you at the start of all this? How without motivation there is nothing.'

He doesn't answer for a long time. 'If it is family, Marlo, it will change them all for ever.'

'I know that Harold, even more than you. And as for the rest, Bill Stone had only been in the state for ten days when he was killed. Apart from the family he left over thirty years ago, it is hard to imagine him making a serious enemy in that time.'

'A murder in the park is a long way from a domestic situation,' he counters.

'Perhaps that's exactly what the murderer thought.'

Silence for a long time. The only sound is the rumble of traffic outside the window and Harold's close breathing. Across the road the last of the light is fading behind the shadows of the trees. Inside, the room is heavy with tension.

I break the silence. 'Do you know who told me to keep going with this?'

He doesn't answer so I finish anyway. 'Emma. She was the one who said it was best to know the truth, no matter who it hurt.'

He looks out through the window, scene of many discussions, both serious and light-hearted.

'Who exactly do you have in mind? I trust you do have someone in mind.'

I have no choice but to keep going. 'I have eliminated a few, at least I think I have.'

'Go on.'

'I refuse to believe that Amy is capable of murder.'

'Amy the magician,' he says musingly and I pick up on his tone.

'What?'

'Just thinking out loud, Marlo. Magic is all about direction and misdirection. To be a good magician you have to be organised, well practised and well rehearsed. I would think

163

these assets would be useful for a murderer and Amy has proved she's got all three.'

I look at him incredulously. 'You can't believe …'

He cuts across me: 'Why not? Magic makes us appreciate how easily the eye can be deceived.'

'She's fourteen, Harold.'

'Yes, and you're right, I don't believe it, but I'm constantly saying things that no one could possibly believe.'

I look at him closely. This is a mood I don't recognise – a little too brittle, a little frivolous. It seems dangerous, as though at any moment Harold might laugh or cry. Instead he takes a deep breath and continues, his tone serious. 'The principle remains – I don't think you can exclude people on sentimental grounds, whoever they are.'

This is something I know too well. Something he knows that I know. The awareness of it buzzes in the air between us. Knowledge and anger. This is Harold at his worst – sanctimonious, smug, constantly right. But I swallow down the retort because, in a way, he is right.

'Go on with your theory,' he says.

'Kristin. Remember she was in Sydney when Bill was killed. Sam told us at the table.'

'I remember it was talked about.'

This is something else that needs to be checked up on. A trip to Sydney can easily be cancelled. People can come back.

'And?' Harold is impatient.

'Sam.'

'Why Sam?'

'The runner.'

'The runner,' he says almost scornfully. 'Back to this.'

I don't answer for a moment. The fixed point for me in all of this has been the runner. That odd moment of stillness in the park and the sound and sight of someone running – a moment of stillness, like the eye of a hurricane, around which chaos gathers speed. I gather my arguments.

'Not just a runner, Harold, but someone running away from

a dying man. Someone who hasn't been in touch with the police. It sounds pretty damning to me.'

'Yes.' He modifies his tone. 'Go on.'

'The only thing I really know about the runner is that they were slightly awkward but very fast. Sam has an artificial leg, which, according to Alicia, means that he couldn't run to save his life. But even if his leg didn't eliminate him, his body shape is wrong for speed.'

'Well, I must say your methods of deduction are original. Anyone else?'

'Jason has an aversion to blood. I'm not giving this as proof, but it is an indication . . .'

'Yes, I see.' The silence is heavy and prolonged. 'So, all of them, except for Rosalyn.'

'Yes.'

The silence stretches on and becomes uncomfortable.

Harold breaks it: 'You don't like Rosalyn do you, Marlo?'

What do I say now? I can hardly deny it and, to be honest, I'm not entirely sure that my dislike of the woman hasn't clouded my judgement. Feelings do confuse things in my experience, no matter how hard you try to guard against them. But I have tried to be objective.

Harold must find his answer in my expression. When he speaks again his voice is very even. 'Suppose what you say is true, Marlo. Why Bill and then me? Why the attack on me?'

'I'm not sure. What you said about being a danger to the murderer is the only thing that makes sense. Maybe whoever killed him thought you knew something or saw something.'

'Well, if they did, they were very wrong.' He looks away and his face and voice are remote. 'So you think Rosalyn?'

'Rosalyn was the one who arranged for you to be at the house. She didn't know I would be there too.' I don't finish the thought – she has made herself pretty scarce since then.

'I told people at work on Friday.'

'Who exactly? Irene?'

'And a few people during the course of the day. Tegan

worked on Friday.'

I don't comment and he doesn't follow it up. It is too absurd. What possible motivation would Irene or Tegan have for attacking Harold. Across the road, the park lights have come on, fuzzy balls of yellow light in the darkness.

'I know it's not a foolproof theory and there's every chance I haven't considered something important. Look, Harold, I'm sorry it's turned out like this. You only took me along out of kindness, as a distraction...'

'Yes.' He turns back to face me and continues slowly: 'But in the circumstances, I'm very pleased that I did.' His tone is softer now and I know where his thoughts have gone: his crumpled body on the cold garage floor, the blood running, his glasses broken at his side..

'I thought that after Jenny and the clear-eyed sleuthing you did then...I thought it might be a way out for you.' A small smile. 'In drinking terms, Marlo, the hair of the dog that bit you.'

'I know and I do appreciate it.'

He is suddenly restless, shifting hs weight from foot to foot. 'Spare me from knowing what is good for people.'

'If it's any consolation, it has helped me, Harold. I enjoyed concentrating on Bill and the mystery of his life. But you are wrong about me being so perceptive. With Jenny I was hopeless, and with this I've been hopeless.'

'You got there in the end. I have no doubt that if you follow this through, you will find out the truth.'

'And what about you? What will you do?'

Silence for a moment and then he almost visibly gathers himself up, seems to stand both taller and more resolute. 'I've listened to what you have to say but, in the end, I refuse to believe that Rosalyn is capable of murder.'

I lean against the desk, feeling momentarily as though my legs won't support me. I have explained my reasons but I might as well have saved my breath. I wonder how much his feelings for Rosalyn have clouded his judgement, how much of this faith in her is blind.

'Let's look at this logically, Marlo.'

'I'm all for logic.'

'Rosalyn was the one who invited us in, if you can call it that. If she was the murderer, don't you think that she would be more careful.' His voice is very measured, very controlled.

'Yes, but if you remember, she called you in to find out if there were any other assets the family were entitled to.'

'Nothing wrong with that...'

'No, of course not. Given the situation, that's what she should have done.' There is pressure behind my eyes, a tiny, pressing band of pain. This conversation is tortuous. 'It's difficult, Harold, because I know you care. All this should be easy because I hardly know these people but, believe me, it isn't.'

'Because of me?'

'Partly because of you,' I say carefully. 'But not just you. Amy. Jason. All of them, really. You just tip the balance. It's hard to be objective because I know how much you have riding on this.

'Let someone else do it.'

I laugh but the laughter falters easily. 'Who exactly? The police? Don't you think I'd like to. I've been to the police often enough but they are happy with their arrest and I don't blame them.'

He nods eventually. 'Marlo, I do understand. I admire you immensely for what you do and what you think. I'm just so...torn.'

'I know.'

'Answer me something.'

'If I can.'

'Do you think Rosalyn asked me to help because she knew I was in law and she thought I might be able to find out information on the police investigation?'

'I don't know,' I say. I don't but I have wondered about this myself.

When Harold speaks he is very formal but I am aware of

a touch of hostility behind the good manners. 'If you'll excuse me, Marlo, I am going to meet a friend. I'll stay there the night, I think, talk it through with an outsider. And then perhaps I'll know what to do. Whatever I decide, I need to talk it over with Rosalyn.'

'Yes.' Talking it over with Rosalyn doesn't sound like a lot of laughs, but he's right, perhaps that's all he can do.

I leave Harold's office, retreat thankfully to my own and close the door. I look at the clock on my office wall. Only twenty minutes have passed since I entered his office, but it seems like a lifetime. The phone rings and I let it go through to voice mail, not sure I can concentrate enough to get past the first sentence. I hear Harold leave. His footsteps in the outer office. The office and street door closing. The heavy silence afterwards.

I stay back to catch up with unfinished work and preparation for tomorrow. Without Harold, there is no need to hurry home and I feel the need to concentrate on small familiar things. I start planning the day and set aside some documents to be photocopied for the files. The photocopy room is between the kitchen and the spare room that Harold set up years ago as a bedroom in case anyone should need it.

I switch the copier on and wait for it to warm up. That curious sweet smell that I have registered on and off lately is stronger in the photocopy room than in the general office area and I wonder if it has drifted in from the spare room. I open the door and the smell is stronger but I can't see the cause. There are no flowers or air fresheners but it is like perfume, as though someone wearing heavy scent has passed this way. Fanciful, Marlo. Too much imagination.

The last person to use the photocopier has left their original under the lid. I set it aside while I concentrate on sorting out my work. When I have finished I order documents into piles for filing and see that the stray sheet of A4 has got caught up with my papers. I almost don't read it. I almost walk away. But something unusual about it catches my eye. Perhaps it is the unusual format – a small clump of text in the middle of a page. I pick it up almost idly and what I see there, takes my breath away, as though I have been punched.

It is a photocopy of a newspaper article from over thirty years ago, the date and title of the newspaper printed on the top of the paper.

The Sun. 20 February 1969.

Assault Charge

A charge for an assault that allegedly took place in the kitchen of an Ashburton restaurant, between Harold Underwood and an unnamed member of the kitchen staff, was dismissed today. The court was told that the accused had picked up a nearby kitchen implement as a weapon in the attack. The charges were dropped through lack of supporting evidence.

I read it over and over again as if the words might change or make sense if I stare at it for long enough. In the end I make another photocopy and leave the original where I found it.

Harold Underwood. Good friend. Business partner. Most sane of men. A shaft of coldness settles in my spine as one particular thought clamours in my head like an out-of-control alarm. A thought inspired by a few sentences in black and white.

I turn away from it, gather up my various folders and head to my own office. Across the road, the brilliant shine of street lights obscures the dark rectangle of parkland beyond – the downward sweep of lawn where a recent murder took place.

That sentence again. I see it without reading it. The snatching up of a nearby implement, the closest weapon to hand. That is how Bill Stone was killed.

I sit at my desk facing the familiar workday things. My desk diary lies open in front of me with my appointments marked in for tomorrow afternoon – a few settlements, some court lodgements. Ordinary things. Utterly safe and commonplace.

So here we are again, the past impinging on the present as it always has done throughout this whole weary business. Harold had known Bill Stone in the past. He told me this himself. Then there was his seemingly uncalled for fear of the police from the very start. His disconcerted air when Rosalyn talked about that restaurant from long ago. And, more tellingly, Harold was out of the office in the minutes before Bill Stone was killed. He was on the street that night, waiting for the courier. There was no need really – the courier was one we often use and they never have any problems finding us. The phone call that I was engaged in at the time was both long and panicky, needing lots of reassurances and back-checking through files. I'm not sure how long it took, but it was lengthy. Harold had been on the street for a long time, just across the road from where Bill Stone was killed. In reality, just metres away. And later, going home, he was the one who had stopped and found the dying man. I didn't hear a thing and my hearing is good.

I remember the inconclusive blood evidence Denton told me about. The killer who would have got blood on their clothing, as Harold did, but not in any conclusive sprays or splatters. I stand up again, stare once more through the window. I refuse to believe it. But last year, I had refused to believe certain things about people who were close to me. Part of the whole sorry business has been coming to terms with the chilling things that people are capable of. Even Denton said it – that given the right triggers . . .

So, disbelief to a wavering credibility and back again. A washing machine effect, round and round it goes. First one way, then the other. Not Rosalyn but Harold.

I want to talk to him. I don't want to wait until tomorrow. For peace of mind, I need to sort it out right now, tonight. I head to his office and go through his diary entries but they are all work related and I have no idea who he is having dinner with. I pace up and down. It is probably just as well. Only the other day, I accused him of interfering in my life too much. I wonder what his reaction would be if I tracked him down at a friend's house and confronted him with something like this.

My only choice is to lock up and head for home. The sky is cloudless, scattered with cold, clear stars and in the air the feel of ice. At home I feed Ebony and close the doors against the world. The phone rings and I let it go through to the answering machine.

Lee's voice. I don't spring to the phone as I usually would, but listen to her bright voice as though it is a thing apart. She sounds even more buoyant than usual, the love affair obviously going well.

I hope that hitting your answering machine means you're out somewhere having fun. I've been away with you know who. It was all very spur of the moment and I've just got your message. I'll talk to you soon.

The silence after the phone call is endless. It seems to me, sitting here in the quiet house, that one of the very few fixed points of my life is threatening to dissolve. And that one essential fixed point is Harold. It strikes me then just how restricted my life has become or, more aptly, how restricted I have allowed my life to become.

I wander through the house, turning with relief to the practical consideration of who would have left that particular photocopy under the lid of the machine. Not that there's a huge field to choose from – Harold, Irene or Tegan. There is only one real contender and I can dismiss any thoughts of carelessness. Irene is not the sort of person to leave things lying around.

I go to bed early, not sleeping much but thinking things through. Without Harold here, it is very quiet and I listen to the house settling into the coldness of night with the familiar creaking sounds I have become used to. I think about love and jealousy and possession; about the possibility of ever really knowing what people are capable of. And it strikes me that if I can believe Harold capable of murder, then I can believe anything.

Chapter 24

I am early for work. That persistent smell of jonquils is there again and after the cold night the office seems warmer than it should be. I wander through the photocopy room and the spare room. Both scent and warmth are more definite here and this little side issue tugs at my mind. I trace events backwards, gathering together all the separate occasions, working it out. Back to the night when I first noticed it. The night of Bill's death.

Someone has been in the office after work. Someone, I assume now, given the warmth of the place and the definite scent, who has stayed the night. Not Harold, not me. It doesn't leave many people, unless Harold has let someone stay without telling me. Irene, I think, but why?

The front door opens. Harold comes in and I forget all about Irene. We look at each other and some complex remembrance of last night passes between us. He looks utterly normal. I'm not sure how I appear but he regards me curiously for a moment. I follow him through to his office and pass him the article from last night.

'What is it?'

'I found this in the photocopier.'

Harold removes his glasses from their case and takes far too long to read a brief two-column extract. He doesn't speak but wanders to the window and looks out over the park. I stay where I am, in front of his desk, the white sheet of paper brilliant against the polished wood.

'It all got out of hand, Marlo. I employed him as a kitchen hand to get us out of trouble over a busy weekend. He was a belligerent sort, quick to take offence, quick to slack off. I told him off one night and, back in those days, I was full of my own importance. I probably came across as pompous and irritating. I must have done because he took a swing at me and I swung back. I didn't do much damage but he hit his head on the way down. He was groggy for a while but no more than that. I went with him in a taxi to the hospital so they could check him out and the hospital sent him home. The next day the police came round and charged me with assault.'

'What happened then?'

'It went to trial but it was my word against his. He told the police I'd picked up a mallet that we use for pounding meat. I hadn't but we were the only two there. There was no one to confirm or deny it and I guess, in the end, I came across better in court than he did.'

It seems so simple, so ordinary. The nightmare quality of last night evaporates into nothing and I feel an instant wash of relief. How easy it is to lose trust when things look grim.

I clear my throat: 'Why didn't you tell me?'

He turns to face me. 'A few reasons. Firstly, I haven't thought about it for years now. Secondly, I didn't think it was anyone else's business but my own. And I guess if I have any vanities left, they are to do with being held in high esteem. Anyway, the whole incident is not something I'm particularly proud of. The only blemish of you like . . .'

There must be something revealing in my expression because he looks at me for a long time and I can see the thought sinking in.

'You suspected me? You thought that this article . . . that this meant I bashed Bill Stone over the head?' He's incredulous.

'Well, yes, I did, but not for long.'

'Not even for a second, I would have thought.'

I return his gaze. 'There were things that confused me. And you were worried, perhaps too worried.'

'What things?' His voice is very quiet but I pick out the different components – anger mixed with a reluctant curiosity.

'I picked up on them, because I know you.' I list them now: his uneasiness at the mention of the Wooden Spoon, the fear of the police that always seemed to be over the top. I don't tell him the rest – the roller-coaster ride that had him lurking on the street the night of the murder; picking up the nearest implement to hand; the blood evidence, that applies as much to him as it does to Jamie Griggs.

'Marlo, Marlo.' He shakes his head as if he can't quite believe where my thoughts have taken me.

'It didn't seem such an amazing leap last night,' I say defensively, but this is more of the same. The pervasiveness of suspicion. When you start suspecting people, analysing every word and action, it can take you nearly anywhere.

We don't speak for a moment, both of us engrossed in our thoughts.

'The thing that worries me the most is who photocopied this,' he says finally.

'Yes, I agree. 'That worried me too.'

He grins easily and I laugh in response, with relief if nothing else. 'Bless you, Marlo. You always keep your eye on the essentials. The only problem we have is that there aren't too many people to choose from.'

'No,' I agree. 'What will you do?'

'Talk to her I suppose. Leaving it under the photocopier could have been a mistake.'

I remember my thoughts from last night. The things you know with complete certainty. 'Except that Irene never leaves anything about.'

He doesn't speak but I know this is exactly what he thinks. When all of this is over, I'm going to take Irene into the back office and strangle her.

Right on cue the office springs to life. Irene and Tegan come in almost together and Harold heads out to keep appointments in town. He is glad to leave – I can tell by the spring in his step and the closed look on his face. I'm not sure I blame him. This business with Irene is a difficult one.

I stay in my office and spend the morning on the phone, setting things up for a series of settlements. A hard little burr of anger has settled in my chest and, between phone calls and spinning restlessly on my chair, I consider my approach.

I hear Irene come back in and exchange some remark with Tegan, then open my office door.

'Irene, can you come into my office for a moment.' She looks at me and I can't read the expression on her face. Contempt? Wariness? I close the door behind her and stand against the window.

'Have you been coming back to the office at night after we leave?'

A flicker of surprise crosses her face. Whatever she thought I was going to say, it wasn't this. I presume she thought I was going to question her about the photocopy, but that is Harold's business. My anger with her doesn't fade. I press on.

'Last Monday night there was someone here, and a few other nights since then.'

She looks at me for a long silent moment. 'Monday night was the night of the murder.' Her voice is dry and rasping.

'Yes.'

Again the long pause. I have no problem reading her expression now. She looks at me with open hostility.

'Harold said you were interested in finding out about Bill. I would have thought you'd had enough of that last year.'

I refuse to be distracted. 'I asked you about coming back to the office, Irene.'

Her eyes flicker and she shakes her head quickly. 'No, I didn't come back to the office. I think your imagination has got the better of you and if I were you I'd keep your nose out of my business.'

The anger simmers between us like a heat haze. I can't pretend that we have ever liked each other but this is the first time she has been openly rude.

'What are you doing, Marlo, accusing me of something?' Her voice is shrill and she almost spits the words at me.

'No, of course not,' I say, taken aback at this sudden unleashing of fury. I keep my voice very calm as a consequence. This is a skill I learned as a child, the very real necessity to diffuse anger, but my mind is racing.

'It puzzled me, that's all. Someone was here and I don't like things going on the office that we don't know about.'

'Playing the detective.' Her voice rises up in scorn. 'Harold thinks you're wonderful, you know. I think you're a fool. I think both of you should wake up to yourselves. He's got his faults you know.'

'Yes, I know. Thanks, Irene.' I speak calmly now. 'It was a simple question. All I wanted was a simple answer.'

She turns away and closes the door behind her with a crash. I am left staring at the rectangle of wood, imagining her progress to her desk. I picture her sitting primly at her computer, her fingers flashing over the keys. I sit at my desk breathing deeply, waiting for my pulse to slow and a more rational, considered part of me to take over. I don't have to wonder about this sudden flare up. I have learnt a few things about anger in my time, both my own and other people's. And with Irene, at least, it is not hard to guess the cause.

Ten minutes later I am disturbed by a knock at my door. I swivel round, expecting to see Irene because my thoughts have been full of her, but instead of Irene I see Tegan.

'Come in.'

She approaches hesitantly, looking concerned. 'I heard you

just now with Irene. I couldn't help it.'

'It did get out of hand. I didn't realise we were so loud.'

'It was me.'

I stand up. So engrossed have I been with thoughts of death that for a moment I think she is confessing to the murder.

'What?'

'It was me who came back to the office.'

I look at her for a long time and she shifts uncomfortably. A sullen blush passes over her round face then fades away.

'I know I should have asked. You see, we've . . . had trouble at home and sometimes I just couldn't bear the thought of going . . . I knew about Harold's bed, so . . .' she trails off.

'I see,' I say mindlessly. I can't think of anything else to say.

'Will Harold mind?'

'I shouldn't think so.' With what Harold is going through at the moment, I'm sure he couldn't care less.

'It won't happen again.'

'No. OK.' I shake my head and she stands irresolute, not sure what to do. I know I should say something to make her feel less awkward about it. After all, it's not such a huge crime. In the end I find both voice and a ready curiosity. 'Tegan, if things . . . are so bad at home, why don't you do something about it?'

She looks at me, surprised that she has to spell it out. 'Money. I need to save a bit more before I can branch out on my own.'

'Yes, of course.' Money is the obvious reason. Sometimes it seems that everything comes back to money.

Tegan looks at me and hesitates. What she finds on my face I'm not sure but she almost backs out of the room. If she had waited just another moment she would have seen me laugh. I lay my head down on my desk feeling exhausted and slightly dazed, as though I have fielded in the sun for too long, and I am aware that my laughter is very close to tears. I know that if I don't stop I will end up crying again. But it doesn't seem to matter any more if I laugh or cry.

178

Chapter 25

In the end I must do some work. I go out and about on my appointments in the city as if I am on automatic pilot. I pick up my photos at the chemist and shop at the market, filling my bag with things that Lucy likes for tea – chicken and salad for main course, cakes and marshmallows for dessert. On the footpath outside the office I meet Harold. Me coming in, him going out to do the banking. I lower my voice, aware of Irene at the top of the flight of stairs.

'Have you talked to her about the article?' It seems a safer subject than most.

'No, not yet.' He looks evasive and slightly guilty and I remember his comments to me – something to do with cowardice and the need to work on our relationships. I swallow it down.

Harold smiles faintly, as though he has read my mind. 'Rich, isn't it, coming from me. Maybe it just shows that we should mind our own business and not presume to know what is best for others.'

'Harold . . .' I begin but he interrupts me, which is unusual for him.

'It's not as easy as I thought. I will talk to her, Marlo, but not yet. I need to see the way ahead a bit more clearly.'

I don't agree but I let it go and walk with him up the street, telling him some of the morning's events. We stand on the corner of La Trobe Street among the metallic rumble of trams.

Looking at something above my head, he says, 'Don't be too hard on her, Marlo, she hasn't had it all her own way.'

I pick up on his words – the promise of information – like a starving child. 'In what way?'

'The usual, the great love that didn't work out. I've got to go, Marlo, or I'll miss the bank.'

Instead of going back to work I head for the gardens. I have no wish to see Irene or Tegan. Have no wish to feel the atmosphere in the office – Irene's anger or Tegan's guilt. Nor do I have any qualms about using Bill Stone's park bench. I sit down heavily, feeling under my hand the metal rail that fractured an old man's skull.

I look around me and see the park as I have seen it in the past, as a place of changing beauty. In the garden beds, spikes of green from bulbs stand in thick, vertical clusters and the great branches of oak and elm have a fragile glimmer of new leaf. Winter is finally giving way to spring. There is something comforting about the seasons – no matter what happens in your own life, they just keep rolling on. Trees here will have witnessed many centuries. I contemplate the history of the park as I know it, from cemetery to signalling station, complete with requisite canon and flagstaff. A lethargy steals over me, inspired by warmth and the unnerving roller-coaster ride of the past days. Bill Stone's bench or not, I feel as though I could nod off where I am and sleep until morning. I had no idea how tiring suspicion could be.

I see Irene leave for the day and watch her walk briskly down William Street, crossing at La Trobe street to the station entrance. It occurs to me that, at a stretch, I could even make a reasonable case against Irene. She has been upset this week, over who knows what, and in my experience Irene usually doesn't let her emotions show. An episode of murder could explain it well enough.

I could cite the great love of her life thirty years ago, with a man who left the area abruptly, a man she has met up with in recent times, hiding out in the Flagstaff Gardens. I could invent an emotional aspect – him hardly caring, hardly remembering; her, the exact opposite. Every day for thirty years, she would wonder why. Of course, she would crack him over the head in such circumstances...

And then there's Tegan, leaving now with her heavy bag over her arm. No brisk stride here but a slow, head-down plod, an almost palpable reluctance to go home.

I'm not sure how I feel about Tegan. If she'd wanted a place to stay for the odd night, all she had to do was ask. But then, if we hadn't been so preoccupied with everything else, perhaps she would have done.

I am shaken by where I have been, the thoughts I have entertained. Given my recent track record, I think with a wry smile, if I suspect Rosalyn, she must be totally and blazingly innocent. Give it up, Marlo. It seems that no matter how far I go or how much time and effort I spend, I am getting nowhere. My progress is slow, like walking through thick mud.

What I have learnt in the last few days is that it is possible to go down lots of different, promising avenues, but speculation is just that. To get any further, it is necessary to have some hard, cold evidence. I sigh out loud. Easy enough to say, almost impossible to do.

There are a lot of people in the gardens now, courtesy of the unexpected warmth. A mix of business people, couples and families. A gardener in green overalls works along one of the beds on the main path. This is the gardener I watched yesterday, when I was talking to Harold about Rosalyn.

I open the packet of photos that I picked up on my travels, but haven't had time to look at yet. The photo of the vagrant on St Kilda pier is as I imagined it. A stunning pearly grey, almost monochrome, photo with the focal point of the unknown homeless man, his body curved against the bin. The other photos are of my walk with Ebony, and the park on the morning after the murder. I look through them idly. Many of the photos include figures I took note of from my window that morning. The slow jogger. A woman with a pram. The gardener in blue overalls.

I look up. The gardener on the hill is moving away, his green uniform dappled as he walks beneath the trees. Blue overalls in the photo. Green overalls on the hill. My thoughts leap and I am on my feet and running.

'Wait!' I call out but he is too distant and I have to sprint up the path behind him. My bag is full of shopping and bumps against me as I run, weighing me down awkwardly. In two strides I have the solution to that strange awkwardness of the runner, an awkwardness that I have just replicated without thought. A heavy bag over a shoulder.

The gardener stops in front of the cottage at the top of the hill, aware of me for the first time. 'Can I help you?' He is surprised at being chased up the hill.

I am out of breath, not so much with the uphill sprint as with anticipation and hope.

I show him the photo. 'I know it's a bad shot, it's hard to tell, but do you know the gardener in this photo?'

He gives the outstretched photo a quick, cursory glance. 'He's not one of ours love.'

He says it with such certainty that I am taken aback. 'Are you sure?'

'Completely. There's not that many of us for a start, and even if there were, this one's wearing the wrong colour overalls. We wear green, most city gardeners do.'

'Yes,' I say. 'I thought so, but he has a trowel in his hand. If you look closely you can see it.'

He smiles. 'Can't help that, love. He's not one of ours.'

'Yes, I see that. Thanks.'

I head back to the park bench, my thoughts racing. This is what struck me the morning after Bill Stone's death. That small sense of something being wrong. I have worked opposite the Flagstaff Gardens for two-and-half years and in all that time all of the gardeners have been dressed in green. I was so focused on the runner after the interview with the police that nothing else registered.

I feel as if I have made some momentous find, like discovering radium or walking on the moon, and a spurt of elation rises up. I find myself smiling at the sheer perversity of things. Give up, Marlo, I had thought, just a few minutes ago, and now here in my hand, are photos that take on a new and significant relevance. Photos taken as soon as the police had left the park. I study each one carefully.

The blue-clad gardener is in one shot only, standing with his back towards the camera, his head bent slightly forward as though looking down at the garden beds, a tiny trowel glinting in his hand. A gardener that doesn't belong to Flagstaff. This is a fact and I hug it to me. Someone came into the gardens as soon as the police left, long hours after the murder. A night had passed and a day begun, and the person in my photo had assumed a disguise. Yes, but why?

I go through it now. Another rich seam of thought opens up but this time I follow it with pleasure, and the flow of energy and interest lifts me again. Bill Stone had commented on the need that criminals have to revisit the scene of their crime. The criminal equivalent to leaving the iron on, checking for something incriminating that they may have left behind. Is this what I am seeing in the photo? But if they were looking for something, wouldn't the police already have found whatever it was? A fragile hope, surely, after the police search. But what else? What other possible reason could there be?

I have seen a family member dressed in blue overalls – Jason. He matches three out of three of my criteria. Physical ability. Motivation. Geography. He has the speed of the runner in the park, the same motivation for killing as the rest of the family, and geographically, as far as I know, he could easily haver been present in the Flagstaff Gardens.

I cannot tell the gender of the gardener from the photo. I expected them to be male because most park gardeners are male, but nothing in the photo offers gender up. The gardener's head is bent forward and lost in shadow. They look as though they are searching a garden bed but on closer inspection, I realise from the angle of the head that they are studying the grass.

My mouth is dry. If Jason is the suspect then Rosalyn will be OK and Harold will be pleased. It's a horrible thought, preferring one family member over another. And anyway, if it is someone in the family, the family will never be the same again.

I take a mental step backwards. No more jumping to conclusions that aren't verified. I cannot make assumptions. And at least this time I have more than just thoughts to go on. A photo can be magnified. With luck, there will be something. A strand of hair to show hair colour. A glimpse of a jaw line. A suggestion of profile. A gleaming fact caught on film.

I check my watch, surprised by how much time has passed since I first sat down and notice how in the two weeks since Bill Stone's death the light has changed. It stays lighter for longer now. Almost six o'clock and the sun is still visible, low in the sky. A frail note of birdsong rises up. I stand up, looking for the source, transfixed, realising that on the street behind me the traffic has stopped. At this particular moment, there are no cars or trucks or trams caught between lights on this particular stretch of William Street. Traffic noise is audible but distant, no more than a faint hum of cars on the roads around the park. It is possible to hear birdsong. It is also possible to hear someone speaking on the middle footpath. It is also possible to hear their footsteps.

The lights change and the traffic flows again, accompanied by varying degrees of noise, the hum of cars, the rumble of a tram. The brief moment of silence is gone. I should not have doubted myself. I heard what I heard. There is a heady sense of pleasure in being right and it swells in my chest. I head to the office, wanting to show Harold the photo and get his opinion.

I am too late. Through breaks in the traffic I see him on the other side of road, walking off with an air of purpose about him and a bag of shopping over his arm. He is in a hurry. He is moving with the light, quick tread of anticipation. It is the bag of shopping that worries me. Today is Friday and Rosalyn is due home.

Chapter 26

Alicia meets me at my front door, with the air of someone who has been waiting impatiently. She has news.

'Marlo, I've done some checking on my own.' She looks alive with information, her brown eyes sparkling, her gestures animated.

'Go on.' I have the horrible feeling I know what she is going to say. The sense of dread thickens inside me.

'Jason is enrolled in a horticulture class at the local college. He has a night class once a week and after I talked to you, I remembered it was on a Monday night. He talks about it sometimes at the market.'

'Yes.'

'I know his teacher slightly. I've met her at different open days and she seems to think Sam and I are . . . well, never mind that. I rang her and asked about Jason's attendance recently.'

'And?'

'He hasn't missed a class all year.'

'Could she have forgotten do you think?' I ask without hope or expectation.

'No. The night of Bill Stone's death, Jason was scheduled to do a presentation. She mentioned it because it was so good.'

'I see.' There is only one thing left to ascertain. 'And the classes are ... ?'

'Between five and nine. Apart from a half-hour break some time in the middle, Jason was there for the entire night.'

Five o'clock is definite. Anyone in class at five o'clock could hardly be out killing someone in the Flagstaff Gardens between half past five and six o'clock.

'That would cover it,' I say lightly. 'You're a marvel, Alicia, finding out.'

'Well, that's what we wanted, wasn't it? To find out.'

'Yes, of course.' I must sound distracted because she looks at me strangely. 'I'll let you get on. Lucy's waiting.'

Lucy and I prepare dinner together – Lucy's choice of chicken sandwiches with lettuce and yogurt spread. I don't care what I eat or if I eat. Our conversations are back to where they have been in the past – Lucy chattering on about this and that, not minding that my only comments are more like punctuation to her words. My mind darts about, thinking about Harold and Rosalyn. The process of elimination.

'What's up, Marlo?' Lucy is looking at me curiously and I come back to the present with a little bump. For Lucy to comment, my preoccupation must have been absolute.

'Sorry, I was thinking about something else.'

She nods and drops more yogurt onto her lettuce. 'You've been doing that a lot lately ... thinking about things.'

I look at her closely, taken aback by her observation. There is a sense of being on the brink of something.

'It's about Jenny, isn't it?' Lucy asks, looking at me levelly. 'And ... Cate? That's who you think about the most.'

Moments of insight from Lucy are rare, or so I thought, and the air escapes from my lungs as though someone has kicked me. I have always known that Lucy is good at the odd curved ball. Just as you settle into regular patterns and complacencies, she delivers something new, something entirely unexpected. I look into her unfathomable, slate blue eyes and wonder, as I have before, what she knows and what she thinks. I have the uncomfortable sensation that perhaps moments of insight are not so rare, perhaps it is only sharing her insights with others that is.

I take a breath before replying. 'Yes,' I say very steadily. 'That's who I think about the most.'

Her voice is very small. 'I miss them too you know.'

'I know you do.' I put my arm around her and feel her thinness and her warmth. It seems as though we have come a long way because, until this moment, I could only guess what Lucy thought or felt.

After dinner, when Lucy is settled with some programme she enjoys, I change and head out on my usual run to Port Melbourne.

Tonight there are no lights in the first-floor windows, no glimpses of company and candlelight. I head for home, relieved, wondering what I would have done if she had been there. Would I have found the courage or audacity to interfere, to knock on the door and tell them what I think? The whole weighty conversation about interfering in other people's lives raises it ugly head. Harold knows what I think. If he is with Rosalyn, he has set his course, acted in accordance with his beliefs, and there is not a single thing I can do about it.

On the way home my thoughts are clearer. The night is pleasant and still, the air almost balmy. A three-quarter moon is reflected in the sea and the strange green glow of its light stains the dark water. The colours are intriguing. Black shot with green, like silk. Shot silk. Two colours blended.

Silk. The piece of material that Jamie Griggs held in his hands that day in court. Material that shifted between green and black. A colour I had seen before, like a shadow on grass, or moonlight on a dark sea, or a camellia leaf in shadow and

188

strong light. A colour I recognise with complete and sudden certainty. The same shade of green as the dancing froth of ribbons on Amy Stone's magic jacket.

I walk on slowly, working out how it could have come together, how the fabric passed from family hands to Jamie Griggs' hands in the Flagstaff Gardens on the night of a murder. I think of a simple man arrested for murder, who collects brightly coloured objects – feathers and stones and leaves. A man who we know was with Bill Stone on the night of his death because Bill's blood was on his clothing. A man who won't or can't talk to the police, even to save his own skin.

I pick up the pace. It is too cold for walking and I feel alive, shot through with excitement and exhilaration. For the first time since this began, I have a particular line of thought that explains a lot of things. The delay of ten minutes between the attack and my sighting of the runner. For the first time I understand why the killer had hung around that night and what brought them back in the morning. I can, at a pinch, explain the attack on Harold.

The way ahead is suddenly clear and logical and I can add to my scant criteria. I need to find out who owns that green-black fabric, or rather who dropped it in the park. I think about Rosalyn with her down-turned mouth, disapproving of the magic show that night at dinner, or perhaps not the show but the jacket. She had missed the fabric before then and had returned to the park in the hope of finding it.

At home I shower and change into warm clothing and wander through to the lounge. Lucy is watching a foreign film on SBS and the subtitles dance across the screen. I'm not sure she even registers my presence. I ring Harold's number but the answering machine picks up. I leave a message for him to ring me urgently, letting him know I have news. Lucy's film moves into shouts and gun shots. It is still only nine o'clock. Not too late to ring Amy.

I am just about to hang up when Amy picks up the phone with a rushed and breathless hello. When she realises it's me, her voice changes slightly. I suspect she was hoping for someone else.

'I haven't heard from you for a few days. I wondered how you were?'

'Fine.' She sounds both surprised at my asking and reluctant to talk.

'Amy, I wondered if I could borrow your magic jacket.'

She hesitates. 'Why?'

What do I say now? Whatever I say, Amy is shrewd and observant. She will notice the lie. 'I want to check the colour out. I wondered if it matches some fabric I have.' It's weak, but it is almost true.

A hesitation before she speaks, as if she is considering her words. 'I can't find it, Marlo. I looked for it the other night but it wasn't there.'

'That's a shame,' I say carefully casual. 'When did it go missing?'

Again the pause. 'I'm not sure. I haven't noticed it around the place but I didn't check properly until last night.'

'Oh well, it doesn't matter. It's a great jacket, Amy, I wondered where you got it from.'

'It's secondhand.' The persistent beeps of call waiting interfere with her voice and it is clear she does not want to chat about clothes.

'Secondhand?' I repeat, ploughing on regardless. 'But not with the ribbons of silk, surely?'

'No. We sewed them on later. Marlo, I've got to go.'

She hangs up and I am left listening to the dialling tone and my own thoughts. I'm pretty sure that with Harold's help I can get hold of the piece of material that Jamie Griggs is so taken with. I need the magic jacket to compare colours and fabric types. Without Amy's jacket as a comparison I have nothing.

I pace the floor. Lucy's film draws to a close and she heads upstairs to bed. I am too restless to sleep so I head to the kitchen to make a cup of tea. Suddenly the phone rings and

I snatch it up, hoping for Harold's voice. Not Harold but Alicia. 'Did you know someone's watching the house? They've been there for a while now but I can't see who it is.'

Her words are like an electric shock. I can feel the current of fear on the back of my neck.

'What are they doing?'

'Just standing there next to the lamp post. They haven't moved for the last ten minutes.'

I take the phone with me and look out the lounge window. I recognise her instantly but from Alicia's windows most of her body would be hidden behind the post.

'Amy Stone,' I whisper into the phone.

It is her stillness that is worrying. No attempt to hide. No attempt to come in.

'Amy?' Alicia breathes. 'What's going on?'

This is the girl that I eliminated from my list of suspects on the strength of her age and a tremor in her voice on the night of the dinner party. That blind bit of faith deserts me now. This is the same girl who lied to me about her grandfather. The criteria I have applied all through these shifting suspicions also apply to Amy. She is physically able. She is geographically able. She has the same motivation as the rest of the family. She is the one who wore the magic jacket with mid-green, black-green silk ribbons.

'I'll let her in and see what she wants.'

'I'll come in, shall I?' asks Alicia.

'Yes,' I say eagerly. 'I'll take her into the kitchen but she might close up . . .'

'That's fine, Marlo. I'll just be there, I won't disturb you.'

I take a couple of deep breaths and plan my strategy for the encounter, considering how much to tell her. I am glad Lucy has gone off to bed, as her presence would complicate matters. I take Ebony outside with me and open the garden gate to the street, aware of the pantomime effect, with Alicia watching from next door.

'Hello, Amy,' I say, with more brightness than I feel, taking in the drawn look on her face and the plastic bag under her arm. 'What are you doing here?'

She doesn't answer, except to look at me with her huge green eyes.

'This is Ebony,' I say to break the silence but Amy is not remotely interested in the dog. There is a tension about her that is ringing.

'How did you know where I live?' I ask.

'I looked it up in the phone book.'

'I'm not in the phone book.'

'I know, I looked. I knew you were a neighbour of Alicia's so I looked her up and when I got here I saw your car.'

Full marks for enterprise then, but I don't much like being tracked down.

'Why are you here, Amy?'

Her eyes flicker and she looks away.

'Come in. I'll make you something hot. You can tell me then.'

I step back for her to pass, closing the door behind us but making sure it is unlocked.

In the kitchen I make hot chocolate in the microwave, adding some of Lucy's marshmallows to the top for both of us. As I do so, I can faintly hear the front door open and Alicia's footsteps moving softly into the lounge. If Amy hears her, she gives no sign. Amy puts her package down on the bench and holds the cup with both hands so that her long fingers mesh around its surface. I wait for her this time. She has walked a long way to talk to me and I don't think she'll disappear for a while.

Silence is interesting. Silence is underestimated. In our chatty world, silence is difficult for lots of people but it is something that I usually have no problem with. And in this encounter silence gives me to time to think.

'Why did you ask me about the magic jacket?' Amy's voice is low and hushed. Ebony is against her legs and her hand strokes the dog's smooth, dark head automatically.

My answer is the truth but not quite the whole truth. 'I

wanted to match the silk.'

'You said that. I want to know why.'

My turn not to answer. This is something I haven't yet solved. Even if I had a month to think about it, I probably wouldn't come up with a hard and fast answer. How much do you say to a child of the family? Something at least.

'I think, Amy, that it might just have something to do with the murder of your grandfather. I think that if I could match the silk with some other piece of silk, it would prove something important.'

'And . . . without the jacket you can't prove it?' Her voice is very low.

'No. Without your jacket, I haven't got a thing.'

Silence again, silence so long and ringing that even I find it difficult.

'You know, don't you?' She says finally, quietly. 'You know who killed my grandfather?'

I turn to face her. 'I know some of it. Mostly I know who didn't.'

'I found it . . . before you rang. I didn't know what to do or what to say.' She trails off. 'Ros asked me about you. She told me you'd gone to her work and then, when I thought about it, you wanted to know too much.'

I don't answer.

'What are you going to do?' she asks after a while.

'Try to find out if I'm right. I don't want to accuse people and be wrong. It's easy to get things wrong, Amy, especially when they're complicated.' I should know. Amy looks at me with calculating eyes and again I have the sense of adulthood, of childhood left behind.

'First Bill . . . and then Harold. And for some reason my magic jacket comes into it.'

I can't deny it and she takes my silence for acquiescence.

'I'd like to help,' she adds simply.

'No, you wouldn't,' I say absolutely. No one on the planet would want to be left with the complexity of thoughts and feelings that go with all of this. 'It's not a game, Amy.'

'I'm tough, Marlo. You saw that at the hockey game.'

'It's not physical hurt so much as mental hurt that I'm worried about. Although that too, of course. I don't want to feel responsible for you.' I should walk away. Amy is only fourteen years old. She is still a child.

She looks at me for a long cool moment. 'Suit yourself.' She flounces away, puts her cup in the sink with a clatter.

'I'll drive you home.'

She doesn't protest and I suspect that walking home through the dark is not something she is comfortable with. Not quite the tough adult she thinks she is. I head down the hall and look into the lounge. Alicia has a library book of photos on her knee. She looks the part. Not intrusive, merely there.

'Alicia,' I say a shade too loudly. 'You know Amy don't you?'

Amy smiles and I sense her relief at finding a friend in a house that she has had to force herself to come to. Alicia greets her with the ease of established friendship and chats momentarily about the market, taking the sting out of the general tension.

'I'm taking Amy home, Alicia. Do you feel like a drive?'

I don't ask out of any need for protection but for Amy's comfort in Alicia's presence.

When we pull up the house is in darkness.

'Where is everyone?' I can't help asking, not just in terms of Rosalyn and Harold but in terms of a fourteen-year-old child being left on her own at night. A fourteen year old who is having a bad time.

'Kristin's at work and Ros is having dinner with a friend.' Her voice is quiet and I don't ask which friend. Somehow I think I know.

'Thanks for the lift.' She slides out of the car and leans against it for a moment. 'I left a bag at your house. I found the magic jacket but there's something else . . . I looked through it so I know.'

'Thank you, Amy.' So the magic jacket is not lost. There is still a way ahead. I tune back into Amy because there is something I haven't paid enough attention to: the sense of immensity behind her words.

'I found them in Rosalyn's sewing basket, hidden among the fabrics.'

Them, not it. What else has she come across?

'You'll see when you get home.' She falters again and licks her upper lip. 'I thought you would know what to do.'

'I'll do the best I can,' I say. 'Try not to worry.' Stupid to use such platitudes, but sometimes it seems like that's all there is. We wait until the lights go on and the front door closes.

'A worried child,' Alicia says.

'Yes,' I agree, still looking at the house, uncomfortable with the entire situation. I don't like leaving her on her own, not sure after recent events if she is safe. And if safety isn't an issue, comfort surely is. In the circumstances, Amy has far too much to cope with.

A sky-blue station wagon sweeps into the driveway and Kristin emerges after a brief moment. She doesn't take any notice of us, parked out the front. She looks different from last time, heavier somehow, weighed down with her bag. Her hair is pulled back and tied in a band, no sign of the wood shaving curls. The front door closes again and I pull away.

'Well, at least she's got company,' Alicia comments.

'Do you know Kristin?'

'Never met her.'

'No goss?'

'None at all. Sam doesn't talk about her much.'

This is surprising. He seemed proud enough of her achievements at the dinner. We are quiet for the rest of the way home, my thoughts shifting between Harold, Rosalyn and the contents of the bag that Amy left at home. I invite Alicia in and she looks on while I empty the contents onto the table – two items of clothing, two jackets.

Amy's magic jacket is on top, a flamboyant, colourful,

eye-catching garment. A garment I would have fallen on with relief at any other time. Now I hardly see it save to register that I was right about the colour. It is the pale beige jacket beneath it that I pick up. I sit down heavily, unsure if my legs will support me. Now I understand Amy's hesitation and the enormity of her thoughts. The last time I saw this particular jacket was on Saturday when Harold and I went to check out Bill Stone's house. I smooth the fabric over my knee, find Harold's wallet in the pocket and pass it to Alicia. She goes through it, reading the owner's name on his driver's licence and library cards.

I imagine Amy doing this earlier. Reading through names and understanding with a rush of fear the implications behind her find. Enough to send her to my house, enough to make her wait on the street, screwing up her courage to show an outsider what she had discovered. Someone to set things in motion.

Chapter 27

I bag the two items of clothing up again, collect Ebony, camera and cricket bag and take them with me. It takes no time to drive to Port Melbourne and when I get there I check out the cars on the street. This time Harold's car is in the carport and parked behind it is Rosalyn's dull gold Mazda.

It is past midnight and Harold's house is in darkness. No glow at all behind the curtains in the bedroom. No lights on anywhere. No cosy couple looking out. I suspect they are even cosier.

I park on the kerb outside his house and consider my options. Short of breaking in and telling him what I have found, there's not a lot that I can do. I take a photo of Rosalyn's car, as much as anything for something to do, and ring Harold's number from my mobile phone. Even from the car I can hear the quiet jingling of it in the downstairs study. It sounds faint, but I know from experience that in the house, it is loud enough. It rings twice before the answering machine clicks on and I hear the faint burr of Harold's recorded voice. Two rings means that he has had other messages tonight. At least one of them is mine.

I ring his mobile, hoping it is there on the bedside table, hoping that whatever he is doing, it disturbs him enough to answer, but a different recorded voice clicks on. I close the phone in frustration. Inside, the house stays dark. The dilemma goes on. The conviction that I have in suspecting Rosalyn is tempered with doubt. There is something that doesn't feel right about this recent, undeniable proof. If I have learned anything about the people involved in all of this, it is that Rosalyn is a planner. Would someone who plans a dinner party down to the symbolism of the flowers be careless enough to leave such damaging evidence lying around? And there is something else. Some flickering fish tail of thought that darts around on the heels of this. Something new and worrying that I am too weary to catch. Something to do with Amy.

My neck aches with tiredness and my thoughts head down familiar, well-worn channels. Harold is no fool and he has a well maintained sense of self-preservation. He was not convinced about Rosalyn's guilt and he said he would talk to her. I could be wrong – I have been wrong often enough. Who is to say that there isn't some perfectly understandable reason for Rosalyn having Harold's things.

I consider my choices. Poor choices, but right now they are all I have. I could go home and try to sleep. I could march through the bedroom door, show him – them – what I have in my possession and where it was found. I imagine it for a moment and quail at the thought. This would be the ultimate invasion. In the end I compromise. I still have a key to Harold's house and I know that Lucy will be safe back home with Alicia. I gather up my camera and my cricket bat and let myself in. My progress is silent enough but I hadn't considered Ebony. In a strange house she is curious, and takes a long time to settle down. I am thankful for Harold's deep pile carpet that silences her claws but, even so, the back of my neck prickles with the audacity of being here.

I lie down on the couch and Ebony finally nestles on the floor by my side. I am aware of every sound in the house. The hum of the heater. The slow creaking of the joists. A passing car. Ebony's soft breath beside me. Quiet sounds, all of them. The tiredness of earlier has evaporated, and for most of the night I am wide-eyed and alert.

I must sleep in the end because the first light awakens me. The house is still silent as I make tea and toast in Harold's kitchen, looking out at the view across the road. I stretch and do exercises and listen some more. Harold is an early riser, sooner or later he will have to come downstairs.

He does so twenty minutes later. I hear his feet on the staircase and meet him at the bottom of the steps. At first he looks puzzled to see me, as though he can't quite take it in, but then his expression changes. Good manners, I assume, stop the explosion of anger in his voice.

'Marlo, what are you doing here? What's happened?'

My voice is very low, aware of Rosalyn in the room above us. 'I rang you over and over and you didn't answer. You should have answered.'

He doesn't answer now but I can see where his thoughts go: I had better things to do.

'I have something to show you. It's in the car.'

He looks at me and I can't read his expression. A general gravity overlies everything. He has dropped his voice too, in response to my own. 'This had better be good, Marlo.'

'Good enough for me to come here,' I say bluntly.

He nods, not quite believing I have lost sight of all propriety, understanding that I wouldn't be here without good cause. I collect my things, close his front door behind us and unlock the car, opening the passenger door for him, the one behind it for Ebony. I take the plastic bag out from under his seat and he opens it warily. He looks at the contents for a long time, his head down.

'Where was it?' he asks, and I realise that he doesn't know about the significance of Amy's magic jacket. It is *his* jacket he is engaged with. I don't tell him the rest because I doubt whether he'd take it in. He has enough to contend with.

'In Rosalyn's sewing basket. Amy brought it round last night.'

I remember the moment of elation last night at the prospect of finding proof. Right now I feel I can hardly breathe, let alone look at the anguish on Harold's face.

'Christ, Marlo, I can't believe it.'

'No, I know.'

'I talked to her. I'm not . . . that stupid.' He says it as though it all happened a long time ago.

I don't tell him what I think – that perhaps we're all stupid when it comes to love. 'What did she say?'

'She laughed and made the whole thing seem absurd. She said that we must have over-active imaginations.'

'Yes, I can understand that.'

A moment of silence in which all I hear is my breath and his breath, out of time, one following the other.

'What will you do now?' His voice is very quiet.

I check my watch. Quarter to seven. 'Call the police.'

It is almost light now. Harold turns his head to look at his house, his face as blank as the closed and curtained windows.

'Where is she?'

'I left her asleep,' he says.

I look out over the sea. The grey of dawn has given way to colour. A blue sky, a blue sea. A cool breeze scuffs the surface of the water in little flurries of white. The colours shift with the play of wind, blue then white, white then blue, like shot silk.

'Come with me,' I say. 'Leave her here until we sort things out. You've still got clothes at my house.'

He wavers. I take a deep breath and wait for his answer.

'Do you know, I think I will.'

Chapter 28

The house is very quiet when we get back. I check on Alicia and Lucy. They are both still asleep, and it strikes me as puzzling that Harold and I seem to have lived through so much while other people have not yet woken.

Harold sits at the kitchen bench and looks out into the back garden as if he has never seen it before. Ebony rests her head on his knee, registering his distress as though she has an in-built emotion barometer. I feel completely inadequate, unsure of how to handle such blows to the heart, which are so far beyond the scope of soup and sympathy. I wish Alicia was up, someone older and wiser who would know what to do.

I make Harold some tea and toast and poach some eggs and all the time he sits there, his hand moves absently backwards and forwards across Ebony's head. I head to the lounge, not sure if he registers I have gone. My call to Denton is diverted to his mobile phone, and this time he answers it straight away. I tell him about Harold's jacket and where it was found and where Rosalyn is, or was, twenty minutes ago.

'I see.' His voice is very steady and I can almost hear him

working it out, making the connection between the woman sleeping in Harold's bed and the jacket in her sewing basket at home. There is a long hesitation before he speaks.

'Yes, I see,' he says again in a different tone.

'Will you ring me. Harold . . . we . . . are anxious.'

'Yes, of course.'

Alicia is in the hallway waiting for me to finish the call. She hasn't changed since last night and her clothes are crumpled and her hair tousled. I should have thought to offer dressing gowns and towels.

'How did it go?'

I tell her about last night and she lets out a long sigh.

'The only thing you can do, Marlo, is to be here for him.'

'Yes, it just doesn't seem very much.'

'Sometimes not very much is a lot. What will you do now?'

First things first. 'I want to get some fabric analysed, to see if it's possible to determine whether the two separate pieces of fabric came from the same source.'

She looks at me but her gaze is unfocused as if consulting a memory. 'I know of someone who might help. She's ex-police but working privately now, and if she can't help, she will know who can. I've got her number at home. Come with me and I'll get it for you.'

This is running ahead because, at the moment, I haven't got the other piece of material that will prove things. I go with her though, and watch as she writes down the number on the back of an envelope.

'I'll come back after work,' she says passing it to me. 'Will you be all right?'

'Yes, of course.'

Harold has finished his tea but the eggs have congealed on his plate. I put my hand on his shoulder and scrape his food into the dog's bowl. His head is bowed and his skin is pale.

Lucy is up, chatting to Harold about this and that, but it is very much a monologue – a run down on her day at work yesterday, the customer who admired the flower in her hair. I make coffee and listen in, taking in Harold's complete lack of engagement with the dartings of her mind. In the end I take some money from my wallet and send her off to the shops for some bread and milk.

I put my empty coffee cup in the sink. 'Harold, I need you to do something,' I say peremptorily

He doesn't answer for a moment but I know what he is thinking – something else, Marlo. Don't you think you've done enough?

Finally he looks at me and asks, 'What is it?'

'I want you to visit Jamie Griggs.'

I explain what my thoughts are, what I think the crime revolves around – the fabric that I need to compare with another piece, the piece of silk that an old man picked up in the Flagstaff Gardens.

Harold looks dismissive, a million miles from being up to the task. But it will do him good to be busy, to think of someone other than Rosalyn.

'I'll come with you,' I say. 'I'd go myself but they wouldn't let me in. That's why I need you to do it.'

He nods, uncaring, 'Yes, I see that. OK.'

'I've got something to do first.'

First of all I wait for Lucy and we drive to a material shop in Chapel Street. Together we buy a little selection of fabrics. There are none exactly the same colour as the silk on Amy's magic jacket but some are close. I buy a strip of green fabric shot with black and another shot with gold. Lucy chooses a few of her own, entranced by the shifting, vibrant colours – blue shot with red, pink with orange.

Back at home, I check the answering machine. No message from Denton. Lucy helps me cut the fabrics up into handkerchief-size patches, which we lay out on the bench, one on top of each other. She plays with the leftovers, entranced with the colours and the sensual feel of silk. When it is time for her to go she packs a few into her bag and heads for home.

The psychiatric hospital where Jamie is being assessed is in Glenroy. Harold is silent for most of the drive but that suits me well enough. Instead of attempting to make strained conversation, I turn the radio on and listen to some music, keeping the tiredness at bay by sheer force of will. The hospital is a large complex of separate housing in the cream and pink coloured bricks of the 1950s. The car park is just off the main road but screened from it by greenery and a carefully tended garden. Harold gets out of the car silently, taking with him the little collection of silks. I try to imagine where he goes and what he sees but my only image of Jamie is of that stiff, squat man in the dock, engrossed in a piece of material. I wonder if he will like the idea of swapping silks.

Harold comes back after a while and sits down heavily next to me. He passes Jamie Griggs' fabric over without a word. I look at it as if it were alive, as if it could talk to me and tell me its provenance. A single mid-green, black-green strip, clean cut on both sides. But when I lay it on my knee to examine it closely, I see that one of the edges is not straight, as though when cut, the scissors bore slightly to the left. And, worryingly, the fabric is less lustrous than I had imagined, certainly less than the pieces Lucy and I had cut up earlier. I see again Jamie Griggs' restless hands in the dock and hope that over-handling explains the difference, and that, for analytical purposes, it doesn't matter.

'How was he?'

'OK.' Harold's voice is closed, reluctant.

I look at him and tiredness settles on me like a weight. My eyes feel fuzzy. I feel like staying here and sleeping.

'He was better this time, not quite so frightened. It was only when I asked him about the silk that he closed up.'

'Did he mind swapping?'

'He didn't seem to.'

I show Harold the photo I had wanted to show him last night. I had forgotten about it in all the drama since then.

'Who is it?'

'Whoever it is, they are not a city gardener.' I tell him

204

the story of the park yesterday, and he looks at the photo more closely.

'So you have two things – a photo and the material,' Harold says quietly as we drive away.

I'm not sure whether he thinks we have riches to prove our point, or poverty. It should be enough, I think, but with recent history in mind, who can tell?

We stop at a photo lab near home and I ask the technician to do whatever he needs to do to produce photos that can help us identify the gardener. Any aspect is welcome – head, hands, shoulders. He promises to do what he can, the results due by the end of the day.

We head for home, Alicia comes over and Harold looks marginally brighter. Still no messages on the answering machine from the police. I take a casserole from the freezer and can't think of anything else I can do at this stage except succumb to sleep.

I wake mid-afternoon, feeling better, the heavy fuzziness in my head gone. As I lie in Lucy's bed, enjoying the warmth and the quietness, that fleeting fish tail of thought from last night leaps boldly to the surface.

This fish is a large one – something worrying to do with Amy. She gave me a little present last night that sent me spinning down a certain path. Her jacket and Harold's, hidden in Rosalyn's sewing basket. If they were hidden, how had she known where to look? One doubt leads to another. I had assumed that Rosalyn helped Amy sew her magic jacket. My aunt, she said, but Rosalyn disapproves of Amy performing magic. Hard to see her encouraging Amy in any way, let alone by sewing flamboyant frills on the sleeves of her magic jacket.

Doubt about Rosalyn's guilt swings back like a pendulum. I find myself sitting up in Lucy's bed thinking the same thoughts over and over. And worse, if I have got this wrong about Rosalyn, what will it do to Harold? My mouth dries at the thought.

★

I make a phone call to Alicia's contact – I need to prove the connection. All I have so far is a theory, and theories have lead me down too many dead ends.

'Gillian Stockton.'

I explain my relationship to Alicia and the nature of my problem.

She hesitates before answering. 'Well, it's a bit unusual for me because I'm a document analyst, but I can't see there'd be much difference between material and paper.' She goes on to mention some long-winded case that she was involved in and my attention wanders slightly. 'But anyway, we can give it a go. If I can't help, I'll refer you on.'

'Thank you. That'd be terrific.'

Her first free time is Monday morning. Monday morning, it will have to be.

I head off to collect the enlargements of the photo of the gardener. The technician has done what he said – enlargements of the hand that holds the trowel, the back of the head and the body itself. I study them closely. In the original, the head was lost in shadow. In the enlargement, the shadow is there still but is recognisable as a black woollen hat. This is all there is. No trace of hair colour, no jawline, no distinguishing features. I sigh out loud but, given the unpromising back view, I'm not really surprised.

At home, someone has obviously discovered the casserole, as I can smell the rich gravy from the street. I show the enlargements to Harold and Alicia. Between them they know the family well, but their expressions remain blank. I pour some of Harold's wine. We are quiet over dinner, none of us bothering to fill the gaps in conversation. I don't tell Harold my latest doubts about Rosalyn.

It is dark when the doorbell rings. Harold looks at me and his expression is articulate – a mix of hope and fear. We go together to answer it.

Denton is on the doorstep, in a strange little repeat of his last visit, almost a week ago.

'Do you want to come in?' I ask.

'This won't take long.' He looks from Harold to me. 'We've talked to Rosalyn Stone and she denies any knowledge of the jacket. I'm inclined to believe her.'

Framed in the yellow light from the porch, he looks larger than I remember and more remote. His words sound like they are coming from far away.

'Why?' My voice is croaky and I clear my throat.

His eyes are unshifting. 'She has an alibi for the morning of the attack on Harold and it checks out.'

'I see,' Harold says, calmly.

I wonder about the alibi and feel a new strand of fear for Harold. Next to me Harold keeps his head averted but his thoughts are obvious. By listening to me, he has given up on his chance of love.

'And before you ask, she has an alibi for the night of Bill Stone's murder. We dug into it all pretty deeply.'

'Yes.'

'Tell me about the jacket,' Denton says.

'Amy brought it round. She told me where she found it.'

'Someone else could have put it there.'

'Yes,' I agree, 'but perhaps not just anyone.'

'We're looking into that, Marlo, going back over things. Talking to them all.' He nods. 'I'll be in touch.'

We watch Denton walk to his car. Harold stands next to me, his face a mask of misery over who knows what depths of thought. This is the biggest set back. This time it has gone too far.

Harold takes himself off to bed, muttering an abrupt goodnight. It is early yet, far earlier than Harold usually goes to bed. He doesn't look at me when he goes and I know that it's not sleep that he needs but privacy and time to think.

Over glasses of wine, Alicia and I talk late into the night. We cover a wide selection of topics, touching on, among other things, love and guilt and responsibility. I feel better for talking, better for listening to Alicia's font of wisdom and experience.

But later, in Lucy's bed, I realise that I was simply doing the opposite to Harold, filling my mind with conversation to avoid thinking. To avoid my own feelings of guilt.

Chapter 29

I wake before first light and the house feels very quiet. There is a note on the kitchen bench from Harold.

Marlo, I've gone home. Thanks for looking after me. I'll see you soon but I need some time to think. H

Harold's notes are legendary, dripping with friendliness, running at times to whole pages for even the briefest of messages. But not this one. I crumple it up and smooth it out again. Throwing it away seems like an act of savagery.

Harold was shaken too, I tell myself. Yesterday morning he had accepted my findings at face value. My findings were worthwhile ones. What else was I supposed to do?

I put the kettle on for tea and my mood is a curious one, shifting between anger, guilt and cool resolution. I have been down lots of different paths. I have been to the police more than enough times. What I need now is something conclusive.

I resurrect my clean slate policy and put two people that I had excluded for various reasons back on my list. In Amy's case, age. In Kristin's case, geography. If Rosalyn didn't sew the silk on Amy's jacket, then Kristin or Amy did. I consider Amy objectively. If greed is the motive, then in Amy's case, it seems impossible. What need has she for wealth? I consider her present to me of Harold's jacket. If she were the killer she would hardly have given it to me. But perhaps she set it up like that. Perhaps all I have done is to play into her hands.

I think of her at the hockey match, lashing out in retaliation at an opposition blow. The unleashed, uninhibited moment of savagery. And Rosalyn with her question after the funeral on heredity and savage genes. Who in the family was she thinking of then? Amy? Harold talked about the art of deception necessary to be a good magician, the sleight of hand, and I remember how quick Amy was to lie about having met Bill Stone. I think about her waiting, poised, outside my house on Friday night, and the little chill of unease that I had felt at the thought of her tracking me down so easily. She presented me with the story about finding the two jackets in her aunt's sewing basket and I fell for it. So not just murderer but manipulator. If this is true, and I emphasise the if, then Amy is a force to be reckoned with.

I won't leap to someone else's agenda. If I need more facts then facts I will get. My own facts, not anything handed to me.

And then there's Kristin. I had assumed on our first meeting that she was suffering from grief at the loss of her father and anger at being forced to socialise against her will. It is possible that on that night of erratic emotions, her behaviour stemmed not from grief, but guilt.

I think about how I can check up on her trip to Sydney. There was no mention of companies or hotels in that brief unsuccessful conversation at the dinner table, so I will have to ask Sam myself or ask Alicia to ask him. And if he does know the name of the company, I won't be able to ring them until tomorrow anyway.

I consider my options. There is something I can do now,

however, and hopefully Sunday morning is a good time to do it. I make breakfast and eat some fruit, planning my strategy.

In the laundry there is an old blue overall that belonged to Jenny, slightly too large for me and unworn in the thirteen months since her death. When I put it on I smell the faded scent of Jenny's perfume. No boots but runners, for ease of movement and silence. I swirl my hair up under a cap and examine my appearance in a full length mirror. The unusual clothing makes me feel optimistic and adventurous and, more to the point, unrecognisable, at least at a distance.

I set out for Riley Street, my mobile phone in my bag, Ebony in the car. It is still very early, only just light and the streets are empty. I drive past the warehouse and park my car on a side street, a couple of blocks away. Ebony is snoozing in the back so I leave one window slightly open.

The factory looks even more cheerless than it did on my last visit. There are no cars out the front, no lights in any of the windows and no sign of a sky-blue station wagon.

I walk around it as I did once before. The railway embankment is higher than I remember and an early train rushes along on its way to the suburbs, scattering air and rubbish as it passes. The same high meshed window that I looked through on my last visit is open now. Easy to pull myself up and swing through. I am inside in seconds.

I stand still for a moment, feeling both alarmed by my actions and curiously exultant. It is even lighter inside than I had thought, the sky-lighting above my head extensive. The space is narrow, not much wider than a corridor and very basic. There isn't much in the way of materials, not much of anything at all really. A large workbench, a sewing machine, a few scraps of cotton, a tin of sharp-bladed scissors, but not much else. It feels a long way from the productive, creative space that I would have expected. In one corner is the cluster of domestic items that I noticed on my previous visit. The bed, a cabinet, kettle and cups.

One of the few things of interest is a curious mound of ash on the floor near the bed, as though a fire has been recently lit, the debris lying undisturbed. I pick some up and rub it between my fingers. Ash is curious stuff – insubstantial, weightless – and in my hands it disintegrates even further. I can tell that it is the soft white ash of burnt paper and I wonder what Kristin burnt and why she didn't bother sweeping it up.

There is also a pile of letters and a camera on the cabinet. Beside it, a bulging plastic bag tied at the neck. I lift it up to check its weight – old clothes by the feel of it. I undo the tie slightly and discover dirty washing. A man's dirty washing. And, more interestingly, under the bed there is a suitcase. I slide it out and it scrapes loudly on the concrete floor. The noise is louder than I anticipated, and I stand very still, listening, alert. There is a faint and distant whisper that I can't place. The sound swells and strengthens, and my heart thuds in my chest like a fist. And then I understand and break into a silly grin. Another train, city bound this time. The wheels clatter past at eye level with a roar like thunder. I wait for the sounds to die completely, then undo the straps and zips on the case

Men's clothes. Not those of a vagrant, but tidy trousers, shirts, jumpers and socks. All good quality. I take a neatly folded jumper from the top layer. It feels soft and luxurious and when I look at the label I discover it is a blend of wool and cashmere.

There is enough clothing in the case for an extended period of time. In the zip pocket I find a passport, a plane ticket to London, traveller's cheques and a thick wad of banknotes. The ticket and the passport are in Bill Stone's name. The ticket is dated 3 August. Ten days ago. If Bill had lived, he would have been there by now, safe and well.

I take some photos, aware of the need for documentation, and put things back as I found them. At the last moment I take the camera and the little pile of letters from the cabinet, stash them in my bag, and then climb out the window the way I came.

*

Even when the focus shifted to family, I should have stuck with my original idea of finding out where Bill Stone slept at night. The correlation between someone putting him up and his death. Someone who cared enough to give him a bed, as opposed to the other family members who scarcely seem to have given him a second thought. Is love a better motive than greed? I ask myself. And if Kristin thought enough of Bill to shelter him, could it have turned suddenly to hate?

I drive to Black Rock and the car park, that looks out over the bay and the historical wreck of the Cerberus. This early in the morning the sea and sky are very pale and the wreck stands out, dark brown against the clear water. I open Kristin's mail. Two letters, both in business envelopes. A bank statement and a power bill.

I read through the bank statement first. On the 31 July, Kristin made a couple of purchases, and I see, with a sense of the inevitable, that the purchases weren't made in Sydney but in Melbourne, one from a supermarket in Richmond, just around the corner from her space. There are no Sydney listings, no hotel bills or taxis. No other geography, save for the geography of inner Melbourne.

The statement ends on the 31 July and there are no details for August. No telling perhaps, if she went to Sydney in the afternoon. It's not proof, I know, and I refuse to speculate. I will ring Alicia tonight and persuade her to ask Sam for the details of Kirstin's trip. Whatever happens, I can't ring a Sydney business until tomorrow. Instead of being impatient at the delay, I am pleased. I have a day to myself. It almost feels like a holiday.

I let Ebony out of the car and we walk past the little cluster of buildings and on to the beach. Ebony darts ahead of me, enticed by new scents and the feel of wet sand beneath her paws. After the close confines of the warehouse it is good to look out on distance and breathe in the fresh, salty air. The coastline sweeps towards the unseen city in a semi-circle of sand and red cliffs, and across the bay Williamstown is a pale smudge on the horizon.

There are people around now, and the day seems to take on a semblance of normality. A little buzz of elation rises up inside me as I walk, like effervescence in my blood. I have stuck with it. I have found out a whole raft of significant details. I have removed, finally, a lot of the confusing clutter.

On impulse I call Shane Black, ringing his number quickly before I change my mind. There is a sense of mending fences, but not just this. I would like to see him again. Predictably, his answering machine clicks on. I laugh at the anticlimax, but leave a message anyway.

The sense of well-being stays with me and for once I spend some time considering the future instead of dwelling on the past. Study and sporting options. I need to talk to Harold about it though, and Tegan. Whatever direction I choose, Tegan will have to be employed for more hours than she is now. Hopefully the extra work and money will be enough for her to strike out on her own.

In the car I make up a little list of things to do and people to ring. I am good at lists and the thoughts flow easily. People tell me that all I need to do is make a start, and perhaps drawing up a list is a start of its own. When I have finished, I put it in my track suit pocket and head for home.

Chapter 30

I get ready for cricket and my positive mood stays with me. My team, the A team, field first. The green grass, the white-clad players, the thwack of the ball, the blue parabola of sky, the smell of spring and the elation of earlier combine to give me a sense of well-being that fizzes through my body like a drug.

The cricket field is a place of contest, an arena I am as familiar with as my own house. The rules are fixed and unbending; they don't change according to the circumstances. Compared to what I've been going through, cricket is easy. The thought stays with me until the change of innings.

I am about to face the first ball. I breathe in the crisp air and feel the bat for grip. Such a familiar, welcome grip, my fingers finding their customary pattern on the handle. The adrenalin floods in at the challenge before me, in the guise of an aggressive fast bowler who makes much of intimidation and game play in her lead up. I strike the first delivery and have the pleasure of seeing the ball loft straight to the outer. Then I have a steady string of shots and running, the score rising faithfully with the runs.

The other side changes bowlers, pitting me against a

demure spin bowler with a wicked touch of cunning in her delivery and a reputation to match. Her length and line are invariably perfect but her deliveries drift away at the last moment, or worse, curl unnervingly back to the wicket. Her technique is so baffling, so honed to perfection, that experienced players quail before her.

I take a deep breath and grin. I am used to changes of tactics, things changing in the space of a heart beat. As Amy said at the beginning of all this, I have good hand–eye coordination. The first delivery is unnerving, a swish at thin air. The second even more so, a snick that doesn't carry, but by the third I am beginning to read the play, see the pattern of her delivery, and I settle down to enjoy it.

I hold out through a succession of bowlers and have the pleasure of seeing my score rising through the decades. Somewhere in the middle of it all, it occurs to me that overcoming those mental areas of lack that have plagued me for so long is perhaps something that I don't need to work on. Perhaps such things are beyond the scope of thought and planning. Perhaps, as Harold said, it really is just a matter of giving it time.

Someone in the crowd catches my attention. A large man with a gleaming crescent of silver hair. Harold, I think, glad that he has come to see me play. The spin bowler is back and I turn my attention to the delivery, hitting out against it.

The second delivery of the new over takes me by surprise. Instead of the curl I had expected, the ball snakes up from the ground in front of me. I hit out but misjudge slightly – not the clean strike I wanted. For a moment I think I have got away with it. The ball lofts cleanly through the air but dips too quickly and I see the fielder on the outer, running, diving, then leaping up again, the ball grasped firmly in her hand. Out for 86.

Now I have the time to concentrate I see that it is not Harold in the crowd. Someone not remotely like him really, save for their size and silver hair, but the sighting reminds me of the complex web of events and I come back to earth with a rough and heavy landing.

I watch the rest of our innings, applauding the runs and the catches equally, taking photos from time to time. The light is good for photos, a low sun creating long shadows and interesting effects. The match finishes and, while I wait for everyone to leave, I spend a few minutes looking out at the oval. Without the cricket, it seems somehow bleak and lonely. I take a final shot and head for home.

Sunday night. I am not hungry but I need to eat. No casserole tonight but tuna salad and a hard-boiled egg. I eat on my own, chewing the rubbery egg determinedly and washing it down with lots of water.

I phone Tegan to ask her to fill in for me tomorrow morning.

'That's fine, Marlo.' She sounds relieved to hear from me, and to know that she still has employment.

'Have you heard from Harold?'

'No.' She sounds surprised. 'Was I meant to?'

'Just wondering.'

I think about Harold uncontactable somewhere, licking his wounds. There is deadlock on two fronts – between me and Harold, and between myself and the people I suspect of murder. I have some idea now of how to go about sorting out the murder, but no idea of what to do about Harold. And I would very much like to discuss the murder with him. There is still something I'm not sure of – something about the weight of responsibility. But even if I could contact him, discussing Rosalyn might not be a viable option. And after all that has happened, I'm not sure if his opinion would be reliable.

I take a deep sigh and ring his number anyway. His answering machine picks up. Apart from anything else, I just want to know that he's OK.

Chapter 31

Morning. I update the computer file, adding my intentions for the day and what I hope to prove. When I have finished I print out two copies, one for Denton and one for me. I eat breakfast, running the scenario through to the end, trying to see the twists and turns, the consequences of my actions. The toast is dry and tasteless and the atmosphere feels close, like air before rain, sultry and heavy.

I make the phone call to set it up before I can change my mind. The tape engages and once again I listen to Rosalyn's soft, well modulated voice. I am halfway through my sentence when the receiver is picked up.

'Marlo.' Even in the space of a single word I can hear her anger.

'I want to see you,' I say.

'Yes, I want to see you too.'

'Meet me on St Kilda pier. I'll be there in ten minutes.'

She disconnects with a heavy thump and I set off, taking Ebony with me.

I wait at the rotunda at the start of the pier. It is early still and the car parks are not yet full. In one direction is the pier and the still waters of Port Phillip Bay, in the other, a semi-circle of grass surrounded by a sweep of road. The gold Mazda drives in and pulls up abruptly. Rosalyn slides out of the front seat, a bulky collection of keys and a business card in her hand.

Beside me, Ebony shifts restlessly, suddenly alert as though sensing the tension in the air.

I watch Rosalyn as she strides towards me. She is not quite as carefully groomed as usual, her streaky blonde hair not so carefully styled, and the wind snatches at it as she walks. She didn't kill her father. I know that now but there are other things to take into account – less obvious things such as complicity and manipulation that I sense but can't begin to gauge. Ebony growls at her approach and I put my hand on her head reassuringly.

'This is yours I believe.' Rosalyn's green eyes are steady and assessing as she hands me my business card.

'I met up with my secretary last night. She said you wanted to know where I was.'

I return her gaze. 'Harold said Adelaide. Amy said Perth. I was curious.'

Her hand sweeps down and her keys jangle with the movement. 'You were checking up on me?'

I can't deny it, so I don't.

'You told the police about Harold's jacket, thinking it was me?'

'Yes.'

'I can see why you would.' She nods slowly, as if pleased to have confirmation of something she has thought. 'I didn't mind that you and Harold were discussing me, hatching wild theories, but I do mind that you told the police.'

'It had to be done,' I say evenly.

She looks at me coldly. 'It took me a while to work it out but when I knew you'd been snooping around at work, I realised what you were thinking. Let me guess – old office, unsure merchandise, premises rundown, the whole business needing an injection of cash and then, like magic, an inherited property.'

219

'That's how I thought it might be,' I say carefully.

Again the steady gaze. 'I won't deny that the business had me tearing my hair out at one stage. However, it wasn't the business that was at fault but the direction I was going in.'

'I don't follow you.'

'I think you've got the wrong idea about modelling schools,' she says crisply. 'They're the new growth industry, flourishing in these unmannered times. Especially in the corporate world, grooming their up-and-coming stars in table manners and social skills. And, believe me, the corporate world is very lucrative.'

'I see.'

'I'm not in the process of closing down, Marlo, but expanding. We already have new premises in Collins Street and I'm setting up interstate. That's why I took a business trip to Adelaide and to Perth. A little network I'm setting up with different partners.' Her eyes glint again. 'We have high hopes for it, no . . . more than that. We, all of us, think it's a gold mine.' She is into lecture mode now. 'You might not agree but there's a lot to be said for putting people at their ease. Oscar Wilde is said to have found his way to the quietest person at a party and in just a few moments made them sparkle.' Her eyes sweep over me momentarily, as though she is still trying and failing to gauge my social skills. I smile at her difficulty. The social contact between us, now and in the past, has been a string of difficult situations, hardly a fair testing ground. But I change the subject. I don't want to talk about deportment.

'I think you suspected someone in the family for a while.'

She doesn't answer so I push the point. 'I suspect that you've been trying to protect them. You knew about Amy.'

More silence. She looks towards the sea and the little forest of masts at the marina. The boats shift in the wind, haphazard and patternless.

'What exactly?'

'That she'd met up with her grandfather. That they spent time together.' This is a guess but an educated one. 'And you knew about Kristin.' Another guess, not yet something I have checked up on, but why not give her something to think about. 'You suspected she wasn't in Sydney.'

She turns back, curious. 'What makes you say that?'

'You dropped a fork at dinner.'

She looks surprised. 'I might be a deportment queen, Marlo, but I am allowed to drop things.'

'Of course, I just don't think you do very often.'

Again the glitter. Amusement? Anger? Curiosity? 'Interesting what people make of things.' She lifts the keys in her hand, slides a finger up and down the shaft of one, looking at it with steady interest. 'So you think Kristin or Amy?'

'I don't think anything any more, Rosalyn. I've paid the price for that with you. And Harold. I've narrowed it down but next time I decide to take things further, I want to be sure.'

'And how are you going to do that?'

I take a deep breath and wait until she looks directly at me. 'I need your help.'

'And what makes you think I'll give it?'

'Because you're still here and talking. You know and I know that for everyone's sake it has to be sorted out. It's uncontrollable and I don't like my friends being attacked. These things tend to flow on to other people. It makes you wonder who might be next.'

She looks back down at the keys in her hand. She doesn't like me but she doesn't have to and she must have thought along similar lines often enough these last few days.

'Tell me something, when you first suspected . . . why didn't you do something then?'

She looks at me for a long moment before answering. 'You forget, I was away all last week.'

Conveniently away. Easier to be empire-building than at home confronting a murderer.

'So what do you have in mind?' She asks finally.

I tell her and she listens closely, her eyes fixed on the distant marina. The wind has shifted slightly and the hollow metal chime of clanking masts and riggings reaches us. A lonely sound that for some reason makes me think of Harold.

'Tonight? All of them? Why don't you ask them yourself?'

'Because I don't think they'd come. You have a lot of influence, Rosalyn. They'll listen to you.' I don't say the sentence in the unflattering way I have come to think of it – too much influence, too much manipulation.

She looks at me levelly. 'And if they won't come?'

'Then tempt them. Tell them that there is evidence of who killed Bill Stone and who attacked Harold.'

There isn't yet. Not quite, anyway. I still have one more visit to make. Rosalyn looks at me curiously, her eyes unreadable. I have the feeling, looking at those green and steady eyes, that I am standing on a precipice, just about to dislodge the first stone that will start the avalanche, that dry-mouthed, head-down plunge into the unknown. The only thing I'm sure of is that there will be reaction.

'Under lock and key,' I say definitely. 'But don't tell anyone my part in it.'

She nods but doesn't answer and I know without doubt that I can't trust her. This is nothing new. I have sensed it from the beginning. She turns away but I call her back, not wanting to ask, to give her satisfaction, but I seem to have no choice.

'What?'

'Have you seen Harold?' I ask, feeling absurd, like a Victorian grandfather, asking an inappropriate suitor about their intentions.

Her eyes glint again and a flicker of something crosses her face and is gone. Malice. Scorn.

'Not since Friday night or was it Saturday morning? Remember, Marlo. Something else you had a little part in.' Her voice is flat and even and I am no clearer about what her intentions are towards him.

'Tonight then? Six o'clock.'

She doesn't say goodbye but turns suddenly on her heel. She drives away, her wheels spinning momentarily in her haste. I watch until her car is out of sight, giving her a silent lecture on the advantages of deportment in our unmannered world, and referring her to Oscar Wilde's little treatise on the value of putting people at their ease. Delay tactics I know. But right now I don't want to think about six o'clock or filling in the hours in between.

Chapter 32

Gillian Stockton works from a house in Kew and opens the door at my knock. She is a thin, older woman, narrow faced, with a friendly, welcoming smile. She leads me into her office, a large area at the back of her house, with immense windows and lots of light.

'Now you have some material to compare, I believe.'

I show her the frills on Amy's jacket sleeves and the fabric that Harold obtained from Jamie Griggs.

'And you want to know if the pieces are from the same bolt of fabric?'

'Yes.'

'Bolts might not be so easy. If they're from a similar part of the bolt, then that's one thing, but bolts of fabric, like rolls of paper, are immense and variations can occur. But let's give it a go. I'll have to undo the frills.'

'Yes, of course.'

She unpicks the sewing around the sleeves of Amy's jacket with deft fingers and smoothes them back. She chooses one ribbon and places it with the sample of Jamie's silk on a sheet of white paper on a baseboard at her desk. The image is transferred, slightly enlarged, to a TV screen on a shelf at the side. The difference is obvious. The fabric from the sleeve is rich green, the sample from Jamie Griggs much duller. She must see the doubt in my face and shakes her head.

'You can't tell from that – one piece is just dirtier than the other – but see here on this edge, where the sample is cleaner.' She indicates with a pen and I feel a little surge of hope.

She puts a scale on the separate fabrics and examines them under light and a magnifier. 'So far so good, the same composition, the same number of black threads to the centimetre.' She concentrates, talking as much to herself as to me. 'I'd say that whoever cut the fabric is fairly deft and used sharp-bladed scissors.'

'How do you know that?'

She passes me the magnifier. 'See how there aren't too many jagged cuts, except at the start where the scissor blades moved a couple of times. For most of the cut the scissors slid through the fabric. Bear with me and I'll show you under the microscope.'

She sits without speaking for a few minutes then shifts her chair to let me in. 'Take a look.'

Under the microscope there are millions of threads, so thick they look like string. She points to a portion of the fabric with a pen. Under magnification the pen is curiously thick, the neat edges of the fabric pieces curiously ragged.

'It's not a pattern because the fabric isn't consistent but it's almost as good. Look at the black threads on this sample and notice how they almost follow through to the other sample, the same spread and consistency.'

'Yes, I see that,' I say, looking up, and she smiles at my pleasure.

'Good.' She discards that frill, picks up another one, and places it on the baseboard next to Jamie's sample. She adjusts the pieces, making lots of minimal changes without comment, taking up a hand-held magnifier from time to time. I'm not sure what she's looking for exactly but follow the progress of the alignments on the screen. After a few moments she looks up, satisfied. 'I thought so. It's a physical fit. See how this piece of fabric from the park fits exactly into this section of the frill. You can see the separate nicks of the scissors where he or she began the cut. See how that tag matches that indent and this one.' Her pen is at work again, pointing out the corresponding nicks and notches.

'Yes.'

'And when the scissors slid through the fabric there was a slight drag to the left. More to the point, the fabric from the park follows the exact shape of the drag. It's what they call a physical fit, when one piece fits in physically with another.'

I look up at her, feeling as though she has presented me with a piece of magic, and she laughs.

'There's nothing new about physical fits. They were first used as evidence in the 1700s. I don't know what the odds of finding one are, but probably a million to one. When I present evidence in court, I work a tiered scale from conclusive down to inconclusive. If there is such a thing as absolutely conclusive, then this is what you have. If this was police evidence they would be delighted.'

I feel slightly queasy, as though I have been too long in the sun. 'Could you write it down and sign it? Will you remember it, if this has to go to court?'

'Of course. I'll take some photos and document it for you.'

She fits a new film into a camera, attaches a micro-lens and sets it up above the baseboard. She invites me to view the image through the lens. The fabrics lie together, separated by a millimetre of white base board and every indent and nick lines up exactly.

'Fairly stunning, eh?' She takes a series of photos, winds the film on and places the fabrics in snaplock bags with labels attached. She makes a few notes on her computer and sends me away with a sizeable collection of evidence.

I walk away feeling slightly numb with relief and then wonder why. Haven't I known it all along anyway? Some-where within myself I have always had absolute conviction that the fabrics would match because it was the only thing that would make any sense. But, even so, it feels good to have the weight of science to back me up.

I drop off the new film at the chemist and pick up Kristin's film, which I left earlier. I go through her photos while I wait for the new film to be developed. In Kristin's film, there are photos of Bill on his own. Interesting photos in that, apart from the stubble, he is well dressed. There are photos of Bill and Kristin together in different restaurants and places around the city. I recognise some of them – St Kilda Pier, The Rialto, the warehouse in Richmond.

There are also photos of Bill and Amy together, both of them smiling. The three of them – Bill, Kristin and Amy. Three generations, the stamp of family on all their faces. I look at Amy's smiling face with mixed feelings. I guessed she had met Bill Stone but feel absolutely no pleasure in being proved right.

In my car, I have a red folder full of the details of the case so far. I add a handwritten note outlining the progress of the day and file it with the rest. A thick folder with clear dates and theories. I glance through it all, surprised at how much has happened over a relatively short space of time. I add the evidence and photos given to me by Gillian Stockton and lock the folder in the boot, aware how precious it is. I also have the second copy, the one for Denton, and I add similar notes to it, along with Gillian's name and address. This document is back up. I want to keep it close to hand for the moment, so I place it in the glove box.

It is still only half past eleven, too many long hours to get through before tonight. My mouth is dry and I feel reluctant and impatient in turns. Harold doesn't ring but I have almost given up on him, not sure any longer how I feel.

I ring both his home number and his mobile. No answer from either. I leave a message both times, telling him what I have set up and asking him to join me. Harold has a calming effect on people and I hope that with him in the room, any tendency to temper or violence might be negated. The only problem is I'm not sure where he is. I think of that moment of complete conviction with Rosalyn this morning. The complete lack of trust. I need Harold there. If he doesn't get in contact, then I will have to think again.

Alicia's driveway is clear of her yellow van and I drive on to her chemist shop. In between customers I tell her what I have put together and outline the evidence I have collected this morning.

'You've come a long way, Marlo. Where is it all now?'

'In the car. Will you come tonight?'

'Of course. Who will be there?

'All of them. You, me and the dog. Hopefully Harold.'

'Is it safe, Marlo?'

'I think so,' I say, going through my recent thoughts. 'I think that both attacks have been pretty much spur of the moment. Even with the attack on Harold, I think it wasn't planned. And with everyone there, it should be safe enough.'

'Hopefully.' She doesn't sound convinced.

'Yes.' I answer her doubt rather than her words. 'What else can I do, Alicia? Lack of resolution is worse, don't you think?'

'Yes, I do. What are you doing now?'

'Filling in time. Getting nervous. Keeping away from home in case they are all blessed with detective instincts. If Amy can find me, anyone can.' I don't voice the other thought – whether Harold, in a confiding mood, will have told Rosalyn where I live.

Alicia checks her watch. 'I finish in half an hour. Why don't you wait for me and we'll have a walk somewhere and lunch on the way.'

'Yes, I'd like that.' The sense of safety is something I crave, and so too is company.

'What will I do with the car?' I explain about the evidence in the boot.

'There's a safe in the office.'

I collect the red folder and Alicia locks it away.

I drive her home and we leave the car in my driveway, setting out on our walk around the coast. When we get past the Elwood Canal, we see the house where we are expected tonight. I point it out to Alicia and we stare at it for a while as if there were no other view.

We eat a sandwich in Brighton and then head for home. Near St Kilda the light changes, sea and sky darkening like dusk. I check my watch, thinking that I must have lived through more hours today than I imagined. But it is only half past three.

'What's happened to the day?' I ask.

'It's the eclipse, Marlo.' She looks at me surprised. 'Didn't you know? People have been talking about nothing else for days.'

I go with Alicia to her house, taking Ebony with me. Alicia heads off to the shower and I think about the back-up document in the glove box, wanting to read it through once more before tonight. I want to consider things like weight and subtlety and the obscure sense of something going on in the background. I don't think I'd make a good criminal. I would be the compulsive sort that Bill Stone had talked about, one of the brigade who have to go back and check on things they might have left behind.

My mobile rings in my pocket. I snatch it out, expecting Harold. Hoping for Harold.

'Marlo. Shane Black. I got your message.' There is something so ordinary about his voice, some link to the time of optimism on the beach when I left my message, that despite the nerves and fear, some of the pleasure washes over me again now.

'Shane.' I head out to the car. 'Have you seen Harold?'

'No. What's up?'

I check my watch for the thousandth time. Just after four o'clock. Two hours to go. 'I don't know where he is. I wanted him to come with me tonight.' I don't know if this makes much sense to Shane. The whole business has occupied my thoughts so entirely that it seems everyone should know what I'm talking about.

'Can I help?'

Shane instead of Harold. Or Shane as well as Harold. The more people, the safer I will feel.

'Yes, of course. Alicia and I are going somewhere and we need a witness.' Not quite a witness, because Alicia and I are witness enough, but an extra presence.

'I see,' he says slowly, and I wonder what he is thinking. Whatever it is, he doesn't comment. 'What time?'

'If you could be here by half past five? I'll explain when I see you.'

'OK,' he says agreeably and I give him my address. 'I'll see you then.'

I close the phone up, feeling light with relief, and open the passenger door of the car, inattentive to the shadow behind me. It is only when I close the door, document in hand, that some awareness of light shifting alerts me. I spin on my heel and my heart thumps erratically in my chest.

'It was you.'

She is standing against the fence, pressed up against it and for a moment the memory of pink eyes and skin leaps up. No pink eyes now, but brilliant green. There is something luminous about them, a kind of magnetism or madness. She is so close, I can smell the sourness of her skin. So close, I could reach out and touch her. I look around desperately, wanting to back away, but I am trapped between the car and the fence line.

Chapter 33

By the look on her face, Kristin had no intention of waiting around for six o'clock. She has come to me. But then I half expected she would. The only flaw in my plan is that I shouldn't be here. I curse myself for the momentary thoughtlessness that brought me to the car and the compulsive need to check what I had written.

Kirstin's hair is lank, streaked with grey, and pulled back so tightly from her scalp, that her eyes seem to protrude slightly and a vein pulses on her temple. She looks bigger than I remember and, out of flowing, youthful clothing, she also looks more solid and impenetrable.

I consider my position. Four o'clock, Monday afternoon. The quiet time before people drift in from work. There is no one on the street. Ebony is in Alicia's house, the front door closed between us. Alicia is in the shower – I heard the hiss of it as I closed her door. Not a good position to be in. I breathe out as though the air has been trapped in my lungs for long minutes and take a small step along the car body.

'How did you know where I live?' I ask, to deflect her

attention from my sideways step as much as anything.

'Sam told me.' A touch of triumph in her eyes and an odd little giggle. 'Relax, Marlo. He told me you were a neighbour of Alicia's and when I got here I recognised your car. I didn't tell Sam I intended paying you a visit.'

Obvious when you think about it. Next time, Marlo, hide completely. Next time, hide the car.

'So why are you here?' I try for a conversational tone, trying to lower the tension.

'I'm here, Marlo, because I got your invitation.'

'I didn't send you an invitation, Kristin; Rosalyn did.'

She grins almost happily. 'Then you don't know Rosalyn.'

'On the contrary, I think I know Rosalyn very well.' That lack of trust was spot on.

'And you know about me, don't you?'

'Yes.' I know two things I could only guess at a moment ago: the identity of the murderer, and Rosalyn's ability to stir things up in the background. Rosalyn has sent Kristin to me as surely as if she had driven her here. Despite the fact that it is Kristin in front of me with her mad eyes, it is Rosalyn I feel a rush of anger towards. Who knows what little lines she fed. Who knows what hatreds she has stirred up. Even if the killer is Kristin, I don't think there's much to choose between them.

I collect my thoughts. 'I know a lot about you Kristin,' I say, my voice very even. 'I know you dropped a piece of fabric in the park. I know you stayed around that night trying to find it and that you went back in the morning hoping that somehow the police had missed it.'

She licks her lips and looks at me blankly.

I go on. 'The old man picked up the material you dropped. You saw him that night didn't you? They arrested him and you were pleased.'

'No, I wasn't pleased.' She shakes her head. 'I just didn't know what to do.' She lapses into silence.

'Why don't you tell me about that night.'

She flashes me a quick glance and I can see the compulsion

to talk fighting with the compulsion to be silent. She licks her lips again and a little bit of her solidity seems to fade.

'I had my work bag with me that night because I wanted to show Bill something I'd been making. The fabric fell out of my bag when I took the hammer out. I didn't realise until I checked. After he fell... I took off but came back again. I didn't know what to do. And that's when I saw the old man. He was kneeling beside him. That must have been when he picked the fabric up.'

There is something quiet about her voice that seems to negate any possibility of threat. Her tone is ordinary and every day, as if this conversation were a normal one. 'And that's when Harold came on the scene. I heard Harold call out and I took off. I didn't know then that he was calling you.'

My mind switches from Bill Stone in the park to Harold lying on the cold garage floor. She seems to follow my thoughts.

'I hit the wrong person that day. I thought it was Harold who was checking up but Ros told me it was you. She said that Harold wasn't much more than a bumbling old man who couldn't see what was in front of his face.'

So the crack on the head was meant for me all along. My heart almost stops and my throat constricts. I wonder who told her I would be there. Rosalyn? We look at each other silently, and I am aware of the rush of our breath, like we have both run a long way. In the background I hear another sound – the persistent eerie whine of a dog. A sound that is so welcome that the hairs on my arms lift.

I slide another step along the car body. Another small and sliding step. Kristin smiles and the smile is chilling. 'Rosalyn says you have some things of mine.'

'What things?'

She searches for the words. 'Some evidence.'

'Yes,' I say evenly, watching her. She moves forward slightly, scraping the gravel, the stones shifting beneath her feet. 'It's in the house. I'll just get it.' My cricket gear is on the porch. A bat. A couple of balls. Things I can chuck and swing and make a noise with. I take another step sideways.

'I don't think so.' Her voice cracks into threat and aggression. I watch her hands as they come towards me. Her sleeves are up and I can see the strength in her wrists. The muscles and sinews in her arms. Bare hands. No hammer, no implement to hand, but for all that the hands look immensely strong. Another step along the car, a frantic shifting this time, but I am held by the wing mirror.

Not flight then but fight. The only thing in my hands is the document from the glove box and my car keys, a cluster of metal and knobbly ends. I sweep them up in front of me and swipe at her face. Behind the blur of metal her eyes gleam and she almost looks surprised.

'What's the matter, Kristin?' I yell like I do at cricket, full throated, hoping that Alicia will hear me above the noise of the shower. Again the odd look of surprise on Kristin's face. 'Different, isn't it, when you haven't got someone old or unsuspecting to contend with?'

In Alicia's house, Ebony's drawn out whine has changed to a persistent growl, like an engine revving up. Kristin must hear it but if she does, she gives no sign. I am fully launched now and the words burst out of me in fear and anger.

'You put the jackets in Rosalyn's sewing basket, didn't you? You told Amy, or you suggested something that got her wondering. She found them. You wanted to blame Rosalyn.'

She smiles then and the smile is sweet and very chilling. 'It nearly worked, didn't it? But in the end they let her go. I thought I was good at setting things up but she was always better.'

Her voice is calm enough and again there is that odd sense of conversation that is belied by the frenzied look in her eyes. 'You see, I couldn't take it . . . she was always telling me . . . taking over, telling me that Bill was worthless and then . . . when I found out he was, it was worse.'

I take a steadying breath, suspended now, waiting for the right moment to run but held by the horror of it and the need to understand.

'Tell me about Bill.'

Her face doesn't change but she lowers her hands, leaves them hanging loosely at her sides.

'What's there to tell? He kept in touch, told me that I was the special one. He always said that he'd help me out when I needed it...' She trails away.

'And you needed help?' I prompt.

'Yes. When the Sydney contract fell through...you probably don't know what that's like. Everything you've ever worked for and someone with a bit of power gives the contract to someone else. All your dreams are wiped away.'

'I do understand that,' I say.

'I thought that if I could start up on my own, then perhaps...not everything would be lost. You see, I'm not getting any younger. I can't afford to keep on waiting for that break. But to set up on my own I needed money, and when I asked...he said no.'

'I see,' I say calmly. 'I would be angry too.'

'Yes,' she says eagerly. 'I was. That night...we were going to have dinner. We used to buy take-aways and eat out some-where, different places, parks or bus shelters, sometimes at the pier in St Kilda. We'd find a different place every night. It was like a game.'

'He liked games,' I say.

Her eyes narrow. 'How do you know that?'

'I know a lot about your father. I've made quite a study of him lately, and I know about his humour because of his name – Bill Stone to Bill Diamond. He was a wealthy man playing a part. He had lots of money, Kristin, he could have helped you easily.'

She doesn't answer and her face is masklike.

'A house in South Yarra. A ticket and money for an overseas holiday. Who knows what else he had hidden away?'

'He said that when he was dead, I would have enough money, and now he is.' Her words are soft, almost dreamy. 'I had my work bag that night, have I said that...?' She looks confused momentarily.

'It doesn't matter. Go on.'

'I usually have it with me. Suddenly the hammer was in my hand. I didn't mean to . . . it was the handle that hit him and he just collapsed. I couldn't believe it when he fell. I think . . . I'm not sure but I think he hit his head on the rail, I heard the . . . and after that he didn't get up.'

Ebony is thundering against the door now, the sound of her claws against the wood like dull jack hammers. Even in the shower, Alicia must hear her, surely.

'Kristin,' I begin. 'It sounds more like an accident . . . the police will know that.'

'I burnt his letters until they were no more than a pile of ash on the floor,' she says, unheeding. 'I'd kept them all you see. All the letters he ever sent me. All of them lies . . .'

'Kristin . . .'

Her gaze is fixed at something behind my head. She doesn't seem to have heard me. 'Ros told me that Harold found his body in the park and that he'd seen someone running away.'

'Harold didn't see you that night – he was too busy looking after your father.'

'But . . . Rosalyn told me.' She looks puzzled, as though she can't understand my words, or perhaps it's the fact that Rosalyn got it wrong.

'She was wrong,' I say, glad to derail Kristin from her track if I possibly can. I watch her closely. My news seems to have stunned her and I press the advantage. 'I saw you that night running away. I told Harold and he told Rosalyn.'

'But . . . I thought that's why he came to tea. I thought he was checking up on me. She told me that he knew about the law.'

'He does but it was just a friendly visit.' I take pleasure in saying it, in seeing the shock register on her face.

'He didn't see me,' she repeats. This seems to be where her mind has stuck. The fear of being seen in the act of murder. I can imagine how compelling it must be. The fear of being found out. She is standing still, as though unable to take it in.

I dart around the mirror, leaping forwards and sideways in two bounding strides, away from the car body, away from Kristin and those reaching hands. In front of me I have air and space and room to move. I sprint to the porch, grab the bat from the bag, and turn to face her. It's not far but it seems to take forever. Kristin has hardly moved, however, has only just begun to come towards me.

I lift the bat in front of me, like I am ready to drive to the outer. She stops dead and her stillness is somehow riveting. Bat in hand, I begin to feel slightly absurd. Instead of menacing, she just looks pathetic.

After all that has happened, I thought I would be angry enough to kill her. I thought that taking the violence back to her would bring some kind of peace and resolution, some sort of vengeance for Harold and events of the past. Instead, in the face of Kristin's bewilderment, my anger shrinks and dies.

Silence. Stillness. Ebony stops her noise momentarily and the silence now is heavy. I turn at the faint sound of a door opening and see Alicia in her dressing gown, her hair dripping wet, her hand on Ebony's collar. Ebony strains against her grip, her eyes almost glowing.

Alicia's voice carries clearly to us. 'I've called the police, Marlo. Shall I let the dog go?'

I look at Kristin but the pathetic look is still there and my anger and fear have faded like mist in sunshine. I feel cold and worn and immensely tired.

'No,' I say, loud enough for everyone to hear. 'I don't think you need to.'

A strange grouping. Ebony's silent, straining tension. Alicia with her dripping hair and watchful eyes. Kristin in front of me like a deflated balloon. All of us still and staring, waiting in this frozen moment until the police arrive.

Chapter 34

The aftermath seems to take for ever. I tell the police about the events and the lead up. Alicia confirms it all and Kristin stays silent and defeated. Eventually they lead her away and I watch her move awkwardly between two uniformed officers. She looks smaller and her walk is strangely dreamy as though she is lost.

I sit on the porch and wait some more, feeling as though my legs won't support me. Ebony sits beside me, calmer now that Kristin has gone, knowing that the threat has passed. But she remains alert still, her head turning at different sounds, watching the shift and play of different people in the yard. I stroke her from time to time but with strangers in the yard, she won't settle or relax.

Alicia must get dressed at some point because when she brings me tea, her hair is combed and she has changed from her dressing gown into a bright red track suit. She sits beside me on the porch and I drink the tea thirstily, enjoying the warmth and the clean, clear taste. During all this, Denton arrives and consults with one of the uniformed officers. He crosses the small garden eventually and sits down next to me. He asks similar questions to the uniformed officers and I answer as clearly as I can. He has retreated behind officialdom, as though the presence of others is somehow inhibiting. This, I realise, is what he has always done, as though he isn't able to decide on the correct response. He does ask after Harold and I tell him that I don't know where he is. He looks at me curiously, as though sensing the rift and the worry.

'I have evidence.' I say, going back to the subject in hand. 'I told the police officers. It's locked up in Alicia's safe at her work.'

'Well let's get it then.'

We all go, an odd little entourage, to Alicia's chemist shop on the crossroads. Alicia, Peter Denton, me, Ebony.

Alicia unlocks the safe and passes out the bulky red folder that I left before lunch. Denton takes it from her and opens it up.

'You've seen some of it before,' I say. 'The early stuff I gave you that morning on the footbridge.'

'Yes, I remember. It all looks very efficient,' he says quietly, closing the folder, the friendliness back in his voice. I don't comment, not caring one way or the other.

'I'll drive you home', he says. 'Where will you be tomorrow if I need to get in touch?'

Tomorrow is Tuesday. A working day.

'Either at home or at work. You know both places.'

'Yes, I know both.'

He drops us off outside the house and Alicia and I watch the police car pull away. Its place is taken by two other cars that pull in almost together. I check my watch because I seem to have lost track of time. Only half past five. An awful lot seems to have happened and not much time seems to have passed.

I watch Harold and Shane emerge from their cars. An older man, heavy but with a light tread. A younger man, slim to the point of thinness. Both of them very different but united somehow by their look of concern at the disappearing police car and the small cluster of people on the footpath.

Alicia looks at me and takes everyone inside to offer explanations. I listen to the conversation going on around me as though I am not a part of it, but when she tells Harold who the police have arrested, it is impossible not to miss the turning of his head and the remoteness in his eyes. I am glad that Alicia is here to tell them because I don't think that I could. I feel as though I have run a long and exhausting marathon. I spend some time trying to define some of what I feel into single words. Completion, Relief. Resolution.

Harold rings out for pizza and opens some wine from the fridge. It is so like Harold to offer comfort in food and wine that I find myself relaxing and some of the heaviness of the encounter with Kristin seems to melt away. When the pizza arrives Harold distributes slices from the cardboard box, with serviettes for the grease.

'You'd never know I ran a restaurant, would you?' He smiles at me and his expression is so normal and so friendly that another layer of heaviness drifts off somewhere. I think he and I are going to be all right.

I watch Shane as he listens to an anecdote of Alicia's about one of her customers. As usual he is very still, but he looks very much at home in the present company. I like the slimness of his body and the blueness of his eyes. For some reason I remember that complicated moment in the car park and his face when he moved to kiss me. With a flush of pleasure, I hope there will be more.

After the food is finished, Harold makes coffee. It's the first chance I have to speak to him alone.

'Harold,' I begin. I need to tell him some of my thoughts regarding Rosalyn. I'll never know how much, if any, of Harold's attack was down to Rosalyn, have no way of knowing the strings she might have pulled behind the scenes. But I do know what she did in my case and Harold needs to know this. What he chooses to do about it is entirely up to him.

'Tomorrow will be soon enough, Marlo. There's a lot we

need to say but you look like you've had it for today.' There is no animosity in his voice and I am glad. He drops a hand on my shoulder.

'We'll talk tomorrow, Marlo. I told you you would see it through.' He sounds as he has always done. Kind and caring. I cover his hand momentarily with my own.

Alicia stands up. 'I must go too. I didn't realise it was so late. Are you all right on your own, Marlo?'

'I'm fine.'

'Ring me if you wake in the night . . . if you find that you can't sleep.' A fleeting kiss and good wishes.

Shane is the last to leave. Another kiss and he too is gone.

I wander through the house, tidying up a few things as I go. The empty wine bottles and pizza boxes from dinner. My track suit dropped on the bedroom floor. When I pick it up a piece of paper crackles in the pocket. I take it out and read through the list I wrote to myself in that moment of optimism on the beach.

I add to it now. Not work possibilities but personal ones. Things like sorting out the house to my liking. Making contact with family members and the difficult but necessary process of talking about Cate with Emma. Things like returning Lee's phone call and picking up where we left off.

When I have finished, I sink down into the warm bed, Ebony on her mat beside me. I am tired beyond belief but strangely content. Tomorrow will do to begin, Harold had said. And listening to Ebony's gentle breath in the moment before sleep overwhelms me, I realise that for the first time in a long while I am looking forward to tomorrow.

Established in 1978, The Women's Press publishes high-quality fiction and non-fiction from outstanding women writers worldwide. Our list spans literary fiction, crime thrillers, biography and autobiography, health, women's studies, literary criticism, mind body spirit, the arts and the Livewire Books series for young women. Our bestselling annual Women Artists Diary features the best in contemporary women's art.

The Women's Press also runs a book club through which members can buy, every quarter, the best fiction and non-fiction from a wide range of British publishing houses, mostly in paperback, always at discount.

To receive our latest catalogue, or for information on The Women's Press Book Club, send a large SAE to:

The Sales Department
The Women's Press Ltd
34 Great Sutton Street London EC1V 0LQ
Tel: 020 7251 3007 Fax: 020 7608 1938
www.the-womens-press.com

Ellen Hart
The Merchant of Venus
A Jane Lawless Crime Thriller

When Cordelia Thorn's sister Octavia, a beautiful and successful young Broadway actress, announces she is marrying fabulously wealthy 83-year-old Roland Lester, Jane Lawless smells a rat ...

'Hart's style is hypnotic. Her action is brisk and riveting' *Washington Blade*

Crime Fiction £6.99
ISBN 0 7043 4718 0

Robber's Wine
A Jane Lawless Crime Thriller

Jane and her irrepressible sidekick, Cordelia Thorn, set off for a well-deserved summer holiday. But with a mysterious death in the local town's most prominent family, the holiday takes a dangerous turn ...

'A classic whodunit with an inventive twist in the tail' *Sunday Times*

Crime Fiction £5.99
ISBN 0 7043 4719 9

Alma Fritchley
Chicken Shack
The long-awaited fourth Letty Campbell mystery

Mourning the end of a relationship, Letty Campbell, chicken farmer par excellence, turns her hand to a spot of property dealing. Aided and abetted by her glamorous sidekick Julia, Letty sells the land she inherited to a Texan outfit who plan to set up a health farm.

Letty's mother has been busy too, announcing her engagement to the fabulously wealthy Colonel Thompson. But when her mother starts receiving mysterious phone calls, Letty wonders what skeletons are rattling in the Thompson family closet.

Meanwhile, back at the health farm, Letty finds plenty to distract her. But is the sleepy Yorkshire village of Calderton ready for colonic irrigation and 'stunt' aerobics? And what is the connection between a freak accident, an escaped prisoner and a load of filthy lucre...

'Alma Fritchley gets better and better' *Eve's Back*

'A talent to watch' *Crime Time*

Crime Fiction £6.99
ISBN 0 7043 4686 9

Alma Fritchley
Chicken Run
The first Letty Campbell mystery

Letty Campbell warily agrees to let her land be used for a classic car auction, but she has a horrible feeling that she should never have got involved...

'Hilarious' *Evening Standard*

'Irrepressibly bouncy' *Pink Paper*

'A breath of fresh air... Alma Fritchley is a talent to watch' *Crime Time*

Crime Fiction £5.99
ISBN 0 7043 4691 5

Chicken Out
The third Letty Campbell mystery

Trapped into arranging an unusual funeral after her neighbour dies in suspicious circumstances, Letty finds herself embroiled in a dangerous case involving mysterious letters, hidden treasures – and a secret lesbian love affair...

'Hilarious' *Evening Standard*

'Alma Fritchley is a talent to watch' *Crime Time*

Crime Fiction £6.99
ISBN 0 7043 4619 2